The Motherhood Mandate

The Unborn Child Protection Act

M.E. Wright

Merrywidow Publishing LLC

ISBN 979-8-9883566-4-6 (ebook)

ISBN 979-8-9883566-5-3 (paperback)

ISBN 979-8-9883566-6-0 (hardcover)

ISBN 979-8-9883566-7-7 (Audiobook)

To Mom
The ideas you shared, the stories you told,
and the support you gave me shaped every page of this book.

Contents

1. Chapter One   1

2. Chapter Two   8

3. Chapter Three   21

4. Chapter Four   37

5. Chapter Five   53

6. Chapter Six   69

7. Chapter Seven   87

8. Chapter Eight   108

9. Chapter Nine   128

10. Chapter Ten   143

11. Chapter Eleven   159

12. Chapter Twelve   176

13. Chapter Thirteen   190

14. Chapter Fourteen   202

15. Chapter Fifteen   215

16. Chapter Sixteen   230

17.   Chapter Seventeen   244

18.   Chapter Eighteen   260

19.   Chapter Nineteen   277

Epilogue   297

Author's Note   307

Acknowledgements   316

About the Author   317

Chapter One

Rylee carefully pulled into the parking lot and scanned for Sam's car. A few vehicles were scattered around the large lot. She spotted Sam's distinctively dark blue hybrid at the far end, near the trail that led through the tree-lined path to Tietjen Beach.

She pulled in next to his car, sighing as she checked her watch. Just after 8 a.m. So much for being early.

Of course, he'd picked the beach. Grabbing a nearby picnic table and talking things out would have been so much easier.

No. Sam was not going to make this easy for her. Nothing said 'we're done' like a forced march along the worn asphalt trail to remind her of happier times. After all, Tietjen Beach had been their special place.

Rylee blinked back tears as she exited the car, automatically locking it and tucking her keys into a pocket as she walked over to the northern trail entrance. She knew where to find him. He would be waiting for her on the farthest access point to the beach, far away from anyone taking an early morning walk.

A slight chill seeped past her loose linen sundress and the damp wind caressed her bare arms. The forecast had called for a chance of rain later in the day, but it had been so warm at home that she hadn't thought to bring a wrap.

Rylee glanced through the window into the backseat. She didn't see her spare sweater. *Dammit*, she thought. By the time she got to the beach, she'd be freezing.

No help for it. Time to get going. With any luck, Sam would agree to continue their conversation over breakfast at a nearby restaurant.

She could feel the random pebbles and irregular pavement through the thin soles of her leather flats as she walked. The trees overhead flickered in the damp breeze, birds happily chirping as they greeted the morning sun.

As she followed the trail deeper into the forest, all Rylee could think of was how crappy it was that Sam had chosen this place to meet. It felt like the ultimate punishment. So many memories, good and bad.

She could feel the tears starting again. She wiped at her face with the back of her hand and kept walking.

The summer beach parties with the robotics team. That time someone had lit up the entire lakefront with a bunch of possibly illegal fireworks.The community barbecue the summer before her senior year, when she first thought he might be interested in her.

Their first kiss had happened right along this trail, during last year's Winter Wonderland Hike. These trees had even witnessed their last fight.

Rylee stopped walking, stretching her neck to look up at the tree canopy. *No!* she thought. She was not going to give him the satisfaction of seeing her break down. Not now.

Maybe she should just go. He didn't love her. Maybe he never did. Maybe all she had been to him was someone who gave him sex on demand, like some anonymous plastic sex doll.

She wiped her face with both hands. *That wasn't true*, she told herself. Somehow, she knew Sam had genuinely cared for her, even if he could never bring himself to say the word 'love'. Cared? Yes. Needed? Absolutely. But never loved.

Rylee crossed her arms, blinking back tears as she rocked back and forth for a long moment. There was only one way to find out if he could help, and that was to keep going. Besides, she could see glimmers of the beach peeking through the trees up ahead. No sense turning back now.

As she approached the beach, she noticed the small details. His vague silhouette stood against the backdrop of the calm lake waters, his faded blue t-shirt and old jeans making him blend in. His dark red hair was a vivid smudge against the shades of blue around him.

Sam stood with his back to the trail, the small waves lapping up against the monochrome shoreline at his feet. He was staring off into the horizon, to that place where the sky kissed the shimmering lake water.

He might have been lost in thought. Or, more likely, he was avoiding even looking at her.

She stepped off the trail and onto the beach, if you could call it that. Sandy pebbles littered the shoreline, with larger stones and pieces of driftwood scattered around as if Mom Nature had had another temper tantrum with the last storm.

"Dammit!" she cried out, bruising her toes as she tripped over a small tree branch. "Why the hell did you want to meet on the beach when there are perfectly good picnic tables closer to the parking lot?" she complained as she got her balance and looked down at her shoe. A shallow scrape marred the dark leather.

She looked up, annoyed. Sam hadn't even noticed her distress. Of course, he hadn't.

Rylee made herself continue walking until she reached his side. "Sam, I'm cold," she told him. "Can't we go someplace else?"

When he didn't respond, she reached for his hand as she tried to make a connection.

He pulled away, shoving his hands into his front pockets as he took a step away from her. "Just tell me what you want, Rylee," he told her, his voice dark with anger. He continued to scan the horizon, eyeing the dark clouds that were gathering out over the lake. "We broke up. It's over. There's nothing more to say."

"It's really chilly out here," she whimpered, rubbing her cold hands against her arms to ward off the chill. "I can't talk when I'm freezing to death!"

Sam knew how sensitive she was to the cold. Once upon a time, he'd cared enough to put his arms around her against a sudden chill. Not now, though. She felt the tears threaten to start again and held up one hand under her nose to try to hold back the sniffle.

Sam turned to her, his hazel eyes blazing with unspoken rage. "Let's go," he snapped. Before she could do more than blink, he grabbed her by the arm and dragged her across the beach to the trail that led through the woods behind them.

She stumbled after him, tripping over another small piece of driftwood. His fingers flexed, painfully gripping her bicep, as he kept her from falling. She struggled to pull away from him and he abruptly let her go as they slowly made their way through the overgrown trail to the stairs that led to the bluff overlooking the beach.

The limestone steps were nearly overrun by wild grapevines, goldenrods, and various weeds. They made it nearly impossible for her to reach the ancient wooden handrails as they headed for the bluff.

As soon as they reached the top, Sam moved to one of the benches that used to overlook the beach below. Over the years, the forest had taken over the bluff, obscuring the once picturesque view.

He sat, leaning back against the bench as if the very sight of her disgusted him. "Tell me what's going on," he growled.

Rylee slumped onto the closest bench. There were so many things that she needed to say, but the words just wouldn't come out. "We can't break up, Sam," she finally told him, brushing her tangled, black hair out of her face. "I–I need you." *I need your help.*

Sam's expression hardened and he turned away, staring at the random foliage around them. After a long moment, he told her the words she didn't want to hear. "Rylee, it's over." He leaned forward, staring at the sandy ground between them. "You broke up with *me*," he spat. "We're done."

His words hit her like a backhanded slap. She sprang from her seat, fists clenched at her side. "No!" she cried out. "You don't understand. We made a mistake!" She choked back a sob; the words 'I think I'm pregnant' stuck in her throat.

Sam leaned back and eyed her, scorn etched into his pursed lips. "How many times do we need to break up before you finally accept that it's over, Rylee?" he asked mockingly. "Two more times? Five?" He glared at her. "Breaking up was your idea." He paused for emphasis, then barked, "Both times!"

Rylee swallowed a sob, screwing her eyes shut as she turned her face upward. "I was wrong," she whispered. She opened her eyes, wiping the tears from her face with both hands as if she could wipe away her fear. "Things have changed, Sam."

He rolled his eyes. "What things?" he demanded. "I'm really tired of this, Rylee! Tell me what's going on!"

She collapsed against the bench as she covered her eyes with one hand. She didn't have the words to stand against his rage. This wasn't him. Couldn't be him. Not the Sam she loved.

Rylee took a deep breath and then looked up at him. It was obvious she couldn't expect any help from him. "It doesn't matter, Sam," she finally told him. "I'm probably worried about nothing."

Sam glared at her for a moment, then sighed as he stood. "Fine," he growled. And, with that, he sauntered away.

Rylee collapsed into tears, wrapping her arms around herself as she cried. Her last hope was gone. He really didn't care.

After a long while, she wiped away her tears and tried to pull herself together. Time to find some answers.

She fumbled for a moment as she pulled her phone out of her pocket, then hit the button for the AI assistant. "Who can help figure out why I have been feeling nauseous?" she asked in a low voice.

"Hello, Rylee," her phone answered. "According to your MediTrack app, your last menstrual period was July 16th. It is highly recommended that you seek out a gynecologist to rule out pregnancy before pursuing an alternative medical diagnosis."

She thought about it for a moment. Her regular doctor was out. Dr. Marrow might contact her mother and she couldn't have that. Not yet. Not until she figured this out. She tapped the app button again. "Where can I find a gynecologist that will see me today?"

There was a pause. "There are five gynecologists within a thirty-mile radius. One of them offers same-day appointments and confidential consultations."

Rylee took a close look at her screen. The Faith and Prayers Pregnancy Crisis Center. According to her phone, it was just a few minutes away in Fox Point.

She stabbed at her phone to make the call. *It was early*, she thought. *Maybe they could get her in now.*

Chapter Two

Rylee glared at herself in the mirror again. The bathroom reminded her of a truck stop restroom off the highway in the middle of nowhere. The sinks were filthy, with a visible layer of calcified dirt on the faucets and brown paper towels littering the floor. The toilets and showers were no better. Even the bath towels provided were a faded gray-white, scratchy, and probably should be replaced.

She picked up her brush and carefully combed it through her hair. It was made of cheap plastic and had been provided to her as a part of the 'welcome to detention' personal hygiene kit. The clear plastic bag had included a brush, a comb, and a simple elastic scrunchy to pull back her hair. She'd used a bit of shampoo from the travel-size bottle to wash them as best she could, but she was still mortified she might be using a previous detainee's cast-off.

She put the brush down on the porcelain sink and got to work French braiding her hair. It had been a long and incredibly dehumanizing weekend. Dealing with other detainees. Forced participation in individual and group 'counseling' sessions. Being forced to sleep on an ancient, stained, incredibly thin mattress with a single blanket and a flat pillow. The food.

And that so-called medical exam. Rylee had never been seen by a male doctor before, not even as a child. It had been so humiliating for him to stare at her, almost as if she was going to star in his next personal jerkfest.

She blinked back familiar tears and glared at herself in the mirror again. Her hair was a mess. Uneven strands of hair buckled against what should be a flat, carefully woven braid. One length behind her ear was threatening to escape.

Rylee leaned forward and scrubbed her hands through her hair, untangling the chaotic mess with nervous fingers. With a careful flip, she stood straight and watched her black hair as it settled around her shoulders.

What the hell was she going to do? She only had ten minutes left before they took her to the courthouse for her hearing.

She nodded to herself in the mirror. *You can do this*, she told herself. *You are going to get your shit together and tell that judge whatever it takes to get released from detention so you can go home.*

Rylee picked up the brush again and carefully pulled it through her hair. *You are a Williams*, she reminded herself. She would do whatever it took to get out of this place. And that started with looking her best with whatever tools she was given.

Rylee sat in the back of the transport van, looking out the window as the early morning traffic streamed by. Mondays in Downtown Milwaukee were always challenging, as cars jockeyed for position on the crowded, narrow streets. It was also the middle of road construction season, which meant that at least one lane was closed, forcing cars to merge at random intervals.

The ride took much longer than she'd thought. It was hard to tell because she still didn't have her phone. After a while, the traffic seemed to blend together and she couldn't tell where she was.

The van finally stopped in the loading zone behind the courthouse. She barely had time to register where she was before the side door opened and a police officer offered her a hand down. She automatically took his hand, grateful she hadn't been handcuffed on her way out of detention. The orange jumpsuit was humiliating enough. Just wearing it made her visible against the drab colors around her.

Rylee carefully walked up the concrete steps, mindful of the police officer who escorted her into the building. She quickly got lost as they walked down one hallway, then another, before she was escorted to a room near the elevator.

A small table with two metal chairs took up most of the room. The door locked behind her. She sat, feeling the strain. She hadn't really slept since being detained.

It had been a surreal couple of days. The doctor at Faith and Prayers Pregnancy Crisis Center had insisted on performing a transvaginal ultrasound to confirm that Rylee was pregnant. She'd finally given in because she didn't trust pregnancy tests.

Having a tube shoved up inside of her to search for a heartbeat had been embarrassing enough. Then, the center's social worker started in on her, refusing to let her leave unless she'd talked about her plans for the pregnancy. That led to the center calling the police, who insisted she talk to a crisis intervention 'specialist' who eventually recommended that Rylee be detained for seventy-two hours because she might be a risk to herself or her unborn child.

Rylee grimaced. The only risk Faith and Prayers needed to worry about was the massive lawsuit coming their way.

There was a knock on the door, almost immediately followed by a police officer, who poked her head in. "They're ready for you," she told her.

Rylee stood. "Is there time to go to the bathroom?" she asked. "Nervous bladder."

The woman smiled. "Baby bladder," she replied. "I understand." She gestured. "Bathroom is just around the corner."

Rylee moved down the hallway as the officer had indicated. It was just a small bathroom with two stalls. She was grateful she didn't have to leave the stall open, but it was still embarrassing to know that the woman was right outside the metal door.

A few minutes later, they were walking back to the elevator. From there, it was a maze of random hallways. They stopped at a door manned by another police officer.

He opened the door to the courtroom. It was a small room with four narrow tables. Sam and his family sat at the closest one, but she only had eyes for her mom and dad. Mom looked like she was almost ready to faint, her head resting wearily against Dad, the tangled blond strands almost obscuring his shoulder. Dad looked calm enough, but she knew that expression. It was the calm before the storm.

The officer urged her forward, and Rylee slowly made her way past the Maxwells, careful to avoid eye contact. She could almost feel Mrs. Maxwell's maternal glare as she passed their table and knew from the shuffling of his feet that Sam was almost as nervous as she was.

Mom launched herself from her chair, smothering Rylee with full-body hugs, almost wrapping herself around Rylee in an effort to soothe her sudden tears.

She glanced down at her dad. He looked sad, but gave a slight nod of his head and joined the family hug before urging them all to have a seat. Rylee found herself between her parents. Her mom scooted her chair over until it was firmly wedged against Rylee's and wrapped her arm firmly around Rylee's shoulder until she shrugged it off.

She looked around the courtroom. Her family sat at the table on the right side of the room. The Maxwells sat on the left. Both faced the judge's desk, and there was a small table on the other side of the room. A man stood near it. She made eye contact for a moment, then he sat and started sorting through the files on the desk. He found what he was looking for and returned the other files to the neat pile on the right side of the table.

"All rise," the bailiff said. "The Honorable Judge Christina Olson presiding."

Rylee stood, swaying a bit with anxiety. Her mom grabbed her hand tightly, her rings biting into Rylee's skin. She quickly shook her hand away, flexing it before discretely clasping both hands in front of her.

The judge slowly walked to her desk, the expression on her ebony face a mixture of concern and contemplation. Her white lace collar reminded Rylee of Ruth Bader Ginsberg. She only hoped that this meant a quick, favorable outcome.

Judge Olson sat, then cracked her gavel. "You may be seated," she said in a quiet voice, looking from the Maxwell family to Rylee's side of the room and back. There was a loud rustle as everyone complied.

She opened the file that lay on her desk, studying it for a moment before looking up again. "Rylee Williams and Samuel Maxwell, you have been brought before this court because your unborn biological child has been declared a ward of the state," she told them. "Under State of Wisconsin statutes, we are here to determine the facts leading up to Ms. Williams' viable pregnancy, enroll you in the Wisconsin Individual Family Education program, and to ensure that you finalize post-delivery financial and placement arrangements for your biological child, which is expected to be born—" she paused and looked down to confirm the date, "—in approximately thirty-three weeks."

Rylee buried her face in her hands, rocking back and forth as she tried to swallow her fear. Thirty-three weeks until she became a mom. Unreal.

Her mom reached out again, but she jerked away. *Enough already*! she mentally screamed. *Leave me alone!*

"Attorney James Mueller has been appointed as your biological child's guardian ad litem," the judge continued. "He is responsible for representing the best interests of your child. This includes a financial resource assessment and participating in child placement negotiations or adoption, if you both agree to it."

"Investigate the facts?" Sam's mom shrieked.

Rylee opened her eyes, trying to peer past her father and attorney as Mrs. Maxwell turned to Sam. She couldn't see him very well, but it looked like he was cowering.

Sam's mom turned her rage to the judge. "We don't even know if this . . . this . . . this . . . girl is pregnant and, even if she is, that it's my son's!" she ground out.

The judge banged her gavel sharply. "Order in the court," she said, annoyed by the outburst. "Mrs. Maxwell, I will have you removed if we have any more outbursts."

"But Your Honor—"

Sam's attorney quickly stood; one hand firmly planted on Mrs. Maxwell's shoulder.

"Yes, Counselor?" the judge asked, quirking an eyebrow.

"Olivia Davis, Your Honor," the attorney said. She looked down at Sam's mom, then back up to the judge. "My client's mother is distraught, and with good reason. May we ask the Court to validate how we know that there is a viable pregnancy? Sometimes tests can be deceiving."

The judge took a deep breath, obviously annoyed. "I'll allow it, Counselor." Davis sat and the judge turned to the guardian ad litem. "Mr. Mueller, was there more than one ultrasound to confirm the embryo's placement and fetal heartbeat?"

The guardian ad litem frowned, squinting a bit as he looked at the judge. "Of course, Your Honor," he told her. "It's a standard procedure to repeat both the pregnancy test and ultrasound as a part of the intake process. Ms. Williams would not have been detained if we had not been able to validate that this was a viable pregnancy."

"Thank you, Mr. Mueller," Judge Olson replied with a sharp nod. "No issues found?"

Mueller looked at Rylee. "Your Honor, my client is approximately seven weeks old and appears to be healthy."

The judge smiled. "That's good news!" she said, turning back to Sam's attorney. "And, in answer to your next, obvious question, this court will rely on Ms. Williams' sworn testimony to determine the child's biological father." She gave Rylee a sardonic look. "I don't believe that I need to remind anyone about the penalty for perjury, do I?"

Rylee buried her face in her mom's shoulder. Of course, no one needed to tell her what the penalty was. Under no circumstances was she going back to detention!

She heard Sam's mom start to sputter, but the judge cut her off. "Unless you have pertinent third-party testimony or another man who is claiming to be the child's actual biological father, final determination will be made after the child is born with a court-mandated DNA test," she said in a firm tone.

Rylee wiped her face and looked over at Sam's mom. Her skin had turned an almost comical shade of red along her jawline. It looked like she hadn't taken the time to blend her makeup. It just stopped. Even her neck was red.

"Your Honor, will the Court allow us to request amniocentesis to test for birth defects and to determine if my client is the biological father?" Davis cut in.

Judge Olson turned to the guardian ad litem. "Counselor, I know that there is a small risk of miscarriage, but will allow it if you agree."

Mueller looked down for a moment. "I will only agree to amniocentesis if Ms. Williams' physician finds just cause. There is no reason to put my client at risk if we don't need to."

"So ordered," the judge responded.

Sam and his dad talked in low tones, but Rylee couldn't make out what they were saying.

The judge cleared her throat, gently interrupting their sidebar. She turned her attention to Rylee. "Ms. Williams, I need you to confirm your date of birth for the Court," she told her. "According to your driver's license, you turned eighteen on December 22nd of last year. Is that correct?"

Rylee bit her lip. "Yes, Your Honor," she murmured.

"Thank you for confirming that, Ms. Williams," the judge replied. "I'm glad we don't have to make a referral to criminal court for statutory rape charges." She paused and looked down at the papers on her desk. "I also see no report of rape or domestic abuse. Can you confirm this for the Court?"

Rylee found herself looking down at her hands. She didn't want to admit it, but she'd had sex with Sam before she turned eighteen. "Yes, Your Honor," she whispered.

The judge leaned forward. "Can you repeat that a bit louder for the Court?"

Rylee lifted her chin to look at the judge. "Yes, Your Honor."

The judge looked back, dark eyes suddenly narrow with suspicion. "I need you to be very clear with me on this," she snapped. "Did Sam Maxwell do anything physically or verbally that might cause someone to reasonably fear physical or sexual assault?"

Rylee swallowed hard. That wasn't it at all. Sam was the kind of guy who had captured the spider someone had found in one of the parish storage closets so he could take it outside. There was no way he would ever raise his hand to someone. She slowly shook her head. "Of course not, Your Honor," she finally said. "I'm not afraid of Sam."

The judge nodded in reply. "Thank you," she said. "Now, there are a few other items to discuss. You are an unmarried couple and, as such, your child's physical and developmental safety is at risk. Until this child is born, neither of you will be allowed to travel more than 50 miles from this courthouse."

What? No travel? What about the Home Mission next month?

"Objection, Your Honor!" Sam's attorney exclaimed. "My client is not pregnant and does not pose a risk to Ms. Williams' pregnancy."

That was the wrong thing to say. "Denied," Judge Olson snapped at her. "The statute is very clear. Your client will fully participate in his biological child's pre- and postnatal development. And he can only do that if he is local."

"She can't do this," Sam's mom grumbled, shooting a glare at Rylee. "Sam is leaving for Northwestern in a few days!"

Sam's attorney leaned forward. "Objection, Your Honor. Undue burden."

"On what grounds?"

"My client is enrolled at Northwestern University in Illinois," the attorney told her, a slight lilt in her voice, as if she was stating the obvious. "He will be forced to withdraw for a full year if he is unable to travel."

The judge turned to stare at Sam. "Counselor, I understand that this will have an impact on his life, much the same as it will for Ms. Williams," she told them, looking vaguely disappointed at Sam's attorney. "However, it is this Court's opinion that your client will be better served if he focused on preparing for the birth of his child. He always has the option of taking online courses or transferring to a local college. Request to travel outside of the state is denied."

There was movement at the Maxwell table. It looked like the only reason Sam's mom hadn't leaped to her feet in protest was their attorney's hand on her shoulder.

The judge banged her gavel. "Bailiff, remove Mrs. Maxwell from the courtroom. I've had enough maternal outrage for one day."

The bailiff walked to their table and gestured with one hand. Sam's mom sat back in her chair with a stubborn expression on her face. The attorney whispered something urgent, and with that, Mrs. Maxwell suddenly picked up her purse and walked out of the room without so much as a glance back.

The judge looked over to Rylee and then Sam. "Next item. I will need both Ms. Williams and Mr. Maxwell to surrender their driver's licenses and passports," she told them in a stern voice.

Rylee's mom gasped, but the judge ignored her. "You will each be given a provisional driver's license so that you can travel to work, school, medical appointments, and your parents' homes until you have rented a place to live. In addition, you will each be fitted with a GPS ankle bracelet to track your location."

Rylee's mom leaned back to whisper to her dad, "What about our Christmas vacation?" she whispered.

Rylee glanced up at her dad. His face was strangely blank as he shook his head. "Later," is all he said.

"As a matter of fact, it is, and we do, Mr. Maxwell," she said directly to Sam, apparently responding to something he'd said. "This Court must always act in the best interest of the child, regardless of their birth status. As an unmarried father, you are also a flight risk, as this Court has learned the hard way."

Sam gulped. "Yes, Your Honor."

Judge Olson pulled another document from the file and glanced at it. "Mr. Maxwell, I see that you have a birthday coming up. The provisional license includes a prohibition on the purchase or consumption of alcohol and CBD edibles," she told him. "Although you will soon be of legal drinking age, please be aware that you will be arrested and referred to criminal court if you so much as step one foot into a bar, dispensary, or liquor store until your privileges are reinstated after the baby's birth."

He didn't respond, so she paused, leaning forward. "If warranted, you may be required to submit to regular drug testing to validate your compliance. Is that clear?"

The judge pulled out another piece of paper from the file on her desk. "I will also be issuing a court order to have all mail and packages for both households be diverted to a special unit of the Children's Court before delivery to ensure that abortifacients are not sent to your homes," she told them. "As you know, abortifacients are illegal in this state. Please note that we are aware that this does not preclude individuals from personally delivering them to the defendants, but the Court will grant a standard request from the guardian ad litem for immediate criminal investigation if Ms. Williams miscarries. This includes an emergency access request for all electronics, including household security systems."

Rylee stared at her, shocked. Criminal investigation? Someone from the court pawing through every package sent to the house to look for abortion pills? Unreal. It was illegal to send those pills through the mail. Everyone knew that you had to travel outside of the state to get them.

"Next, you will be enrolled in a program designed to facilitate your transition to parenthood," the judge continued. "These classes, including prenatal, childbirth, and postpartum recovery, as well as essential parenting skills, will be taken jointly and at your own personal expense, unless your income falls below a certain threshold." She looked down at another paper in the file. "The good news is there are several low-cost programs that meet statutory requirements, and some online courses are included. These courses, along with weekly participation in motherhood and fatherhood support groups, are mandatory. Failure to complete these requirements within the timetable provided will result in mandatory jail time.

"Last item before you are fitted for your ankle bracelets and released into your parents' custody," the judge said, glancing at her watch. "Ms. Williams, you are required to provide this Court with the names of all medical providers within the next three weeks. I will be issuing a court order so that your physician can legally provide copies of your medical visits and test results to the Court."

Rylee stared at the judge. She didn't know what to say.

"This is a standard waiver of pregnancy-related HIPPA that allows the state to monitor your pregnancy," the judge told her. "You do have the legal right to appeal this request." From her tone, Rylee knew that any appeal would be in vain. It was like the transvaginal ultrasound all over again.

"Any questions?" the judge asked. "If not, we're adjourned."

Rylee wiped her face against the fresh onslaught of tears. She was going home. Finally!

Chapter Three

Rylee sat on the edge of her chair, staring at herself in the mirror. The remnants of her attempt to find something to wear lay discarded haphazardly across her bedroom floor. The small transmitter just above her ankle seemed to defy every effort to hide it under comfortable clothes.

Rylee had spent the better part of an hour trying to get dressed. The plastic band around her ankle had enough 'give' to be able to pull a thin sock underneath it, but otherwise, it rubbed, especially if she wore tapered pants. Shorts or capri pants were completely out of the question.

She had finally settled on a pair of blue high-waist striped trousers that had wide pant legs draping past her ankles. She was just about to pick out a shirt to go with it when there was a knock on her door. Her mom peeked into her room.

"Family meeting, sweetie," her mom told her, eyes carefully averted. "Your dad's office when you're ready."

"Be there in a minute," Rylee told her. She moved deeper into her closet, stepping over clothes that littered the floor until she reached her seasonal tops. She quickly grabbed a white scoop-neck t-shirt and a pair of low heels and hurried down to the first floor.

Heart pounding, Rylee paused long enough to grab a bottle of artesian still water from the under-counter fridge just inside the kitchen before heading down the hallway to her dad's study. The main house was roughly T-shaped and his office was set at the farthest corner of the house. It gave him a clear view of both the guest house and Mom's extensive flower garden.

Dad's desk was near the door at the front of the room. Her sister Chloe and her mom sat on the couch in front of the bay windows. Two of the family attorneys sat across from them, with another woman standing near the fireplace.

What was Chloe doing here? Rylee wondered. This didn't have anything to do with her.

"Thanks for your assistance, Governor," her dad said, cupping his office phone against his shoulder with one hand and gesturing for her to join them with the other. He was all business. "I appreciate your staff's quick response."

Rylee moved past his desk as he hung up, taking the remaining seat on the couch. She placed her bottle of water on the floor next to her feet. Her dad cleared his throat, pursing his lips before looking at Rylee, an uncomfortable look on his face.

"I know you're just getting settled after a trying weekend, Rylee," he said in a gentle voice. "But we need to make sure that we're all on the same page as to what happened and determine what the next steps are."

Rylee reluctantly nodded, trying to swallow the sudden wave of nausea crawling up her throat as she looked at the attorneys and the woman.

"It's okay, Rylee," her dad told her. "Take your time." Her mom reached for her hand, gently squeezing it in support.

One of the attorneys leaned forward. "What can you tell us about the events that led to your detention, Rylee?" he asked intently. "What exactly happened last Thursday?"

Rylee bit her lip and closed her eyes with a slight nod. "I had taken a home pregnancy test about a week ago, but didn't really trust the results," she told them. "Too many false positives, you know?" She opened her eyes, staring unseeingly at the antique mahogany coffee table in front of her. "My phone recommended Faith and Prayers as a place where I could see a doctor that day, so I made an appointment."

"Sweetie, why didn't you come to me first?" her mom implored. "I could have taken you to our family doctor. None of this would have happened if you had just come to me!"

Rylee pulled her hand away, slowly rubbing it against her pants. "Because if the second test came back negative, it would have been okay. No need to talk to anyone about it."

Her parents exchanged a guarded look.

"Understood," the second attorney interjected. "Please continue."

"After it came back positive, the nurse at Faith and Prayers insisted on doing an ultrasound to confirm that I was pregnant," Rylee told them, looking up at the wood panels that hugged the office walls. "Pregnancy tests can be wrong."

One of the attorneys cleared his throat, looking at the woman standing near the fireplace. She shook her head in denial.

"And that's where they found the heartbeat, right?" the unnamed woman prompted.

Rylee nodded.

"What happened next?" the woman gently coaxed.

"They insisted that I talk to a social worker, who wouldn't let me leave," Rylee complained. "She kept telling me she needed to confirm what my plans were."

"Wait," one of the attorneys interjected. "Wouldn't let you leave? Were you locked in the exam room or somehow restrained?"

"No," Rylee admitted. "I was told that I wasn't allowed to leave until I answered all of her questions."

"What questions?"

"Name, address, birthday, marital status," Rylee told them, that feeling of being trapped closing in on her again. "I told her I didn't believe that test was accurate. There was no way I could be pregnant, and their repeated insistence that I was didn't help."

The attorney nodded encouragingly. "And then?" he asked, gently.

Rylee looked down at her hands. Her fingers were tightly clenched around her knees. "She insisted on getting me help. For what, I don't know. After that, they called the police," she told him. "They kept pushing me to tell them if I was married and what my plans were for my baby. And I kept telling them that I just wanted to go home!"

"So, just to confirm, the social worker implied that you couldn't leave until you'd answered all of her questions and agreed to some sort of assistance." He tsked. "A delay tactic, rather than outright confinement. Just skirting the law."

"You mean I could have just left?" Rylee demanded, feeling a deep flush warm her cheeks.

"Yes," she was told. "If the center had physically restrained you or locked you in a room, we might have been able to make a legal case for unlawful detention. However, because you could have left the building at any time, we don't have a basis to directly sue either Faith and Prayers or the doctor."

Rylee threw back her head, closing her eyes against sudden tears. "So, if I'd have just pushed my way past her and left, we wouldn't be here right now," she whispered.

"Not necessarily," the other attorney reassured her. "They did detect a fetal heartbeat and, if there was reasonable concern that you might seek an out-of-state abortion, they could have notified the authorities and you may have still been taken into custody."

"I didn't say anything about an abortion," Rylee protested. "I just couldn't believe that I was pregnant!"

"Interesting," the attorney muttered. "And you didn't indicate that you wanted an abortion to the police officers who took you into custody or anyone at the detention center?"

"No!" Rylee exclaimed. "I didn't know what to think! I just wanted to go home!"

Rylee's mom put her arm around her, pulling her close for a hug. Rylee broke down, sobbing as she clung to her mother in frustration. All of this could have been avoided if she'd just left!

After a long moment, Rylee pulled away. Chloe grabbed the box of tissues off of the end table and offered it to her. Rylee dabbed her eyes and blew her nose, then tucked the tissue into a side pocket.

Her dad cleared his throat. "Let's table that for now," he said, drumming the fingers of his left hand idly against his desk. "The Governor has agreed that the best course of action is for DHS to restrict access to the records of any woman detained under Act 292 due to privacy concerns," he told them. "It will take a few days, but they will only be accessible through a Freedom of Information Act request."

The woman nodded. "That will help," she told them. "By the way, Rylee, I'm Samantha Brown. I've been retained as your strategic crisis manager to help guide your family through this."

"Oh."

"I know that the questions we're asking can be . . . uncomfortable," she said. "But the information you provide will help me create a framework to address the situation. If the media gets a hold of this, they might blow it completely out of proportion, given the current political climate."

She waited until Rylee nodded. "Let's start with some basics," she said. "When did you and Sam start dating?"

Even though Rylee had expected the question, she couldn't help but blush. "Last fall," she admitted.

Rylee's mom gasped. "What? I thought you started dating in January!" she exclaimed.

"We weren't a couple until then, Mom," she replied. "Sam was coming home almost every weekend. We kept bumping into each other at random community events and robotics meetings. It just seemed to happen!"

Mom pursed her lips, huffing a breath out of her nose in frustration. "I see."

Brown picked up her iPad from the coffee table and used the stylus to take notes. "So, this started with you going out with a group of friends autumn of 2027, and you started to officially date in January 2028."

"That's right," she responded, hesitantly. *Please don't ask me when we started having sex*, she thought. *Not in front of Mom and Dad!*

"Next question: according to your medical records, you were on birth control pills. These were prescribed due to a diagnosis of polycystic ovary syndrome. Your doctor also suspected fibroids, as this runs in your family." She paused and looked up. "When did you stop taking them?" she asked.

Rylee gaped at her, feeling her mom stir next to her. "I'm sorry; why do you need to know this?" she demanded.

"That isn't true!" her mom hissed. She turned to Rylee in confusion. "Is it?"

Chloe snorted, looking down at her coffee mug.

"The doctor's notes from DHS state that 'the patient admitted to voluntarily stop taking birth control pills in the weeks leading up to her viable pregnancy'," Brown read to them. "If your conception date was around the middle of July, then I would have to assume that you stopped taking them sometime in the spring." She paused to look at Rylee. "Is that a correct statement?"

Rylee covered her eyes with one hand. "I don't remember," she told them. "Sometime in late spring, I think."

"That makes sense," Brown replied. "Thank you."

"I still don't understand why you need to know this," Rylee whined, dropping her hand to glare at the woman.

Brown smiled. "Just trying to establish a timeline," she told her. "As I understand it from your parents, you and Sam broke up sometime in March and picked up again in May. Do I have that right?"

"I think so," Rylee moaned. *This was so embarrassing*, she thought.

Brown looked up from the note she was making. "Why did you break up?" she asked.

"He cheated on me," Rylee told her in a flat tone, scooping up her bottle of water and slowly unscrewing the top. "I found out when some . . . girl . . . answered his phone for him while he was supposed to be attending an out-of-state tennis match."

He never trusted me with his phone, she thought bitterly, taking a quick sip of water. It explained so much. Why he had stopped coming home on the weekends. Why he had ghosted her for days at a time. The pictures he'd been tagged in on random stranger's social media posts.

"When he came home at the end of the semester, did he apologize or offer any explanation as to how she got access to his phone?" Brown asked.

"Not really," Rylee confirmed, slowly screwing the lid back on her water bottle. "He told me she was a teammate. She grabbed his phone by accident."

Brown nodded, her eyes narrowing for a moment. "And you believed him, right?"

"Yes." What else was there to say?

"Right," Brown said. "So, you started going out again. Were you exclusive during that time?"

Rylee blushed, putting the bottle back on the floor. "I guess that's what you'd call it," she admitted. "I wasn't seeing anyone else. I didn't think that Sam was, either."

Brown moved in front of the fireplace and made eye contact with Rylee's dad. "There are a few ways we can spin this, sir," she told him.

Her dad nodded. "What are your thoughts?"

"The easiest story is that Sam and Rylee are a committed couple," Brown told him. "They'd planned to get married and move out east after Sam graduated so that Rylee could continue attending Wellesley. They'd done the normal thing. Looked at engagement rings. Talked about how to let friends and family know about their relationship. The point is that having a child while they are still in college doesn't change anything."

She shrugged. "They will just have to move up their wedding day. Rylee will have to either transfer to Northwestern so that their young family stays together or delay college until after Sam graduates so that they can move to Massachusetts."

Rylee shook her head in furious denial. "I'm not delaying college," she exclaimed, furious at the idea. "If anything, Sam should transfer to a college near Wellesley!"

Brown looked at Rylee. "That's also a possibility," she allowed. "This scenario does require Sam's buy-in, though."

Rylee looked at her father. He was staring off into space, a slight frown accentuating the lines around his blue eyes as he considered the idea.

Oh, my God, Rylee thought, horrified at the idea. He's actually considering the idea!

Her mom finally broke the silence. "Please don't do this," she quietly told Rylee's dad. "Now is not the time to even think about a wedding."

"Thanks, Mom," Rylee breathed. "I don't want to marry Sam."

Her dad closely looked at Rylee, that frown smoothing out as he studied her. "Agreed," he finally said.

"Besides," Rylee added, looking first at Brown and then back to her dad, "Sam and I broke up."

"Ah!" Brown breathed. "And this was public knowledge?" she asked.

Rylee shook her head in confusion. "It's not like we sent out announcements or anything," she said. "I told a few friends. Sam probably told a few friends. I stopped going to most of the community events." Especially the Tietjen Beach parties. "People probably noticed, though."

"Got it," Brown told her with a quick nod. She looked mildly disappointed. "Our next option is a bit more complicated." She paused, looking down at the carpet for a long moment. "We say nothing for now."

Her mom leaned forward. "Our family's reputation is at stake," she said, outrage dripping from her voice. "How does that help?"

Rylee leaned away, grabbing her water bottle from the floor again. Of course. It always came back to the family's reputation. "We set the standard for our community," she muttered as she unscrewed the bottle top and took a sip of water.

Brown forced a smile as she looked at Rylee's mom. "We need to put some distance between Rylee's detention and her pregnancy," she told her. "The less these events are publicly linked, the more likely her detention is to fade away."

"Only up to a point," one of the attorneys reminded them. "Rylee will still have to attend the WIFE program courses. Someone will notice."

"That program is open to the public," Brown replied. "Not just Act 292 detainees. If someone asks, we can put it out there that Rylee felt the program would help her as she transitioned to becoming a mom."

Rylee's dad nodded. "What do we need to do?" he asked. "Obviously, Rylee will need to stay close to home and won't be able to travel for the Canton Home Mission."

"That, plus wearing clothes that don't call attention to either the monitor or her pregnancy," Brown told them.

She turned to Rylee. "Assume that any conversations you have in public may become public knowledge," she said. "Do not confirm or deny anything about the pregnancy outside of a preselected list. Don't talk about your relationship with Sam or being taken into custody. That sort of thing."

Her mom sighed and started peppering the crisis manager and attorneys for more details. She reminded them that they had no control over what Sam did or how his family was dealing with the situation. For all they knew, Wendy Maxwell had already announced Rylee's pregnancy to the world, and it was inevitable that there would be a swarm of paparazzi camping outside of their front gates.

Rylee cupped the bottle of water between her hands, only half-listening to the conversation around her. No one cared about how she felt about any of this. She was just another cog in the Williams Family wheel.

She finally stood up and got her dad's attention. "I haven't eaten much for a few days," she told him. "I'm going to grab some lunch."

Chloe stood. "I'm hungry, too," she said. "I'll come with you." Their dad nodded, more focused on the conversation around them.

Rylee fled down the hallway. Chloe trailed after her, her slower pace giving Rylee just enough room to have the illusion of privacy.

Unbelievable, she thought as she stomped her way past the entrance hall, the sound of her steps muffled by the long area rug that covered the granite tiles. Marry Sam? He had abandoned her at Doctors Park and had refused to even listen to what was going on. No fucking way in hell was she going to marry that asshole!

She cut left to the back entrance of the kitchen. She paused for a moment, letting her eyes adjust as the sunlight streaming through the windows hit her face. "Jeeves, close the blinds in the kitchen," she said.

"Okay," the house virtual assistant responded. The cellular blinds slowly unfolded, transforming the glare into a more manageable level.

Rylee walked across the room, ignoring the cheery bowl of fruit that sat on the island as if eagerly awaiting its photoshoot. The sink gleamed with the same fingerprint-free stainless-steel sheen as the Bosch appliances. It didn't so much beckon friends and family to enjoy the food created in this space. It was simply a testament to how much perfection money could buy.

She stopped at the fridge, looking behind her. "Sandwich?" she asked Chloe.

"Sure," Chloe responded. She opened a cabinet and grabbed a few plates. "What kind of bread?" she asked.

Rylee studied the contents of the lunch meat drawer. "We've got roast beef, some ham, and something that resembles chicken," she told her, wrinkling her nose. "I'd go with whole wheat or sourdough." She pulled the packages out of the drawer, then grabbed a few different sliced cheeses to lie on the counter behind her.

Chloe pulled two loaves out of the bread box. "Got it," she said.

"Mayo, mustard, or just some butter?" Rylee asked.

"Just grab the mayo," Chloe told her. "That goes with everything." She moved to the other side of the island and started setting up places for them to eat.

Rylee reached over and grabbed her plate. Then she opened up the bag with sourdough bread, pausing long enough to grab a whiff of overly fermented dough before pushing it away. "That's disgusting," she breathed.

Chloe smiled. "Yeah, I remember those days," she told Rylee. "Either something in the house smelled like it had died or was about to. And don't get me started on cravings!" she added with a laugh. "You always hear about the whole 'pickles and ice cream' trope, but no one ever talks about brownies and ham salad!"

Rylee snorted. "Brownies and ham salad?" she asked, drolly.

Chloe nodded. "Some days, all I could choke down was that ham salad from Brew City Bites. I always followed it up with some of their frosted brownies. A simple reward for managing to keep it all down."

Rylee grabbed the whole wheat bread. She held her breath as she grabbed two slices and placed them on her plate. Then, she clipped the bag shut and took a careful sniff. Smelled okay. Then, she opened the ham, and added a few slices to the bread, along with a slice of Swiss cheese and a slight dab of mayonnaise. She sliced the sandwich on the diagonal and placed the plate on the placemat next to Chloe.

Chloe grabbed the meats and cheeses and took them back to the fridge. She pulled out a bowl of fruit salad and a container of vegetable slices. "Interested?" she asked.

Rylee shook her head. "Let me see how the sandwich does."

Chloe nodded and brought the fruit salad back with her. She gave herself a few heaping spoonfuls and dug in.

Rylee looked down at her plate. Her stomach rumbled, but she resisted picking the sandwich up for a moment. It seemed so ordinary. So normal. For a moment, she wanted to pretend that this was just another Monday and her weekend detention was just a nightmare she could walk away from.

"Hey," Chloe said, gently nudging her with her elbow. "It's going to be okay. Honest."

Rylee picked up her sandwich, shaking her head sadly. "How so?" she asked, then took a tentative bite. The tender meat had a slightly salty undertone that seemed to bring out the mild nuttiness of the cheese. She shook her head in amazement. It might be her hunger, but this sandwich was amazing!

"Look, Mom and Dad mean well, but they don't understand, do they?" Chloe said, authoritatively. "Remember how they wanted me to travel to Switzerland to get a second opinion on IVF after we'd found a great doctor in the Twin Cities? Switzerland, for heaven's sake!"

Rylee nodded. "I remember," she said, then took another bite.

"My point is that your life is going to change in the next few months," Chloe told her. "Mom is going to overload you with random advice about health, nutrition, and exercise. She means well, but most of what she's going to force on you is outdated and useless."

Again, with the lectures, Rylee thought as she got up to grab the milk out of the fridge and two glasses from a nearby cabinet. *Chloe always acts like she knows everything about, well, everything!* she thought. Just once, it would be nice if she could just be her sister instead of a judgmental Ashley clone.

"My best advice is to listen to your body and ignore the rest," Chloe told her. She thought for a moment. "That monitor means that you're going to need to update your wardrobe sooner rather than later," she told Rylee. "Focus on pants with wider pant legs, and no dresses until you're ready for people to see the baby." She paused to take another bite of her sandwich, rapidly chewed, and swallowed. "I'd also recommend that you start shopping now so that you can have a nice mix of colors and fabrics. My skin got very sensitive during my last trimester and I had a difficult time finding anything that didn't make me itch."

Rylee continued eating, only half listening. She vividly remembered Chloe's complaints about how her skin felt and how it was unfair that she couldn't enjoy her pregnancy because of how painful the itching had been—that and how her feet and ankles were so swollen in the last few months.

"One thing that helped me was to get a personal spa trainer that specialized in helping pregnant clients," Chloe told her.

"A personal trainer?" Rylee asked. "Why? I go to the spa regularly."

"When I was pregnant, they recommended a daily exercise regime and a weekly massage that *really* helped with my lower back pain," Chloe told her.

Rylee snorted. Just because Chloe had had a difficult pregnancy didn't mean that she would. She put her sandwich down. Her pregnancy. No matter how many times someone said that word, it just didn't seem real to her.

"Hey," Chloe said, gently nudging her with an elbow. "You'll thank me later. Trust me on this!"

"Okay, Chloe," Rylee reluctantly replied. "I'll make an appointment for next week. I promise."

"Good," Chloe said. "Last piece of advice: pick an obstetrician that you can trust. Not that the family doctor can't give you a good referral," she hastily added. "If you'd like, I can give you the number of my doctor. Dr. Zastrow is very knowledgeable, answers every question no matter how silly you think it is, and his staff is top-notch."

Rylee picked up their plates and headed for the dishwasher. "I'd like that," she said as she dumped the last of her sandwich. "Thanks."

Chloe picked up her phone and sent a text with the doctor's contact information. Rylee's phone chirped an alert. Rylee grabbed her phone and moved the phone number into her contacts, then put the phone back in her pocket.

"Glad to help," Chloe told her. She came over and hugged Rylee, rubbing at her back briefly before pulling away. "I have to get going," she told Rylee. "I left a bottle for the nanny, but I have a feeling Patrick's going to be fussy unless I'm there to nurse him myself."

"I'm sure," Rylee told her, smiling back at Chloe. Patrick might be ten months old and already eating bite-sized finger foods, but he still insisted on nursing the old-fashioned way.

"I'm going to say goodbye to Mom and Dad, then head home," Chloe told her. "Call me if you need anything!"

"I will," Rylee assured her. Then, she put their dishes in the dishwasher and wiped up the random crumbs from the granite countertop.

Truth be told, she was relieved Chloe was being so nice to her about this pregnancy. Chloe had struggled with fertility treatments for several years, including three rounds of IVF before getting pregnant with Patrick. She felt a twinge of guilt. It didn't seem fair that she'd had to go through all of that.

She headed down the hallway and went up the stairs to her room. Time to sort through her clothes to find out what would work with the ankle monitor and what could be packed away for now. Plus, maybe Chloe was right and some spa time would help!

Chapter Four

Rylee nervously waited in the church narthex. She focused more on keeping her breakfast down and less on the fact that her parents were there. Her mom had insisted Rylee seek 'spiritual counseling' from Pastor Chapman because, as she'd put it, Rylee's absence on the upcoming Home Mission would drive the rumor mill into overdrive. The family needed counseling and support so they could find a path with the congregation.

The last week had been rather surreal. Both of her parents had pointedly ignored her pregnancy. The conversation focused mostly on the mundane: the upcoming school board election, proposed changes to the Wisconsin Right to Work laws that might incentivize the company to set up a second solar panel plant in Sun Prairie, and even updates to the family social calendar.

Sometimes her pregnancy came up in the strangest conversations. Once, Ashley started pulling items out of the refrigerator at random and insisted that Rylee smell everything on the counter so she could get rid of anything that might be contributing to Rylee's nausea. A few days later, her dad ordered HR to conduct a comprehensive review of all pregnancy-related policies and insurance coverage to ensure that they were 'family-friendly.'

Even worship service was surreal. It was as if the Maxwell family had staked out the north side of the church sanctuary before worship began, forcing the Williams clan to sit in the south side pews. Wendy Maxwell had planted herself in the middle of the first row and spent the entire service glaring in their direction. In response, Mom had gathered her closest friends and allies around them, most of whom were blissfully unaware of the tension.

After an incredibly long wait, Paster Chapman walked down the long hallway and into the narthex. "Hello, Rylee," he said. "I believe we have an appointment this morning."

Her mom stood up, hastily grabbing Rylee's hand to pull her forward. "Yes, Pastor," she said. "We do."

The receptionist looked up from her computer, a bemused look on her face. Dad shot her a look and the older woman turned away and began sorting a pile of mail on the back counter.

Paster Chapman smiled. "Sorry, Ashley," he replied. "My calendar says the appointment is with Rylee, not the entire family." He looked at Rylee, who shrugged her hand away.

Her dad stood and tucked her mom's hand into his elbow. "That's right, Pastor," he quietly replied, then looked at her mom. "Rylee's appointment is for an hour," he told her. "Why don't we get some coffee and pick her up when she's done talking to Pastor Chapman?"

Her mom's lips thinned in frustration. After a moment, she looked up at him. "That's fine," she said with a sigh.

Without another word, Pastor Chapman beckoned Rylee to follow him down the hallway to his office. As they passed the offices on the left side of the hallway, she felt as if time had stopped. Staffers paused what they were doing and looked up as they passed by. Even the volunteers who were pulling autumn decorations from the storage room stopped to look at her.

He stopped and gestured Rylee into his office. She slowly walked into the small room, looking from the floor-to-ceiling bookcase that covered one wall to the couch and the contemporary wingback chair next to the windows. Soft light filtered through the blinds, casting a warm glow on the wooden furniture.

"Why don't you have a seat," Pastor Chapman told her. "Can I get you anything? Maybe a bottle of water?"

Rylee sank onto the two-seat couch, one hand brushing against the soft dark blue fabric. She shook her head. "No, thank you."

Pastor Chapman nodded as he took a seat. "How can I help, Rylee? From the very brief conversation I had with your father, it sounded rather urgent."

Rylee ducked her head. Her hands protectively moved to cover her stomach as she tried to gulp back tears. One escaped, slowly rolling down her cheek. "I don't know if you can, Pastor," she whispered. More tears followed the first until they dripped into her blouse.

The pastor grabbed the box of tissues on the side table between them and offered it to her. She blindly grabbed a few and wiped at her face.

"Why don't you start at the beginning," he gently encouraged her. "This is a safe space. Nothing you tell me will leave this room."

Rylee gulped back a giggle. *Start at the beginning*, she thought. *If only it was that easy!* She coughed, then blew her nose. She pushed the rumpled tissue into a pocket.

"I don't know how to say this, Pastor," she slowly said, unable to look at him. "I'm—pregnant!" She covered her face with her hands, unable to stop the sobs from coming out. It just didn't feel real.

"Is it Sam's?" Pastor Chapman gently asked.

Rylee nodded. That paralyzing fear hit all at once, threatening to suffocate her. Just the idea of how the close-knit fellowship would react when they found out she was pregnant triggered a fresh wave of nausea.

She shifted in her seat, and that was enough to force the tracker to rub against her ankle. She glanced down, convinced it was peeking out from beneath the retro bell-bottom jeans she'd picked out today and that was it.

Her throat ached as she started to wail, her body convulsing. She felt the pastor move to sit next to her on the couch. He reached for one hand and then the other, holding them as he murmured sympathetic nothings.

She pulled her hand away and wiped distractedly at her face. Pastor Chapman offered her more tissues, then got up and grabbed a bottle of water from the small refrigerator tucked at the bottom of the bookcase. He opened it and passed it to Rylee before sitting back down on the chair.

Rylee took a sip, then another. The cool water helped soothe her sore throat. She looked up at the pastor, mortified by her emotional outburst. He gestured to the side table, and she put the bottle down. He waited patiently for her to continue.

"I honestly don't know what happened," she told him. "My doctor told me I wouldn't be able to get pregnant without help, like Chloe. Like my mom." She gulped. "This shouldn't be possible!"

Pastor Chapman took a deep breath, then let it out slowly. "I understand this must be incredibly difficult for you and Sam. Can I ask why you came here without him?"

Rylee swallowed, slowly shrugging one shoulder as more tears fell. She didn't want to admit that she wasn't on speaking terms with Sam right now.

"It's okay," he told her. "Let's talk about how you feel about this pregnancy." He paused, searching her face for a moment. "Rylee, there is no judgment here. All of us are imperfect and God's grace is infinite."

Rylee nodded, wiping away more tears. Pastor Chapman moved a small waste can from one side of his chair to the other for Rylee to dispose of the tissues.

"I just don't know what to do," she whispered. "I went to a crisis center to confirm if I was pregnant. They called the police, and I was detained for several days because they thought that I might be a danger to the baby . . . " Her voice trailed off.

"Ah," he said. "I'd heard that the law had been expanded to protect the unborn from the threat of abortion."

Rylee put up a hand in protest, more tears streaming down her face. "I never said I wanted an abortion," she protested. "I was just shocked they insisted that I *could be* pregnant and I still don't know why they took me into custody!"

"It's okay, Rylee," he told her. "Most of us jump to that conclusion when we hear about an unexpected pregnancy."

She nodded rapidly. "I am so stupid," she told him. "I stopped taking my birth control pills because that stupid doctor told me I couldn't get pregnant. That when I was ready to start a family, they'd be able to give me some drug to make my ovaries work, just like Chloe!" She whispered the last part, that guilty feeling creeping back in. Chloe had gone through so much to have Patrick. It seemed like a cruel joke for her to get pregnant without medical intervention.

Pastor Chapman sat back, a sad smile on his face. "Rylee, it sounds like you might be feeling just a bit guilty about this pregnancy," he told her. "Feelings are neither right nor wrong. They simply *are*. And sometimes what we feel in the moment can mask our deeper emotions."

Deeper emotions? She shook her head. "I don't understand."

"We all make mistakes that we wish we could change," he told her. "The guilt you're feeling about Chloe and this pregnancy isn't going to resolve without a lot of work and prayer."

Rylee nodded.

"Based on my limited understanding of the current law, Sam would have been notified about your pregnancy," he mused. "Is that correct?"

Rylee looked down. "We had to appear at Family Court," she admitted. "The baby was assigned a guardian ad litem and we have to take mandatory parenting classes."

"Even if you decide to give the baby up for adoption?" he gently asked. "That is a viable option."

Rylee turned away, unable to find the words she felt to protest. She was going to Wellesley next year, and then probably her MBA after that. Move to Manhattan. Lean in, maybe start a company of her own. Become her own woman, finally. And it was all at risk because of a tiny embryo that had a heartbeat fluttering inside of her like a firefly stuck inside a glass jar.

"I'm not sure that I'm ready to become a mom," she told him. "But at the same time, the idea of not keeping this baby . . ."

"I know this is a big decision, Rylee," Pastor told her in a reassuring voice. "God loves you and His grace is there for all of us. Sometimes an unexpected stumble in life can lead to a surprise blessing."

Blessing? "What do you mean, Pastor?" she asked.

"This child is a gift from God," he told her. "It may not feel that way right now, but keep in mind that God's love—and wisdom—is unchanging." He smiled. "'And we know that in all things God works for the good of those who love Him.'"

Rylee looked down at the tissues crumpled in her hands, then up. "A gift? From God?" she asked.

"Yes," Pastor Chapman told her. "This may be an opportunity for you to grow in a way you didn't expect. To experience God's plan for you in ways that you might never have imagined otherwise."

"Oh," Rylee breathed, suddenly confused. This pregnancy felt more like a punishment than a blessing.

Pastor Chapman sat back in the chair. "It's something to consider, at any rate," he told her with a soft smile.

Rylee placed the crumpled tissues into the waste can, then carefully brushed her hair back away from her face. She felt something. A glimmer of hope, maybe? "Thank you," she murmured.

"I'm happy to meet with both you and Sam to discuss this further," he told her, then held up a hand to still her protest. "Or, we could keep it between us, if you'd prefer. The important thing is that you take some time to explore this opportunity, Rylee. You need to be open to whatever God has in store for you."

She nodded. She stretched her neck to the left and then the right, feeling the muscles begin to unknot. *Maybe it was going to be okay,* she thought.

The house was quiet. Dad had taken Chloe with him to Madison for a few days to meet with ranking members of the state legislature's economic development committee. Mom had just left for the Janssen Legacy of Hope Foundation monthly board meeting. The housekeeper wasn't due to arrive until after lunch. A perfect time to get organized.

Rylee quickly made her way to the family library and spread the packet of information that the attorneys had given her about the Wisconsin Individual Family Education program across the drafting table. It was a combination of printouts from the program website, random brochures from different nonprofits offering competing classes that met program criteria, and, of course, a simple one-page summary of the Court's expectations on completion.

Her phone rang. "Kathryn McMillan," it announced. Rylee stared at the phone for a moment, then put it on speakerphone. Might as well get it over with.

"Hey, Kathryn," she said.

There was a pause. "Hey, Rylee," Kathryn said, sounding cautious and maybe a bit sad. "I haven't heard from you for a while, so I'm just checking in."

Rylee took a sip of cappuccino and pushed the mug aside as she stared at the colorful mess of paperwork.

"I know," Rylee responded. "Life has been, well . . . "

"Yeah," Kathryn breathed. "I don't know how to ask, but . . . are you okay?"

Rylee shut her eyes for a moment. *Am I okay?* she thought, feeling overwhelmed by competing emotions. *Maybe.*

The silence stretched between them. "I think so," she finally allowed.

"My brother told me he didn't see you at last week's youth group meeting," Kathryn told her. "I was getting worried. You didn't respond to my text, so I let it be. You know, to give you a bit of space to try and figure things out."

Rylee nodded. "I'm okay," she told her. "Yeah, I'm still wicked pissed that you forced me to take that damn pregnancy test, but what happened isn't your fault."

"What are you talking about?" Kathryn demanded. "What happened? The unspoken question lay between them: did you go to Illinois and get it taken care of?

Rylee sighed. "It's complicated," she told her. "Very complicated." She could feel the tears starting again as she struggled to find the words.

"Is it Sam?" Kathryn breathed. "Do you want me to come over?"

Rylee sniffled, then wiped her face with both hands as she tried to calm down. "It wasn't Sam," she admitted. "Apparently, the state of Wisconsin takes pregnant women into custody if someone suspects that they are going to get an abortion."

Kathryn gasped. "You were arrested?"

"Detained," Rylee corrected. "The baby was declared a ward of the state, and Sam and I have to attend some program for new parents."

"I don't understand," Kathryn told her. "You were detained and you have to learn how to be parents? Those don't go together!"

"Hang on a sec," she told Kathryn. "Lemme grab something our attorney gave me on this."

She sorted through the pile until she found the one-pager. The Wisconsin Individual Family Education program's tagline seemed simple enough: Supporting new parents and building strong families. But the summary told a different story.

"Okay," she said. "Here's what I have: 'The Unborn Child Protection Act, also known as Act 292, was signed into law by Governor Tommy Thompson in 1998. It was designed to protect unborn children from drug and alcohol addiction due to an expectant mother's habitual lack of self-control.'"

"Lack of self-control?" Kathryn said with a slight laugh. "I don't remember addiction being described that way in Health Ed class!"

"I know!" Rylee replied. "Addiction is a disease, not something you can just stop doing. There's more, though. 'Following the changes to the state of Wisconsin's constitution that confer citizenship at an unborn child's first heartbeat, the Act was amended to include protection from domestic violence and mental health issues that might lead the expectant mother to seek an abortion.'"

Rylee sat back, dropping the sheet back to the table in disgust.

"Wow," Kathryn breathed. "Of course, they linked mental health to abortion," she said, her voice dripping with sarcasm. "All women desperately want to be a mom. And any woman who doesn't have that as her absolute life goal must be insane, right?!"

Rylee sighed. "Obviously," she replied. "I mean, yeah, I want to have a family someday. Just not now."

"Tell me everything," Kathryn demanded. "You got detained, and then what?"

Rylee gave her the short version: how the Faith and Prayers Pregnancy Crisis Center had called the police. About how she'd been forced to take yet another pregnancy test and an incredibly dehumanizing transvaginal ultrasound by the creepiest man she'd ever met. The issues her attorney had raised. The crisis manager. The Wisconsin Individual Family Education program.

"Dang," Kathryn said as she finally wound down. "I'm so sorry!"

"Not your fault," Rylee reassured her, trying to swallow that lingering feeling of bitterness. Kathryn may have pushed her to take a pregnancy test, but there was no way of knowing that all of this would happen. She turned over the sheet for a summary of the required parenting courses. "I'm looking over the courses we need to take," she told her. "Looks like the first trimester has the most classes." She quickly counted them. "Eight in the first trimester, four in the second, and only three for the third trimester."

"Is all of that geared toward first-time parents?" Kathryn asked. "Seems like a lot."

"I guess," Rylee replied. She picked up another sheet of paper. "Looks like there are several optional courses, too. Most of these are online." She scanned the list. "Emotional well-being during pregnancy, navigating childcare options, and something called baby-wearing and bonding." At the bottom of the page, there was a QR code that pointed to additional courses offered by various Christian, Muslim, Hindu, Jewish, Native American, and Pagan organizations.

"Baby-wearing?" Kathryn asked with a laugh. "How do you *wear* a baby?"

Rylee took another sip of her cappuccino. "I have no idea," she admitted. "One of those baby harness thingies, maybe?" She vaguely remembered that Chloe got one at her baby shower but never used it.

"Listen, Kathryn, I need to focus here," she said, gently rubbing at the spot near her ankle that was chafing because her sock had fallen down. "Can we talk later this week, maybe?"

"Sure," Kathryn replied, sounding relieved. "Maybe we could grab some coffee or something?"

"Sounds good," Rylee said. "Talk to you later."

Okay, time to get organized, she thought as she pushed the phone away. She quickly sorted the paperwork into first-, second-, and third-trimester courses. Next, she sorted the mandatory courses from those that were optional. She glanced at the documents and grabbed the step-by-step program overview to review.

Step one, she decided, was to make an appointment with the social worker. She got up and grabbed her iPad from the sideboard charger. *Simple enough,* she thought as she loaded the browser. Finding the website was easy enough. Now, she just needed to create an account.

Wait. The site required the case number. Rylee grabbed the one-pager and scanned for it. Nothing. She turned to the paperwork piled in the middle of the table. The official court filing. It had to be around here someplace!

Ah! She found it. Case number 2028FA50403-23912. She quickly typed in her name, home address, birth date, and case number. She carefully read the privacy policy and terms and conditions before clicking on the acceptance button.

The welcome page reminded her of a generic learning site. It was kinda glitzy, with a background picture of colorful building blocks on the floor of a random nursery. She studied the page for a moment. There were three portals, one for each trimester. The second and third trimesters were grayed out. The navigation menu allowed her to update her profile, browse available courses, and track her progress through the required program. There was also a link to the mentoring program, links to additional community resources, and a chatbot.

There was even a button for linking her account to Sam's, so they could attend in-person courses together. She clicked on the link. He didn't have one. Easy enough to fix so she quickly set up an account for Sam, still amazed it didn't have the usual two-step verification set up. It automatically sent the login information along with the password that she'd created to his email address. *Cool*, she thought. *One less thing to have to worry about.*

She paused to make sure she hadn't missed anything, then logged off the site. She didn't want to sign them up for courses or meet with the social worker until she had a chance to talk to Sam. She made a mental note to call him this evening. Maybe things had settled down at his house.

In the meantime, she still needed to make that appointment with Dr. Zastrow. Hopefully, he was still accepting new patients.

Rylee set aside her journal with a sigh. Time to call Sam. Between her mom lecturing her about eating better for the baby's sake, sorting through the program requirements to create a decent schedule, and navigating the new patient intake process with Dr. Zastrow's office, she was exhausted.

Sam answered his phone on the third ring. "Yeah?" he demanded, angry as he huffed out of breath.

Rylee sniffed, struggling to hold back sudden tears. Of course, he was angry at her. He blamed her for getting pregnant. "Is now a good time?" she finally asked.

"Sure," he panted. "What's up?" She could hear the breeze battering his earbuds.

"I've been going through the program information online and there's a lot of things that will need to be scheduled," she told him. "I created a calendar to help us keep track of this. I can share it with you if you'd like . . . " she let her voice trail off, uncertain. Sam had his own way of doing things. It involved covering the wall with a rainbow of color-coded sticky notes, but it worked for him. Mostly. She still remembered finding a bunch of them littering his carpet, his desk, and the window.

"What's on the list?" he asked, sounding uninterested.

"We need to meet with a program social worker," she told him. "And sign up for the parenting classes." She considered reminding him that she'd signed them up for the WIFE account, but he should have already seen the email. "I mean, most of them are online and only take a few hours, but it looks like the in-person classes can be combined in a single day for each trimester or broken up into four-hour classes. We need to get these locked in so we can plan other things around them."

"Like my regular classes?" he asked sarcastically.

"That, and medical appointments," she responded, sharply reminding him of the reason for what was happening. "I made my first appointment with the doctor."

"Oh." That took the wind out of his sails. "When is it?" he asked, curious.

"September 12th," Rylee told him. She heard him mutter under his breath. "It's the earliest I could get in," she said defensively. "The nurse said there's a lot of paperwork that we'll have to complete online before we go. Because of the courts, you know."

Sam sighed. "What kind of paperwork?" he asked.

"I don't know," Rylee admitted. "She was kinda vague on the phone. Probably medical information from both of us. I know that I'll need to have blood work done and probably another ultrasound."

"Geez," Sam said. "How much do they need to do to make sure you're really pregnant?"

That was it. She couldn't hold the tears back any longer. "I don't know, Sam!" she sobbed. "I'm just not ready for this!"

"Calm down," he demanded, irritated. "Look, I've been thinking. Maybe we can have someone pop over the border and pick up some of those pills the judge was talking about?"

What? She stared out the window, appalled he was suggesting that she have an abortion. "I don't know, Sam," she finally replied, wiping at her face with one hand. "My lawyer told me if I have a miscarriage, we could face premeditated murder charges."

"But it's just a cluster of cells that can't even look human at this point," Sam fumed at her. "How could they charge us with murder?"

A sudden wave of dizziness washed over her and she fumbled to find a pillow to hold on to. "You heard the judge," she wailed at him. "She said that if I miscarry, there would be a criminal investigation. I even have a list of stuff I'm not allowed to take without supervision. Like herbs I've never even heard of and even stuff like acetaminophen!"

"That's insane!" Sam yelled. His voice was tinged with outrage. "What if you have a headache?"

"I know!" Rylee whimpered. "I can't believe this is really happening!" She clutched the pillow to her chest, clinging to the phone with her other hand as she struggled to catch her breath.

"Rylee, it's going to be okay," he finally told her. "See if you can get a friend of yours to call one of those clinics just over the border. Maybe all they need is for someone to drop off something from the doctor, confirming that you're pregnant." She found herself focusing on that last bit. As if it would be easy to convince anyone they knew to risk being charged as an accessory to murder.

"That won't work, Sam," she whimpered. "They're watching our every move. Maybe even listening to our phone calls."

"The pills won't show up in your bloodwork, so there's no way they can charge us with something if we're careful," he told her in a gentle voice. It reminded her of when he was in the mood for sex.

Rylee pulled the phone away to blow her nose. She wanted to tell him about the conversation she'd had with Pastor Chapman but knew Sam would just keep pushing until she pushed back. "I'm not taking any more pills, Sam," she whispered. "I gotta go. My mom's calling me."

"Okay," Sam bit off, angrily. "Talk to you later."

Rylee dropped her phone on the floor, whimpering as she fell back against her bed. How could this baby be a gift from God?

Chapter Five

Rylee laid back against the exam bed. A sharp feeling of déjà vu overwhelmed her, even though it had been almost three weeks since she'd been to a doctor's office. She glanced at Sam, who sullenly hunched over his phone as he ignored her.

Rylee sighed. Of course, he was ignoring her.

The nurse entered the room. She smiled brightly at Sam, who glanced up with a scowl before looking away, then at Rylee. "Let's take a look at your baby," she said, moving across the small room to the ultrasound cart.

Instead of pulling out that white plastic wand, the nurse picked up the bottle of goop and carefully squirted a small amount of warm gel across Rylee's belly. Then, she placed the curved transducer firmly against her skin and began to move it, pushing the gel around almost at random.

After a long moment, she paused. "And there's the baby," the nurse told them cheerfully. Rylee looked over, craning to see, vaguely aware that Sam was leaning forward as well. "That's the gestational sac and if you look closely, there's where the baby is! Nine weeks strong."

Rylee took a deep breath. "It's so tiny," she whispered to herself. Were nine-week-old embryos supposed to be that small?

She glanced over at Sam. He was glaring at the screen as if the baby was a lie.

"If you look over here, you can see the heartbeat," the nurse said, slightly moving the transducer. Rylee pushed up on one elbow, trying to see the screen. The nurse punched a button and the view widened. Two tiny threads rapidly flickered, lighting up the screen as if God Himself had said 'Let there be light!'

The nurse did a quick measurement. "Your baby is twenty-two millimeters now," she told them. Rylee glanced over at Sam. He pulled out his phone again, alternating between glaring at the sonogram screen and his phone.

The nurse abruptly pulled the wand away and handed her a cloth to clean the goop off of her skin. Then, she cleaned up the wand and put it next to the monitor. "Be right back," she told them.

Rylee sat up and pulled the sheet higher on her lap, trying to hide that naked feeling from Sam. She looked at him, a protective hand on her belly. "It just doesn't seem real," she told him.

Sam's expression softened, but before he could respond, there was a knock on the door, almost immediately followed by the doctor and nurse entering the room.

"I'm Dr. Zastrow," the doctor said, as he moved to sit at the desk. "I understand you were referred to us by Milwaukee County Children's Court?"

Rylee looked down as she nodded. "That's right," she said, "but my sister recommended you because you really helped her after she finally got pregnant with her last IVF."

"I see," the doctor said, a slight frown ruffling his eyebrows. "You would be our first court referral, Rylee," he said. "Looks like there's a lot of paperwork."

He looked at Sam and raised one eyebrow, looking perplexed as Sam glared back at him. Rylee shifted her weight on the table, looking over at the nurse. She stood next to the door, looking uncomfortable, almost as if she wanted to help, but didn't want to intrude.

After a long moment, Dr. Zastrow cleared his throat and looked down. "Normally, we'd offer to walk you through the services our center has to offer, including a birthing doula, wellness and nutritional classes, a birthing class, as well as prenatal and postnatal exercise classes to help you prepare for your child's birth and aftercare."

He cleared his throat again, shifting his weight as if he was uncomfortable. "It looks like some of this will be covered by the mandatory parent training classes. I can give you our package information, but I'm not sure how much overlap there will be or how much your BadgerCare insurance will cover."

Rylee frowned. "But I don't need BadgerCare," she told him, slightly irritated by the very idea that her medical coverage had been called into question. "I'm on my parents' insurance."

Dr. Zastrow shook his head in confusion. "The paperwork refers to BadgerCare," he told her. "But you should be able to keep your regular insurance as a secondary insurance."

Rylee gave a quick nod of her head. Primary insurance. Secondary insurance. Insurance was insurance, right? "I was hoping to get a doula. Chloe really liked hers," Rylee told him. She could feel tears forming in the corners of her eyes. She needed a doula to get through this.

"Well . . ." the doctor said, looking away uncomfortably. "Why don't you talk with your caseworker to find out what is and is not covered," he finally told her. "We can always move the doula to your secondary insurance, or you can pay for it out-of-pocket if you'd prefer. Going forward, I'll need to see you every four weeks until you're in your thirty-second week, so please get those scheduled before you leave."

Caseworker? Rylee thought, a bit panicked. *Did he mean the social worker? Or was this another person to keep track of?*

The doctor looked at Sam, then back to Rylee. "Do you have any questions or concerns to discuss today?"

Rylee pursed her lips as Sam turned to look at the nurse, who was still hovering near the door. She took two steps to her left, crowding in to stand next to the exam bed almost protectively.

"Okay then," Dr. Zastrow said. He stood up and handed Rylee a folder. "Please let the nurse know if you have any questions. See you in four weeks." He headed out the door, the nurse trailing behind him.

Sam met Rylee's eyes, looking relieved that the exam was over. "Now what?" he asked.

Rylee thought about it for a moment. She needed something mindless. No real decisions. "That's easy," Rylee answered, her face relaxing into a soft smile. "Let's go shopping!"

Rylee looked out her window, mindlessly staring at the landscape as it buzzed past the entrance ramp to the freeway. Sam wasn't exactly speeding, but he seemed eager to leave downtown Milwaukee behind them.

She shook her head as she tried to find something to say. She didn't want to go home. Not yet, anyway. Mom had been so disappointed Rylee hadn't included her and probably had a million questions that she didn't want to deal with right now.

Sam stared out the windshield, distractedly, almost as if he was pretending Rylee wasn't there.

"Winter stuff has been out for weeks," Rylee said, desperately trying to fill the silence. "There might be some great stuff on sale!"

Sam glanced over, annoyed by the comment. "You're only nine weeks pregnant," he gruffly reminded her.

"I know, but it doesn't hurt to start getting ideas," she replied tartly. "I have no idea what I should be wearing."

Sam shook his head. "Okay."

Rylee pulled her phone out of her purse, unlocked it, and started scrolling through Instagram. She'd started to follow a few pregnancy influencers who seemed to have some really good ideas.

"Oh," she said. "I didn't realize maternity jeans could be considered to be a foundational garment." She stopped, a quick swipe of her finger bringing up the comments. "I think I really do prefer the black stretchy band to the nude color. I'll have to bookmark that site," she muttered.

She looked over at Sam. He continued to ignore her. "Breast-feeding shirts?" she continued. "Huh. Oh, I love this one! It's called a skin-on-skin top." She traced her fingers along the screen to make the image bigger. The baby was snuggled directly under the soft shirt, long ties wrapping around both of them so the newborn was in what they called 'the optimal position' for nursing.

Rylee paused for a moment. She would be breastfeeding, right? She gave herself a small nod. Something to add to the list of things to discuss with the doula.

Sam sighed, then reached over to turn on some music. She rolled her eyes but kept going. It was probably too much for her to expect him to actively participate in a conversation . . . even if it was about the baby.

She was so intent on her screen that she almost missed the gentle nudge that told her Sam had moved onto an exit ramp. She looked up, seeing the traffic lights in the distance. *Brown Deer Road,* she thought. "What are you doing?" she demanded.

Sam shrugged. "Dropping you off at home so you can go shopping," he told her.

"Uh, no," Rylee responded sharply. "You have to come with me."

He sighed. "No, Rylee. I'm not taking you shopping. Period." He sounded aggravated.

"I need you to come with me!" she scolded him. He was abandoning her again!

"Rylee—" he ground out, glaring at her for a microsecond before looking back at the road.

"No, Sam," she told him, sharply. "I mean it. I need you to come with me."

He jerked the wheel sharply to the right. She gasped, feeling the seatbelt tighten protectively around her. Sam slammed the car into park and hit the flashers before he turned to her, the murderous look on his face causing her to instinctively shrink back against the door for a moment.

"Why?" he growled at her. "Why do I have to come with you?"

"Because it's not fair!" she snapped, refusing to back down. "This was supposed to be my gap year. I was going to take some time to really relax before next year. To travel and maybe see what's out there before I spend the next four fucking years *networking my ass off* at Wellesley. I planned to spend my junior year overseas, Sam. An entire fucking year!" *Well, maybe not a whole year,* she thought. *But it was on the list!*

"You were?" he asked, looking confused.

"Yes, Sam. I was!" she spat. It was obvious that he never listened.

Sam blinked. "Okay," he slowly drawled. It was as if he didn't know what to say.

She could feel the tears starting again, but refused to back down. "So, if I don't get a choice about how I'm going to spend my gap year, you don't either!"

He glared back at her, not saying a word. She crumpled in the face of his rage and found herself sobbing uncontrollably. She hunched over, ashamed, and buried her face in her hands.

She felt Sam unbuckle his seatbelt and pull her against him in an awkward hug. "I'm sorry, Rylee," he finally said. "I didn't know you wanted to travel."

She leaned forward, pushing her forehead against his chest as she sobbed. "This is your baby, too!" she told him dejectedly. "I can't do this alone, Sam. I just can't!"

He tucked his cheek against her head. It had been such a long time since he'd held her this way and she found herself relaxing into his warmth. "So, where do you want to go shopping?" he gently asked.

Rylee wiped her face against his shoulder. "Can we start at the By-The-Bay mall?" she quietly asked. "I don't remember if they have a maternity shop, but it would be good to just get out to walk around for a bit, you know?"

She felt his lips brush against the top of her head. An almost kiss. "Sure, Rylee," he said. "Let me turn around."

Rylee reluctantly scooted back to her seat. For just a moment, it had felt as though he loved her. Maybe.

As they walked through the outdoor mall, Rylee pulled Sam along, trying to find ways to prolong that feeling of being loved for just a bit longer. He allowed her to hold his hand for a few minutes, then put some space between them.

They stopped at Orchard Oasis for something to drink. *It was a beautiful day,* Rylee thought as she sipped her spiced cider. Lots of places to explore, even if they didn't find a maternity store. The important thing was to reconnect.

They stopped at a small specialty shop. Rylee looked around, trying to find something that might work for her when she started to show. Sam pulled up the mall website on his phone and pointed out that the mall didn't have a maternity store.

Rylee shrugged, handing the cute cashmere scarf she'd picked out to the cashier. "After this, we can head home," she told him. Then, she waited patiently for the woman to ring it up. Sam went back to looking at his phone.

After that, they went back to the parking garage. Sam eased the car back onto the freeway and headed home.

There had to be maternity shops around here, someplace, Rylee thought as she pulled out her phone. A standard search brought up articles like 'Top Ten Best Maternity Wear In Mequon' and 'The Best Maternity Clothes To Wear While Pregnant.'

She sighed. "Chloe told me that, if there was one thing she'd change, she'd have started looking for maternity clothes early on," she told Sam, scanning the article for brand name links. "Obviously, not everything needs to have a designer label, but it needs to be comfortable with styles that are easy to coordinate. Chloe said she's still wearing a few pieces and Patrick's over ten months old!"

Sam grunted.

"Ah!" Rylee crooned. "Found it!"

"Found what?" Sam asked. He sounded annoyed.

"Graceful Expectations," Rylee told him. "Chloe and I went there a few times while she was pregnant. They have a great selection!"

It was Sam's turn to sigh. "Where?" he asked.

"Right off Main Street," she told him. She pulled up the directions, and they were on their way.

It was in that small strip mall, just as Rylee remembered. She peered into the window, trying to see past the early afternoon glare. Sam stopped and looked down at his phone.

"I have a voicemail from school," he told her. "I'll meet you inside."

Rylee nodded. As she approached the entrance, she was greeted by a tall, older woman.

"Good afternoon," she said with a warm smile. "Welcome to Graceful Expectations. I'm Evelyn, your personal shopper for today." She extended a friendly hand. "Is there anything specific you're looking for or are you just getting some ideas for the coming months?"

Rylee shook her hand, slightly embarrassed by the warm welcome. "I'm not sure what I need," she told Evelyn. "It's very early in my pregnancy."

"I understand," she told Rylee, ushering her into the store. "We're here to make this special time of your life as easy as possible. Would you like to start by exploring the latest arrivals, or would you prefer a guided tour of our curated collections?"

Rylee looked around, feeling a bit overwhelmed. "Why don't you walk me through the curated collections?" she finally asked.

"Absolutely," Evelyn replied, waving her hand off to the right. "Why don't we start with our 'Opulent Origins' designs."

"Sounds good," Rylee said, following her deeper into the store.

"Some of our clients prefer the capsule approach," Evelyn told her, gesturing to the wrap dresses on the left. "This collection includes versatile foundational pieces for you to mix and match with."

Rylee pulled out a black wrap at random. "Ah," Evelyn said, taking it from Rylee. "That silk maxi wrap is designed with a lightweight, sheer fabric overlay. Adjustable back waist to ensure a flexible fit that will adjust as you grow." She looked at Rylee. "An excellent choice."

"Thanks," Rylee said with a small smile. "But I'm not sure I need to get that immediately."

Evelyn nodded. "That will work well for the holidays. Would you like to have one set aside for you?"

"Sure," Rylee replied, moving down to the next rack. "I'm more interested in daily wear for now," she told her.

"Great place to start," Evelyn assured her. "Why don't we move to the 'Harmony Haven' collection? We have a fine selection of leggings, slacks, and skirts that might meet your needs."

Evelyn continued to pepper Rylee with questions about her style preferences and comfort as they walked, occasionally pulling items out for Rylee's approval. Rylee found herself relaxing into it. No real decisions to make, just a yes or no on each piece.

After Evelyn had collected five pieces, she ushered Rylee back to the dressing rooms. She placed the pieces onto a side table near the door. "I'll leave you to it," she said with a smile. "Let me know if you need anything."

Rylee hesitantly stepped into the dressing room. It was a bit larger than she was used to, but it was more than that. One wall was covered by a mirror and recessed lights dotted the ceiling. The overhead lighting reminded her of that tiny room at the courthouse. She shook her head, forcing herself to get undressed. Sam was probably getting antsy by now.

She pulled the first pair of pants on. She struggled with the side zipper for a moment as she tried to adjust the front panel that covered her soon-to-be baby bump, then gave up. Too complicated.

She quickly traded the pants for a longer skirt and she found herself furtively studying her reflection. She didn't look any different. Not really. Same black hair carefully brushed away from her face. Same dark blue eyes. Same perpetually pale skin that required gobs of makeup every morning.

She pulled on the matching cashmere top. Her stomach barely hinted at the coming changes. She turned to the side and tried to imagine that elegant curve a pregnancy was supposed to give her.

Rylee sighed. She still couldn't see it.

The skirt hit right below the knee. If she paired it with some nice boots, it might work. She quickly tried on the remaining pieces and got dressed. She took one last look in the mirror, grimacing, as she closed the door behind her.

"Ah, Rylee," Evelyn said as she popped into the dressing room area. "How was the fit? Anything we need to swap out?"

Rylee shook her head. "I'll take these," she told her as she passed the clothes to Evelyn.

Evelyn gathered the pieces in her arms. "Excellent," she said with a bright smile. "Why don't we get you a copy of our concierge form so that I can have items ready for your next visit?"

Rylee smiled, then followed her to the register.

Sam walked in, brushing by the personal shopper who greeted him at the entrance. "Find anything?" he asked Rylee, pointedly ignoring Evelyn as she carefully folded the clothes and wrapped them in white and gold tissue paper.

"A few things," she told him. She signed the receipt that Evelyn handed her, and then accepted the white fabric bag with the company's logo etched in gold.

Evelyn handed her the concierge form in a slim folder. "You can either email me with your preferences or bring it with you next time," she told Rylee. "Thank you for shopping with Graceful Expectation. I look forward to assisting you during your journey to motherhood."

Sam snorted. Rylee glanced over at him, then back to Evelyn. "Thank you," she told her. "I appreciate your help."

Sam held the door for her on the way out, then waited for her to place her bag in the backseat. As she settled into the front seat, she tried to brush away that lingering, sad feeling. Maybe she would feel better once she started showing.

Maybe.

That evening, Rylee sat down at her computer. Something bad had happened today. She couldn't put her finger on it, but Sam had obviously gotten some bad news from Northwestern.

She thought about it for a moment. Should she text him? Maybe there was something she could do to help. But, on the other hand, Sam might just blame her for whatever was going on. *Like mother, like son*, she thought, ruefully.

Rylee opened the baby calendar. She'd updated it with her upcoming medical appointments but saw nothing else. She shook her head in disgust. Had he even *looked* at the calendar? Or, had he decided to just ignore it?

Only one way to find out. She opened a browser and logged into the WIFE portal. There was an alert. *Interesting*, she thought as she clicked on the mail icon. The message reminded her that a mandatory appointment with a social worker was required for both participants.

She sat back and stared at the screen. Sam hadn't even looked at the portal. Maybe he had just ignored the welcome email that had been sent out when she'd signed them up. Or, he assumed she would make the appointment for them.

She sighed, then scrolled through the site to try to find the link to make the appointment. She'd almost given up when she found a link to an appointment calendar. There were a number of options and she rapidly scanned the list for something that might be related to Family Court or the program. Behavioral Health Service? Nope. Energy Assistance, Disability Services, Housing Assistance, BadgerCare . . .

Ah! Wisconsin Individual Family Education. Finally!

She clicked on the link and found a simple form. The appointment was called the 'WIFE program touch-point', which is why she'd missed it. A forty-five-minute meeting. In-person only. Choose date/time only, she was advised. Social workers are assigned cases based on location and client need only!

Rylee groaned. There had to be a backlog of so-called 'clients', so God only knew how long it would be to get in to see a social worker. She clicked on 'first available' and was pleasantly surprised to see there was an appointment available on the morning of September 21st. *Score!* she thought as she quickly locked it in.

She double-checked to make sure she had an email confirmation before transferring it to the baby calendar. Then, she went back to the home page and was pleasantly surprised to see that the First Trimester portal now included links to sign up for both the mandatory and optional courses.

Rylee thought about it for a moment. Sam had a completely different way of dealing with life. He was perfectly content pushing whatever project he was supposed to be working on until the last minute or pulling an all-nighter to catch up on a deadline. If she relied on him to sign himself up for these, he might end up taking back-to-back classes. Which might clash with his college courses. Which would cause even more havoc in their lives . . .

She pulled up another tab and found the Northwestern academic calendar. She scrolled through the obligatory 'Fall 2028 Classes Begin' information and 'Last day to drop a course for Fall term' to find the important dates: what date did the Fall, Winter, and Spring terms end and when were the final exams?

She quickly copied these dates into the baby calendar so that she could try to avoid any conflicts. She also calendared a reminder for Sam to update the calendar with his major project deadlines and midterms so that she didn't double-book him by mistake.

Next, she went back to the First Trimester portal and looked over the dates for the in-person coursework. After a few moments, she decided the half-day options might be their best bet. That Overview course had a few openings left on the afternoon of September 21st, so she quickly reserved seats. From there, it was easy enough to grab spots for the other in-person courses and to sign herself up for the optional courses, as well. Update the baby calendar and done!

Rylee rubbed at the back of her neck and took a few deep breaths to try and clear her head. *This is why Mom has a good PA*, she thought. Someone else to do the heavy lifting.

Time to log out for the night, she thought, feeling suddenly exhausted. She got up and slowly walked back over to her bed.

She thought about going to bed early, but even though she felt exhausted, she knew that it was too early for her to try to sleep. She sat down and pulled her journal out of the bottom drawer of her nightstand, then grabbed a pen and laid down to write.

Rylee had fallen in love with journaling in middle school. At first, it was mostly about stickers and sparkly washi tape and poorly sketched drawings of horses, flowers, and guys she secretly crushed on. But later, it had become more about diving deeper and trying to find herself. About trying to bust out of the shell that her family and even her friends had forced her to hide behind. About what it would take to explore the world around her beyond the sharply defined boundaries imposed on her by all sides.

"*Who am I?*" she wrote as the headline for tonight's entry. "*What do I really want?*" She looked at the words for a long moment. A month ago, the answer would have been simple. She wanted to travel and shed the strict parental oversight that kept her safe but forced her into the 'baby girl' mode. She wanted so much more than that and this gap year was supposed to be hers for the taking.

Instead, here she was, almost completely confined to the family compound and under the Ashley Williams microscope. Was this baby a miracle granted to her by God or just a big mistake?

That was the place to start. "*I want to understand what having this baby will really mean for me, my future, and for my relationship with Sam,*" she wrote. She stopped and looked at the words for a moment. She felt so lost.

"*The best place to start is with the parenting courses . . .*" she wrote. She nodded to herself. The words started to flow and she just let them come. There would be a time to look this over and see where this led her, but for now, she just kept going.

Chapter Six

Rylee glared around the packed lobby again. So many children, all of them running around and screaming as they played some sort of game that only they seemed to understand. Their mothers and grandmothers seemed content to watch the mayhem instead of trying to corral them. It was painful to watch.

The Milwaukee County Social Service office was packed. She leaned forward, trying to get comfortable. The stale air reeked of body odor overlayed by floral deodorant, some kind of citrus body wash or perfume, wet leather from the storm outside, and diapers that were in urgent need of being changed.

Sam had buried himself in his phone again, completely ignoring Rylee's discomfort. "Didn't we have a 10:30 appointment?" she asked him, although she was certain that was what was on the calendar.

He nodded distractedly, much more interested in the article he was reading than the chaos around them.

She sighed as she looked around. "Maybe we should ask how much longer," she told him. "I mean, that's what you're supposed to do when your doctor is running late, right?"

He gave her a slight shake of his head and a shrug. It didn't seem to matter to him. They could sit here all day as long as his phone still had a charge.

Enough. She stood, looking down at him for a moment. "Fine," she said, glaring at him. "I'll go ask." Sam continued to ignore her.

Rylee looked over to the reception desk, trying to find a path between her seat and the desk. An older woman, her dark brown hair randomly streaked with warm blond highlights, dodged another group of kids tossing a stuffed animal around and came to stand next to the reception desk.

"Rylee Williams and Sam Maxwell?" she called out, scanning the crowd as she held a large folder against her chest.

"Finally!" Rylee breathed. She took a few steps forward, then looked back over her shoulder. "You coming?" she demanded. Honestly, Sam seemed to spend more time looking at his phone than he did at her!

Sam stood up, walking right past her as he casually tucked his phone into his back pocket. "I'm Sam," he told the woman.

Rylee took a few quick steps, carefully avoiding yet another child who raced across the room. Sam quickly dodged the child.

"Hi," Rylee said to the woman as she caught up. "I'm Rylee. And you are . . . ?" she asked, struggling to remember if the appointment confirmation had included the social worker's name.

The woman smiled, pushing a stray lock of blond hair behind her ear. "Beth Hoffman," she replied. "I've been assigned to be your caseworker to help you navigate the Wisconsin Individual Family Education program." She took a step to the right and gestured for them to follow. "If you'll follow me to my office, we can get started."

Rylee and Sam followed her. The building seemed to hum with the murmur of dozens of conversations being held behind the closed doors that lined the wide hallway. The paint on the walls had been recently updated, but you could still see nicks and dents here and there that revealed a patina of teal blue paint from decades ago. Rylee felt a gap in the linoleum and glanced down. The faded tiles were cracked in places, forcing her to watch her steps.

Beth stopped at one of the partially open doors on the left and waved them in. It was a small room. Two mismatched plastic guest chairs sat directly in front of the worn metal desk and a fake bookshelf sat under the window.

Sam moved past her and took the seat on the right. He carefully pulled it as close to the wall as he could, looking as uncomfortable as Rylee felt. She settled into the seat beside him, placing her purse on the floor next to her.

Beth carefully closed the door and moved to sit behind the battered desk. She placed the folder on her desk, then pulled a random assortment of paperwork out. "Alright," she said, sorting through the documents and brochures. "It looks like you've already been assigned a guardian ad litem and had your first court date."

Rylee snorted. It seemed the social worker, the person who was supposed to be helping coordinate their participation in the Wisconsin Individual Family Education program, had not even looked at their file before this moment.

Beth made several piles as she spoke. "Our next step is to provide an overview of the parenting preparation program, make sure you've validated your BadgerCare account with updated contact information, and talk you through the program requirements," she told them.

"Why do we have to go through this?" Rylee demanded. "Isn't it bad enough that I can't go anywhere without permission? We're being treated like criminals!" She pointed at her ankle. The monitor peeked out from under her conservatively tailored pants.

"I understand your concern, Ms. Williams, and I share it," Beth calmly replied. "However, the state of Wisconsin has a vested interest in ensuring all of our citizens have a right to a fulfilling life, even the unborn."

"Then why am I under house arrest?" Rylee growled. She felt rather than saw Sam lean up against the wall, almost as if he was trying to warn her not to make a scene. It didn't matter. This woman might not be personally responsible for the decision to hold her hostage, but she was done with this nonsense!

Instead of responding in kind, the social worker gave Rylee a tired smile. "Ms. Williams, you are not under house arrest," she told her. "The state is monitoring your movements because, under current statutes, we are required to ensure that you carry your embryo to term."

Sam stirred, finally interjecting. "What about me?" he asked. "I'm not pregnant!"

Rylee ground her teeth, slowly turning to glare at him. Of course, his only concern was himself. That and his phone!

Beth also looked at him. "No, you're not, Mr. Maxwell," she allowed, a slight frown puckering her eyebrows. "Unmarried fathers-to-be are considered an automatic flight risk. And, as such, we need to ensure that you *fully participate* in all aspects of your child's gestation and birth."

She paused and looked back at Rylee for confirmation. Rylee gave a slight nod.

"So, that being said, let's get started, shall we?" Beth asked with a smile. She pulled out two packets from the pile in front of her and pushed a copy to each of them across the desk. "Here is an overview of the parenting prep classes you're required to take," she told them with a condescending smile. "The Court provided you a link, but we've found this guide to be particularly helpful for new clients. There are several programs to choose from based on your current home addresses. As you can see . . . "

Rylee tuned her out. She'd received a similar packet from the attorneys. She looked down at the piles of paper on the social worker's desk. Some of the printouts appeared to have been downloaded directly from the education website. *Oh, my God,* she thought. *Why waste so much paper?*

She mulled over the particular phrase Beth had used with Sam. She'd told him the state expected him to 'fully participate' in caring for their unborn child. *What did that mean,* Rylee wondered as Beth pulled out the next set of forms to go over with them. "As you can see, the program includes automatic enrollment for BadgerCare medical as well as short-term disability insurance."

"I already have insurance," Rylee objected. "Why do I need this?"

The social worker gave her a patronizing look. "BadgerCare is required for all program participants," she told her. "This allows Wisconsin to standardize maternal care across the entire state. But," she held up a hand to stop Rylee's objection, "you can retain your current plan as a form of secondary insurance if needed. Keep in mind the short-term disability insurance, which is also a part of BadgerCare, will cover time off from work for up to twelve weeks of pay, although some participants receive this coverage through their employer."

Rylee looked at Sam, then back to the social worker. "I'm on my gap year. I don't need a job!"

Beth nodded, pursing her lips in disapproval. "I understand, Ms. Williams." Obviously, her usual clientele wasn't college-bound.

Then, the social worker turned to Sam. "We also offer BadgerCare for fathers-to-be," she told him. He absently nodded, looking over the forms as she handed them to him. "However, this coverage is optional, as most men already have some sort of insurance coverage through their current job. You must make less than 200 percent of the federal poverty level to qualify.

"Last item. Here is some information about your mandatory support group meetings," Beth told them as she handed them even more paperwork. "These are scheduled to start the first week of October. You'll want to sign up as quickly as possible as these groups tend to fill up fast. They're small, usually less than ten people, and each group is assigned a mentor who can act as a liaison between yourself and social services."

Rylee nodded, placing the paperwork on her lap without comment. *What a waste of time*, she thought. *This could have easily been handled by email or a quick video call.*

Sam, on the other hand, glared down at the stack of brochures and small flipbooks in his hands. "Exactly how much is this going to cost?" he asked suspiciously.

"Good question, Sam," the social worker told him. "Some of the courses are free as they are a part of BadgerCare. Others are means tested and you'll have to provide information regarding your annual income."

"Does that apply to my personal income or to my family's income?" Sam asked. "I'm a college student. I don't really have an income."

Rylee snorted. "Neither do I," she said as she slowly shook her head.

The social worker looked at Rylee, then Sam, a bit confused. It made Rylee wonder what happened to the information they'd provided the court. There should have been a note or something about them being students.

"Contact the program sponsors for the courses you're interested in. I'm sure they can advise you as to how they determine annual income," she finally replied. "Make sense?"

She stood. "Do either of you have any questions?" she asked, already moving to open the door. "If not, I suggest you get started on this paperwork. You can complete them here and turn them in at the front desk. Or, if you'd rather sign up online, there are websites listed at the bottom of each form. Please remember these are due to be completed one week from today." She ushered them down the hallways and out into the reception area.

Sam looked at Rylee. "Now what?" he asked, one hand already going to his back pocket for his phone.

Rylee looked at him, perplexed. "Lunch, then the program overview course," Rylee reminded him, mentally going over the list of decent restaurants in the area.

"How did you—" Sam stopped, sorting through the mess of brochures as he tried to find the class information.

"I signed us up for the first-trimester in-person parenting classes over the weekend," Rylee reminded him. "It's in the baby calendar. I thought you knew that."

Sam looked up at the ceiling and sighed. Rylee took a deep breath. He hadn't read any of the emails she'd sent him.

She put her hand on his arm. "I'd rather get this over with as quickly as possible. It's the introductory course, and it's only a few hours."

Rylee grabbed the check off of the table at the restaurant. It was just about time for them to leave. Sam continued to ignore her, his eyes glued to his phone as he relentlessly shoveled carbonara into his mouth. She pulled her credit card out of her wallet and casually held it up so the waitress could see they were ready to leave.

As their waitress settled their bill, Rylee sighed. She'd thought they could take some time to talk out what their next steps would be, but Sam didn't seem interested. If anything, he'd become more withdrawn. Any attempt at conversation had been rewarded with the occasional grunt, minimal eye contact, and short responses. It was almost as if he wanted her to take control of things. There was no way to tell.

She quickly signed the receipt, adding additional gratuity because of the quick service. Then, she looked up at Sam. "Ready to go?" she asked, watching him scrape the remaining sauce off of his plate with a scrap of fresh bruschetta.

He nodded, popped the bite into his mouth, and tossed his napkin onto his plate. "Sounds good," he told her. "I can't wait to get this over with."

"Me, either," Rylee replied.

The walk to the center was uneventful. It was a beautiful day. As they passed the theater, she idly wondered what might be on the upcoming 2029 calendar.

They stopped at the light, watching as the sleek white streetcar, called The Hop, with its iconic blue and gold stripes, made a brief stop in front of the center.

They quickly crossed the street and entered the building. The foyer had that left-over corporate vibe, with a glassed-in conference room on the right and a single elevator. The directory next to the elevator advised them that the introductory module was in classroom 4A.

They rode the elevator up and quickly found themselves in a glassed-in foyer. A welcome sign directed them around the corner and to the right.

The instructor, an older woman with gray hair and a stern look, greeted them at the door. She held a basket in both hands. "Please turn off your phones and place them in the basket," she told them in a no-nonsense tone.

Sam hesitated.

"This isn't optional," she said.

Rylee reached into her purse, found her phone, and turned it off before handing it over to the woman. *Almost like high school all over again*, she thought.

She paused in the doorway, trying to look nonchalant as she searched for a place to sit in the large circle that spanned the room. The windowless room looked like it had seen better days. She chose a seat against the far wall. Sam sat next to her, slouching as he tried to find a comfortable spot on the hard chair that must have been leftover from some corporate shutdown long ago.

The room filled up fast. She counted the seats, scanning the group as they settled in. Most of them were around their age, although she spotted a few older couples in the group. All of them wore the same resentful 'Why am I here?' look.

The instructor handed out large binders, and the participants struggled to balance them on their laps as they leafed through them. Rylee shook her head in frustration. This could have been easily downloaded from the education site and loaded onto a phone or iPad. Why waste so much paper . . . and their time?

"I'm Janelle Olson and I'll be your facilitator this afternoon," the woman told them as she settled in the open seat at the front of the room. "As you can see from the agenda, we have a lot to cover in the next four hours, so let's try to hold your questions until the end. I understand that you might already have a good understanding of FMLA and how medical and short-term disability insurance work, but there have been some updates in state and federal law recently and these topics are a requirement for the program." She paused and looked around the room, brushing her uneven, dark gray bangs out of her eyes.

There was no response, so she plunged right in. "Let's start with an overview of what FMLA is and why it is a requirement for US-based businesses," she told them. In that moment, she shifted into an almost robotic tone as she recited what qualified as a medical event under the federal Family Medical Leave Act.

Rylee found herself studying the group. None of this applied to her personally. She vaguely recalled her dad and Chloe sniping about how having to manage both federal and state FMLA entitlement was a pain. The Williams Group offered very generous leave packages, both paid and unpaid, so tracking these entitlement programs was a waste of time and corporate resources.

Some of the participants seemed to be drinking it in. One girl, maybe her age or even younger, was writing notes in her binder, carefully circling specific items with a red pen. Another sat with her binder closed, but was carefully listening, nodding her head as she agreed with what Olson was telling them.

Sam, on the other hand, slouched down in his seat, hands fidgeting restlessly. Rylee doubted he was even listening.

"Next, we're going to review updates to the State of Wisconsin FMLA statute," the instructor told them. She held up the next worksheet from the binder to guide them.

One of the guys on her side of the room groaned as he juggled the binder on his knees. "Why do we need to know this?" he quietly asked. "Federal FMLA supersedes anything that the state has put out there." A few people nodded, mostly the professionals.

Olson shook her head. "Not true," she told them as she brushed her uneven bangs to the side again. "State and Federal FMLA may run concurrently, but our state has several 'buckets' of FMLA coverage, and the eligibility criteria is completely different. If you'll turn to page three of the FMLA section . . . "

Rylee flipped through her binder, listening to the groans that swept through the group. "As you can see, the state of Wisconsin recently updated state FMLA law so that both parents are allowed up to eight weeks for unpaid family leave time," she said, then paused for a moment. "This includes the birth of a newborn. Please note there is an important difference between federal and state FMLA. Serious health conditions now include prenatal care appointments for both parents in the state of Wisconsin."

The girl with the red pen circled something in a large loop, adding what looked to be large exclamation points to the sheet. She nudged the older guy sitting next to her and pointed her pen at it. He shrugged distractedly, almost as if to say, 'I heard her the first time.'

The Asian guy sitting next to Sam leaned forward, shifting in his seat. "Which is fine, if I really wanted to go," he softly whispered.

"I know," Sam responded in kind.

Asshole, Rylee thought, clenching her teeth. She was beginning to understand what the program had meant by 'fully participating'.

The trainer glared in their direction. "It's important to remember that, in order to qualify for state FMLA, you must have worked for the same employer for more than fifty-two consecutive weeks *and* been on payroll for at least one thousand hours in the rolling fifty-two-week period."

A woman across from Rylee raised a tentative hand. "What about pay?" she asked, a nervous look on her face. "My boss told me I can take off as much time as I need, but he doesn't have to pay me for time not worked."

Olson frowned in disapproval. "That's correct," she told her in a gentle voice. "However, BadgerCare does include short-term disability insurance to help defray some of your lost wages. You should have received a copy from your social worker, but I've included a copy of the form in the back of your binder. You only have a few days left to sign up."

"Yo!" a Hispanic guy called out from the far corner of the circle. "What if I can't afford to take all of this time off?" he rasped. "How the hell am I supposed to have money to eat and a place to live?"

"Sounds like this is just pro-birth, not pro-life!" the Asian guy muttered.

Rylee gasped, leaning forward to glare at him. His girlfriend, who sat on the other side of him, grabbed his right arm and hissed something at him. He patted her hand and she turned away in disgust.

"I believe there's information about financial support in the appendix," the instructor told them as she rapidly flipped through her binder. "Ah. Here we are." She shifted the binder so that it sat open on her lap for them to see. "In addition to community-based assistance and means-tested grants, each set of grandparents may provide up to $15,000 per year to support their child as they transition into parenthood."

Sam glanced over at Rylee. She frowned, then slowly shook her head. She didn't remember seeing a limit to what their parents could provide.

"My parents can't afford to give me $15, let alone $15,000!" one girl blurted out.

"Yeah!" another guy yelled. "I can't afford this!"

There was another round of angry muttering. The instructor glared at the individual offenders, her mouth pursed in disapproval, as she waited for them to calm down.

"Parenthood is costly," she told them in a firm tone. "No ifs, ands, or buts about it." She looked down and her expression softened. "You should have all met with your caseworker prior to this class to get an overview of what the state can do to help you with your next step. The good news is that this program includes an appointment with a financial adviser, who will help you assess your financial resources in the next few weeks. By the end of October, you will have a good start on creating an individual plan to support your child."

She looked around the room again, a sad look on her face. "Part of the program includes helping each couple determine if they are ready to raise a child." She held up a hand to try to still the chatter around her before it got out of hand. "There are a number of options, including sharing post-delivery expenses, even if you don't live together," she told them in a louder voice. "One parent may decide to give up their parental rights in exchange for paying all expenses until their child is twenty-one.

Or, both parents can agree to give their child up for adoption and will only be responsible for costs up to childbirth."

At that, Sam straightened up and shot Rylee a look. *Adoption?* He seemed to be telling her. *We need to do that!*

Rylee leaned back, outraged that he might even think that was an option. Sam looked away.

"Quiet down," the instructor finally told them, her loud voice cutting through the conversation around her. "I know this can be overwhelming, but we're here to help. Please turn to page three of the FMLA section so we can review your rights and responsibilities under state and federal laws."

Rylee's head was buzzing by the time they were given a short break. "We're heading into the next module, so don't be late," Olson warned them. "I'd like to end on time today."

Rylee got up and slowly walked out into the hallway. She avoided looking in Sam's direction. It still pissed her off that Sam was even considering adoption. It felt like the ultimate betrayal; like the only reason he was even considering it was because he could walk away from her.

She looked around. Not one woman was standing in the hallway.

She ducked into the bathroom. All four stalls were occupied, but the rest of the group had crowded around the sinks, socializing.

One of them, an older African-American woman, with a silk decorative head wrap of dark blue with white geometric shapes covering her hair, gestured for Rylee to join the group. "I'm Zara," she said with a warm but wicked smile. "Welcome to this side of hell." Zara was about a half-head taller than the group.

Rylee giggled and took a few steps forward. "Thank you," she replied. "I think!"

"Here's the thing," the short redhead told the group. "I don't believe that what they're doing here is necessarily legal, but . . ." She let her voice trail off for a moment as she looked around. "I'm kinda happy that the boys are being forced to help out, you know? I mean, I had to take Mark to court several times before he even coughed up four hundred dollars a month. This time, it sounds like they're forced to act like a dad!"

The sound of toilets flushing cut her off, but a few of them exchanged nods of agreement. Rylee took advantage of the open stall, intently listening to the continued conversation.

"From what I heard, they're responsible for half of all of our expenses," a chipper voice told the group. "No more living in the cheapest apartment I can find. Nope. I've already started looking for a proper two-bedroom place in Brown Deer."

"Really?" another asked, hesitantly. "I thought it was only expenses related to the baby." There was a murmur of confusion and Rylee missed the response as she flushed the toilet. She quietly shouldered her way to the sinks to wash her hands, looking at the group in the mirror.

"I think you need to reach out to Family Court to see if your firstborn qualifies for a guardian ad litem," Zara told the shorter woman. "If not, there should be someone who can help you at the Child Support Service agency. It's impossible to raise a child on four hundred dollars a month." She lifted her chin in outrage. "Daycare costs more than that, let alone rent!"

"Yeah," another girl said, moving toward the door. "I had no idea the state could force Darion to step up when I applied for BadgerCare coverage."

"Really?" Rylee asked, following her out. "Did they put you in detention, too?"

The girl turned right, putting as much distance between them and the gaggle of guys that crowded the far end of the hallway. "Nope," she told Rylee. "I'm already in my second trimester. One day, they're asking me for Darion's name and address. The next day, we're in court. They tagged us and set us loose." She looked around. "I'm Naomi, by the way."

"Hey, girl!" one of the women said as she joined them.

Rylee turned. The voice was familiar, but she couldn't quite place it. She looked a bit closer. "Brittany!" she squealed. "What happened to your hair? I almost didn't recognize you!"

Brittany shrugged. "I cut it all off," she told her. "After what they did to us in detention, I couldn't stand to look at it another minute. Besides," she said, twisting around so Rylee could see the fresh tattoo on the back of her head. "It gave me a chance to add a fresh tat, you know?"

Rylee winced but found herself nodding in agreement. She couldn't stand the idea of someone repeatedly poking at her with a needle. No way.

Other girls joined their small group and before she knew it, they were checking out each other's bellies to guess how far along each of them were. Naomi came in at a whopping eighteen weeks. Brittany, a meager ten weeks. Zara told them that she was twelve weeks along, but hadn't realized it because she was going through what she called 'quite the messy divorce'. Ava, the angry redhead, was fourteen weeks and pissed. She'd been detained because her boyfriend didn't want her to get an abortion.

"Jokes on him," she told the group. "He expected me to come home crying and beg him for forgiveness. Nope. If I'm forced to have this baby, I'm going to take him for every dime the court can give me!"

As they talked, Rylee looked down the hallway. Sam and that Asian guy were standing next to the cooler, talking. She couldn't put her finger on it, but she didn't trust that guy. She felt bad for the girl who was carrying his child. She stood off to one side of their group, glaring at the man as if she wanted to push him into traffic.

Rylee looked back at the guys. Both of them were chuckling over something. Probably comparing notes on how to get out of taking the classes.

The instructor appeared at the far end of the hallway. "Break's over," she announced as she walked through the crowd. She made vague shooing motions with her hands as she moved.

Zara smiled at the small group. "Like herding cats," she told them, listening to the woman trying to get more of the men to walk faster. "Let's go. I don't want to be late."

Rylee followed the group and took her seat next to Sam. She paged through her binder and found the next module. It was her turn to ignore Sam.

The module on medical and short-term disability coverage was fairly simple. Everyone in the program was signed up, and the coverage lasted through their child's six-month birthday.

After that, the instructor separated the group by pregnancy trimester and passed out additional information that hadn't been made available on the education portal yet. She also reminded them they needed to complete the first-trimester courses, including the ones offered online, set up a meeting with their court-appointed financial counselor, and sign up for the mandatory support groups.

"Remember, your course load is based on your trimester," the instructor said as she passed the basket around so people could claim their phones. "For those of you that are in your second trimester, I strongly encourage you to schedule the rest of the first-trimester courses immediately before moving on to the required second-trimester courses. I've also included some optional reading for those of you who are first-time parents."

She looked around the room, nodding to herself for a moment. "Have a lovely weekend!"

Chapter Seven

Rylee dropped the banana peel into the garbage and slid the drawer closed with a sigh. Her new schedule was challenging. Monday, Wednesday, and Friday mornings were spent on one-on-one yoga, followed by her mindfulness coach. On Tuesdays and Thursdays, she mixed it up with a prenatal Pilates class, strength training with light weights, and even the occasional low-impact aerobics class.

Saturday afternoons, though, were set aside for spa time. There was nothing like a deep muscle massage, followed by a nice facial and manicure to help her feel normal again. Sundays, though, were set aside as a rest day. Worship service, time to catch up with family, and to try to connect with her friends.

Eleanor, Brie, and Clarissa had extended their stay on the Canton Home Mission and wouldn't be home until the holidays. Madeleine was spending some much-needed time traveling with her family. Claire and Krystal had only taken the Fall semester off, so they had very little time before they had to pack things up for campus.

That didn't explain why she didn't get any responses on her invites, though. There were occasional texts and very brief phone calls, but it felt like her friends were slowly abandoning her.

She walked over to the kitchen table and picked up a copy of the email Sam had sent over, along with every single apartment listing he'd attached. She'd gone through it briefly last night, but knew she needed to take a closer look. Most of what he'd sent her was barely livable.

Rylee grabbed her juice and walked through the house, listening to the housekeeper run the vacuum on the stairs leading to the second floor. She briefly considered settling down in the family room to study the list of apartments, but hurried down the hallway when she heard Mackenzie's voice coming from the library.

She pushed the door wider, staring as her older sister paced along the windows, jabbing a finger to something off in the distance. *When had Mackenzie come home*, she wondered. *And what was she pointing at?*

Mackenzie turned around. Her sister was holding a meeting in virtual reality. From a distance, it looked like she was wearing a pair of oversized sunglasses, but on closer inspection, you could see the unobtrusive gray power cable running from the right side of her opaque glasses to a battery pack on her belt. She had on her second-generation Visor headset.

Mackenzie waved at Rylee, apparently using passthrough mode so that she could see into the room. "Alright, everyone," she said. "Great job on the proposal. James, make sure you run it past Dave, Ron, and Nate before submitting it to the zoning department. We don't want to have to pull this back at the last minute. Miguel, can you double-check the contract language to make sure we stay in compliance with local and state regulations? Great! Jeff and Kris, keep working on those potential cost overruns. We need to come in under budget. Heather and

Ryan keep pulling the strings on our stakeholders." She turned and walked toward the bookcases lining the back of the library.

Rylee walked over to the wall fireplace and turned on the gas. There was a slight pause and then blue, red, and yellow flames started dancing behind the glass. She settled down to wait, her juice and papers spread over the coffee table in front of her.

"Okay, folks," Mackenzie told her team. "Going offline. Keep up the great work!" Then, she pulled the headset off, folded it up, and tucked it into the side pocket of her cargo pants. "Hey, sis!" she said as she crossed the room to take a seat across from Rylee. "How're you doing?"

Rylee leaned back and took a sip of juice. "Keeping busy," she told her. "Sounds like you've got your hands full. New project?"

Mackenzie smiled. "Yeah," she said, licking her lips mischievously. "I'm taking a four-day weekend so I can walk the ground for that mixed-use building project in Mount Pleasant."

"Is Dad okay with that?" Rylee asked. Mackenzie had just started her junior year at Cornell. Dad didn't mind that Mackenzie spent time working on their tiny property management company, but he was pretty firm on getting the most out of their educational experience, and that included networking with alumni and future business partners.

Mackenzie nodded. "It's not like I'm doing this alone," she reminded Rylee. "It's called Three Sisters, LLC for a reason."

Rylee grinned back. "It probably should be called 'Chloe's Company' since she thinks she's the one in charge!" she said.

Mackenzie rolled her eyes. "And yet, I do all the work!" she exclaimed. "So, seriously, are you okay? Is Mom done with the whole 'you made a promise at the purity ball!' guilt trip yet?"

"Not really," Rylee admitted. "I haven't been able to get out much because the crisis manager wants me to lie low for a while.

The only time I get out of the house is to go to Omega Spa, and the attorneys had my personal trainers and anyone affiliated with the spa sign an NDA about my pregnancy. I know it's going to get out eventually, but I don't understand why this is anyone else's business!"

Mackenzie shrugged, dark blue eyes looking at the paperwork on the coffee table. "Say, what's that?" she asked, adroitly changing the subject.

Rylee told her, leaning forward to grab one of the sheets. "Apparently, the law says we have to live together from my third trimester until the baby is six months old. Sam has already started looking for something and everything he's found is a dump!"

"Why?" Mackenzie demanded, her nose wrinkling in outrage. "There's plenty of good apartments on the market. You should know. We own a few of them!"

"I honestly don't know," Rylee responded. "I've looked at two-bedroom places in Mequon, Shorewood, Whitefish Bay, and even Bayside. Nothing too pricey or over-the-top, but Sam seems to be stuck on price, not amenities. Everything he's sending me is so rundown and cheap. I just don't know what to say."

Mackenzie cocked her head. "What about the townhouses in Mequon?" she asked. "We have a few units that are due to be renovated over the next few months. I can have the property manager hold one for you. No problem."

Rylee thought about it for a minute. "That's the one that has attached garages, right?" she asked.

"Yup," Mackenzie confirmed with a quick nod. "Remember how Chloe insisted on building a clubhouse with a billiards room and golf simulator." She giggled. "Dad was *livid* because of the added cost!"

"Yeah," Rylee replied. "But the contractor came in under budget and we had a waiting list for rentals." She looked down at the listing in her hand, feeling a bit sad. "Beats what Sam's looking at."

"Well, run it by him and see what he says," Mackenzie told her. "It can't hurt."

Rylee nodded. "Part of the problem is the budget we're preparing for our so-called 'financial counselor,'" she told Mackenzie. "Sam is going nuts trying to figure out how to create a budget when neither of us has a real income. I mean, yes, he's picking up hours as a driver on DoorDash, but I can easily match whatever he's making."

Mackenzie stared at the flames dancing in the fireplace. "Let's just say $3,000 for a good apartment and another $1,000 for utilities and other expenses," she said, then looked over at Rylee. "That's about $2,000 for each of you."

"Exactly!" Rylee exclaimed. "I'm sure Sam is pulling in good money, and if necessary, we can always use some of the money our parents are allowed to give us."

"How much?" Mackenzie asked, curious.

Rylee shrugged. "Each of us gets a whopping $15,000 when we move in together," she told her. "It's not a lot, but I'm sure we can stretch that through the nine months we have to live together." She thought about it for a moment. "That covers the rent for all nine months. Sam is worrying about nothing."

Mackenzie smiled. "Of course, he is," she replied. "Show him the apartment. If the rent is too high, we can always lower it to something more manageable. I mean, you are a partner, right?"

Rylee grinned back. "Sounds like a plan," she replied, already excited about the prospect. Smaller than she was used to, but close to home and better than what Sam had found. She grabbed the paperwork off the table and walked over to the shredder. One less thing to worry about.

Rylee hurried across the street to the same nondescript building where she'd attended the introductory course a few weeks ago. It was just after 10 a.m. and she knew she was running late.

She entered the building and looked at the directory next to the elevator for her mentoring circle location. First floor, it said, but didn't give her a room number.

She looked around. The door to the conference room on the left side of the lobby was slightly open, and she could see a woman walking around a small circle of chairs. She turned and saw Rylee, then gestured for her to come over.

"Ah, Rylee, is it?" the woman said as Rylee hesitantly opened the door. She nodded and stepped into the room. All but one seat was taken.

"Come in, please!" the woman told her, urgently. She was a short woman, with brown eyes and gray threads starting to make their way through her dark hair. She gestured to a small table near the door. "We're just starting the introductions. There are some refreshments on the table. Why don't you grab something and join us?"

Rylee gave the table a quick glance before claiming her seat. Electric kettle for hot water, a basket full of individual tea and coffee servings, and some paper mugs along with a few small bottles of water. "No, thank you," she murmured.

She looked around the room. Zara inclined her head in welcome, looking festive in her beautiful ivory head wrap. She spotted Brittany, who was still rocking her one-inch buzz cut, although the colors had been updated to a wild mix of indigo blue and deep purple.

"As I was saying, I want to welcome all of you to our Monday morning mentorship meeting," the woman told the group. "I'm Erin Meyer, and I will be leading this prenatal mentoring circle. Once you've given birth, you will transition from my care to the postnatal support group."

She looked around the circle with a smile. "Why don't we introduce ourselves? It looks like a few of you have already met." She turned to Zara, who sat on her right. "Why don't you start? It's Zara, right?"

Zara nodded. "That's right. I'm Zara Nelson and I'm currently in the middle of a nasty divorce," she said, tipping her head to the side as she glared into the distance. "That's probably why I'm here. Matthew has a temper and has been trying to get as much of our money locked up so that I won't leave him." She frowned. "I wasn't put into detention, like most of you, but being pulled into court for the rest of it was one of the most terrifying things I've ever gone through."

Erin leaned over and patted her on the arm. "I can imagine," she said. "Anything else to add?"

"Just that Matthew is going to be a daddy again, whether he likes it or not! And I'm going to get him for every single penny he has to his name!" Zara stated, her firm voice causing a small ripple of laughter. A few of the women nodded in agreement.

Zara looked at the girl sitting next to her. The girl took it as a hint. "I'm Devi," she told the group. She was a slight Indian girl with a small, maroon dot precisely placed between her carefully manicured eyebrows. She was huddled in her chair, looking forlorn and alone.

"Hello, Devi," Erin said, her voice warm. "Is there anything you'd like to share with the group?"

Devi frowned, then shook her head. She looked ashamed.

"That's okay," Erin told her, then turned to Brittany. "And your name is . . ."

Brittany shrugged with a frown. "Brittany Martin. I live with Noah and I still have no idea how I got here. One minute, we're looking over contractor bids to redo the second floor of our condo so that we can put in a small nursery and the next minute I'm being dragged into detention because I 'could be a threat to my unborn baby.'"

Rylee gasped, and she wasn't the only one taken aback. "Wow," she breathed.

"We can discuss the language of The Unborn Child Protection Act and how it's actually being implemented another time, Brittany," Erin told her. "Anything else to share?"

"Nope!" Brittany said, then sat back. She looked at the woman next to her.

They continued to go around in the circle, each of them sharing pieces of the same story. Girl discovers she's pregnant. Some seek assistance from a clinic, like Rylee. Some decide to take their chance by seeking an out-of-state abortion. Either way, girl ends up in custody, dragged into Family Court, and loses not only the ability to make decisions about her own body but is also forced into a dystopian nightmare where the state of Wisconsin treats her like a temporary host for the unborn child she's carrying.

As each woman told their story, Rylee felt increasingly uncomfortable and overdressed. Most of them came from low- and middle-class families and a few of them had stared at Rylee with more than just a hint of envy.

"Thank you, everyone," Erin told them, then carefully took another sip of her tea. "There are a few things we need to cover today. Don't worry about taking notes," she said as one of the girls, Zoey, leaned down to pull a notebook out of her purse. "I'll be sure to send out post-meeting notes at the end of every session.

"In the last few weeks, you've had a lot of information thrown at you," Erin continued. "From having your movement restricted so you don't leave the state for an abortion, to learning that you'll be jointly responsible for all expenses associated with raising your child until age 21, to even having a guardian ad litem assigned to your unborn child."

"Mmm-hmmm," Zara said. "I wasn't expecting that!"

"Here are a few additional items to consider, ladies," Erin told them. "First, for those of you who do not currently live with the father of your baby, you will be required to live together from your third trimester through your child's six-month birthday."

There were a few gasps of protest. Rylee nodded, looking around the room. Was she the only one who read through the documentation online?

"Second," Erin continued. "Grandparents are not allowed to provide any financial support beyond the $15,000 they are allowed to give you by law. This includes babysitting unless the guardian ad litem allows it."

"I'm sorry," Rylee interrupted. "What does that mean?" She could hear the brittle edge in her voice, but refused to dial it back. She didn't have any other source of income!

Erin looked closely at her. "It means that you are required to cover the other half of all expenses associated with raising your child," she stated, that firm tone at odds with her gentle expression. "Rent, utilities, maternity clothes, prenatal and birthing courses, medical bills, postpartum care supplies, and *everything* that baby physically requires, whether it is a one-time purchase, like a stroller, or weekly supplies, like diapers and baby wipes."

"And anything that's not specifically related to the baby, like paying for my education, is something my parents can help with, right?" Rylee asked, doing her best to suppress her outrage, but failing.

Erin dipped her head in acknowledgment. "That's correct," she said. "But I need to make this clear for the entire group: you must provide proof to the Court that you can provide for your child." She paused to look around the circle. "One of the most important parts of my job is to ensure that everyone has access to whatever federal, state, and community-based resources they need. So, over the next four weeks, I will work with each of you individually, and as a group."

"What if we don't need anything?" Brittany asked. "Noah and I run our own business."

"I still need to do the assessment, Brittany," Erin replied.

Brittany shrugged, looking down.

"The last thing we need to review is the ankle monitor that you were all fitted with," Erin continued. "Please be mindful that the tracker periodically transmits your location through the closest cell tower. If you go beyond the fifty-mile limit from the courthouse, it will automatically send an alert to the nearest sheriff's department. If it fails to 'check in' because you are in a cellular dead zone, an alert will be sent to law enforcement in your last known position."

Rylee blinked. She glanced around the circle. Most of the women looked angry, muttering between themselves. Devi, however, seemed to perk up, almost as if that small piece of information was important to her somehow.

There was more, of course, but what stuck with Rylee was the huge disconnect between the minimal information the social worker provided, what was available online, and the information that Erin was providing them. Her attorneys had done a good job in gathering all of the publicly available information in one place, but there was so much missing that it made her wonder how much of this program—and the law that it was based on—was still open to interpretation.

She made a mental note to contact the lead attorney. It was obvious she wasn't going to get a job to cover her half of the expenses, but she wasn't sure if Three Sisters should pay her a salary or if the money from her trust fund was available. Or, if state law allowed her parents to continue paying for her expenses. If not, would she be forced to temporarily go on public assistance?

She sat back and studied Erin for a moment. She needed answers. The family had a law firm on retainer. Time for them to earn their money.

Rylee nervously sat down, smoothing her napkin over her lap as she gazed across the dining room table at Sam. She grabbed her glass of water and took a quick sip, then glanced from one end of the table to the other, trying to gauge her parents' moods.

"I hope you're hungry, Sam," her dad told him with a relaxed smile. "We're having one of Rylee's favorites: lemon chicken with roasted potatoes."

"Sounds great, sir," Sam responded quietly. Then, he toyed with his knife, almost as if he wasn't sure why it was on the right side of his plate.

Her mom's lips tightened in disapproval. She looked across the table at Rylee's dad. "We don't want this to get cold, Brandon," she scolded lightly. She held out her hands to Sam and Rylee. "Shall we get started?"

Dad nodded. "Of course, my dear." He held out his own hands. Rylee immediately grasped both her mom and dad's hands. Sam hesitantly followed suit and bowed his head.

"Lord, we are so grateful for the food that You have set before us," Dad said, his soft voice almost melodic in prayer. "We know that not everyone has what we do and we thank You for everything You have given to us. We pray for the poor and hungry in this world who lack resources. Please be with them and sustain them." He paused for a moment, then continued. "We now join in the common table prayer . . . "

"Come, Lord Jesus, be our guest and let these gifts to us be blest," Rylee said, joining her voice with theirs. "Oh, give thanks unto the Lord for He is good. For His mercy endures forever."

"In Jesus' name, we pray. Amen," her dad said.

"Amen," Rylee breathed, hearing the echo of her mom and Sam. She picked up the bowl in front of her and spooned a generous portion of oven-roasted potatoes onto her plate. She handed it to her dad and quickly accepted the platter of lemon chicken breasts from Mom. After that came the glazed carrots. Slow-baked and drizzled with maple syrup that always made them taste like a special treat.

"I appreciate you joining us after service, Sam," her dad said, looking intently over at him. "There are a number of things we need to discuss."

Sam handed the potatoes to Rylee's mom, distractedly nodding at her dad.

"My top concern is navigating our joint financial obligations," her dad told them. "The current legal framework is very specific about splitting costs equally."

Sam nodded. Rylee wasn't sure if he understood just how important this moment was: Dad was talking to Sam directly instead of talking to his parents. Dad was treating him like a man.

Rylee cut a small piece of chicken, studying her plate carefully. Her mom had several formal dinnerwares and rotated through them based on her personal agenda. Today's plate was Italian white porcelain with a yellow Herbarium motif. That usually meant she was angry, but when Rylee looked at her mom for confirmation, her face was bland. She was more focused on Rylee's dad than on her lunch.

"According to our legal team, there are some rather strict rules about money," her dad continued. "Anything related to the baby must be accounted for and the receipts submitted to the guardian ad litem's office every month for review."

Sam frowned. "Monthly?" he replied. "Does that include my car? I haven't been keeping track of mileage, gas, or how often I'm charging my car."

"Why are you worried about your car?" her mom asked, clearly irritated.

"I've taken Rylee to the doctor and shopping a few times," Sam replied. "If they're looking at income and expenses, that might include my car, since they insist I take her to medical and in-person classes."

Dad nodded. "Understandable," he responded, that slight quirk of his upper lip telling Rylee that Sam had a valid point. "I'll reach out to the lead attorney to double-check this, but I think it's safe to say this is not included in the current regulations."

"Thanks," Sam said, cutting a piece of roasted potato to eat. He nibbled on it, looking a bit lost.

"We do, however, need to look at Rylee's spending," her dad said, glancing first at her mom, then at Rylee.

"We do?" Rylee asked. She put her fork down on her plate, perplexed. She hadn't done anything out of the ordinary that she could think of.

Her dad nodded. "Unfortunately, yes." He took a bite of chicken and slowly chewed, looking as if he was uncomfortable. "There is a bit of a gray area in the law regarding minors who don't have an independent source of income," he finally told them. "According to our attorney, the most reasonable action is to provide the Court with an estimate of what we are able to provide you, Rylee, based on what we gave you in the last fiscal year."

Rylee clenched a fist under the table. "But I was a senior in high school last year!" she protested. "I didn't have an apartment to furnish or rent to worry about!"

"Understood, Pumpkin," her dad said. "But we need to keep your spending within a reasonable limit. And that includes everything related to your future living arrangements."

"Meaning?"

Rylee's mom set her fork down with a soft clink against the china. "Meaning that the furniture order you placed with Luminaire will have to be canceled," she stated in a flat voice, gray eyes flashing in anger.

"That's not fair!" Rylee squeaked. She balled up her napkin and tossed it onto the table, narrowly missing her lunch.

"Rylee, there's a legal limit to what we can do," Dad told her, his voice deepening as he tried to interject a note of reason into the discussion.

"Don't you tell me that!" Rylee shrieked, feeling her face flush with anger. "I am allowed to move furniture and my belongings from my home to this new apartment." Her father started to object, but she overrode him. "All I want is a few pieces for the bedroom, kitchen, and living room! Why is that too much to ask?!" Considering how much her parents had spent on out-fitting Chloe's house in Lake Geneva, she'd been downright frugal.

Rylee's mom threw her napkin on the table, almost hitting Sam's plate. Rylee glanced over, catching his startled look, before she turned back to her mom.

Mom leaned toward her, long fingernails digging into the dining room chair's fabric arms. "You should have asked before you bought that kitchen set, Rylee!" she hissed, outrage etched into her flushed cheeks. "Our lawyer has repeatedly told you that your credit cards are a part of court records. That means you just ate into the small amount of money we can give you!"

Unbelievable! "I have my own money, Mom!" Rylee spit at her. "I can spend it any way I want!" She seethed at the insult. After all, hadn't her parents told her that this was the time of her life when she was supposed to learn from her financial mistakes?

"And where are you going to store that kitchen set until you find an apartment?" Rylee's mom demanded, matching Rylee's rage with her own.

Disgusted, Rylee threw up her hands. "I don't know, Mom," she hissed. "Maybe I'll just rent a heated storage locker!" Or, she could store the furniture in one of the unused garage bays. Why heat the space for nothing?

"We are not renting you a heated storage locker, young lady!" Rylee's mom hissed back. "Every single penny you spend must be reported to the Court. We are not wasting one penny on storage!"

Rylee blinked, eyes almost bulging as she glared at Mom. "What?" she shrieked. "Since when have you ever worried about wasting money?" She jabbed an accusing finger at a piece of furniture across the room. "That sideboard was imported from Italy!" she yelled, then spread her fingers over the table. "And this china? Gucci Herbarium doesn't come cheap!"

Rylee's dad cleared his throat. "Rylee, you need to understand the position we're in," he told her as he tried to cut through the raw argument. "We are—"

"Pillars of the community," Rylee growled as she looked down at her plate. "Yeah, I got that. That's all I am, someone who is supposed to set the best example for others to follow!"

Out of the corner of her eye, she saw Dad cover his eyes with one hand. "Sweetheart," he finally said. "We need to be very careful about our next step, that's all."

"We're already in the spotlight, thanks to Sam—" Rylee's mom interjected.

"Mom!" Rylee gasped, glancing from her mom to Sam, then back again. That comment was completely uncalled for.

Sam pushed away from the table and stood, swaying from the sudden movement. "Sorry," he mumbled. "I should go."

Oh, my God, Rylee thought, *he's leaving*. "See what you've done?" Rylee hissed at her mom. Then, she stood and moved around the table. "Sam, you don't need to leave," she gently told him. "We can figure this out."

Sam moved to the other side of his chair to avoid touching her, then quietly pushed his chair in. He looked at the table, carefully avoiding eye contact. "Thanks for having me over," he said with an almost terrified look on his face. Then he fled through the kitchen door and out to the back driveway.

Rylee looked after him for a moment, then wilted into her chair. "Thanks, Mom," she whimpered.

Dad carefully wiped his mouth and pushed away from the table. "Let's regroup in a few hours," he told them. "I need to make a few calls."

Rylee settled down in the family library. She gnawed at the inside of her lip nervously as she waited for her father to join her. He'd been on the phone with the legal team for almost an hour before he'd firmly shut the door to his office.

She grabbed the remote and turned on the gas fireplace. It was raining outside, and she couldn't seem to dispel a feeling that the damp air was seeping into the house.

The door to the library opened. She glanced over, disappointed, as both of her parents entered the room. Her mom had that annoying fake smile plastered on her lips. Her dad carried his iPad and a mug of hot coffee.

Dad sat down on the leather couch across from Rylee and set the iPad down on the coffee table. Her mom grabbed a coaster from the nearby sideboard, placed it on the coffee table, and then settled down next to him. It was almost as if they were going to have 'the talk' with her again.

Her dad set his coffee mug down, then moved his iPad on the couch's arm before looking over at Rylee. He gave her a somber look before glancing at Mom. She nodded at him, then settled back against the cushions behind her, apparently content to let him take the lead.

"I had Dobson do a bit more digging into what the legal requirements are for managing your finances," he told her. "I am still concerned because there isn't much guidance available, but I believe we will be able to work within the law."

Rylee leaned forward, trying to get comfortable. "What did he say?" she asked, curious.

Her dad cleared his throat, looking down at the iPad. "Instead of your monthly allowance, you will receive income from your Three Sisters company and draw funds from your current investment portfolio, if needed," he told her. "In addition, we're going to transfer the $15,000 allowed by the state into a joint account for the two of you."

Rylee frowned. "Joint account?" That went against everything she knew about personal finances. Never, ever, combine your money unless you have a prenup and some very specific legal documentation in place.

"Sam's father thought it would be a good place to keep money specifically related to the pregnancy and childcare expenses," he replied. "Everything else should remain separate, and I agree."

"That makes sense," she told him. "I don't feel comfortable giving Sam access to my money."

Mom stirred, a soft smile lighting up her face in approval. She glanced at Rylee's dad and then back at Rylee.

Her dad looked down at the iPad. "I've created a simple spreadsheet to track all of your projected income over the next twelve months," he told her. "Chloe and Mackenzie are comfortable with the business paying out $5,000 per month for the next nine months and, with your investment income, I believe we can easily cover your expenses."

He handed Rylee the iPad. She glanced over the figures, feeling a bit relieved to have something concrete to rely on. Wait. Her trust fund.

She looked up. "According to this, my trust fund is still locked," she said. "Why don't I have access to it?"

Her father leaned forward to grab his coffee mug. "That fund needs to remain separate for now," he told her. "Donovan is investigating. It may take a few weeks to get an answer." He took a sip of coffee. "It was originally set up to pay for expenses related to college and your post-graduate life. You may be able to tap into it, as this is a significant life event, but we'll need to wait for direction from the Court."

Rylee felt herself pouting and tried to pull on a more neutral expression. That was her money and hers alone. It didn't have the same restrictions her other accounts had. Chloe had been given full access to her trust fund before she'd graduated. Mackenzie had been allowed to tap into hers to give her a majority stake in Three Sisters. Why was her dad denying her the same access?

"Don't worry so much, Pumpkin," her dad told her. "Your trust fund is safe and we will do whatever we can within the legal limits to ensure that it remains that way." He smiled and took another sip of coffee.

"In the meantime," her mother interjected, "we need to talk about how much money you're spending."

"What?" Rylee asked, feeling that anger stirring again. "Tell me one thing that you think I shouldn't have bought—except the apartment furniture!"

"Your mother's right," her dad told her. "Take a look at the 'purchased' tab. It's a running total of what you've bought since September 1st."

Rylee pulled up the tab and looked over the list. Clothes, especially longer pants and short boots, to cover up that damn tracker. Print and audiobooks about pregnancy and early childhood development. Journaling supplies. Make-up, lotions, shampoo, conditioners, and assorted purchases at Omega Spa. A solo trip to the movies. Lunch downtown after the mentoring meeting. And, of course, the furniture.

"I'm not seeing anything that stands out," Rylee admitted, looking at her parents. "I need clothes and boots that are going to hide the tracker. I don't think I went overboard."

"Under normal circumstances, this wouldn't stand out," her father told her. "However, we'll need you to be more mindful in the future."

"That means focusing on a capsule wardrobe for your pregnancy, rather than an ensemble," Rylee's mom told her. "Cost comparison rather than top-end designer items, especially for the baby."

Rylee frowned. *Capsule wardrobe? Cost comparison?* she thought. *Where the hell did that come from?*

"Everything pregnancy-related must be reported to the court," her dad reminded her. "And that means that Sam is responsible for half of every single expense. I'm fairly confident his family is running through the same exercise and determining exactly how much money he will have access to until graduation." He paused, looking grave. "You will need to deposit equal amounts into the joint account and only use that money for approved items. Nothing more."

"So, if Sam can't afford to pay for half of the item, we can't buy it?" Rylee asked, incredulous. She'd known he was responsible for half, but had assumed both of their parents could cover their expenses.

Her parents nodded.

She looked down, vaguely feeling cheated. "Fine," she said. "I will cancel the furniture order tomorrow. I didn't think that furniture fell under the 'baby' umbrella since I wasn't buying anything baby-related."

"Good," her dad said. "You haven't even picked out a place to live yet, so it doesn't make sense to look at furniture yet."

Rylee smiled ruefully, looking over at her mom. Her mom smiled back, shaking her head. Rylee could almost hear the word now: men!

"In the meantime, I suggest you and Sam have a meeting of the minds and focus on finding a place to live," her dad said. "I know you have a few months before you have to formally live together, but it may take some time to find something in Sam's price range."

Rylee nodded. Time to compile a list of decent apartments in the area, including the property in Mequon. Hopefully, she could convince him that they could afford the lower rent.

Chapter Eight

A few days later, Rylee texted Mackenzie about the place in Mequon. *"I think it's time to take a closer look at the East Home properties,"* she wrote.

She puttered around the kitchen, looking for something to nibble on. She'd had a great yoga session this morning, an iffy one with her mindfulness coach, followed by a rather bland chicken Caesar salad that left her wanting more.

She opened the under-counter refrigerator to take a look. Usually, she could find something snack-worthy. Her mom kept the mini-fridge stocked with some Greek yogurt, cheese, individual servings of hummus, bags of grapes, and orange slices. But today, nothing interested her.

She walked into the pantry, trying to find something that might work. Nuts? No. Crackers? Rylee looked over the shelf, trying to see if anything worked for her. Nope. Kettle corn it is, then!

She pulled out a two-serving envelope and placed it in the microwave. While it popped, she grabbed a bowl and then settled down at the breakfast bar to wait. Hopefully, Mackenzie would reach out soon. She needed to talk through what her options were.

She was emptying the popcorn into the glass bowl when Mackenzie texted back. "*Gimme 5 mins.*"

"*K,*" Rylee texted back. Then, she grabbed her bowl and headed for the library. She'd printed out all of the new apartments Sam had offered her, as well as those in the area that met her personal criteria: close to home, three bedrooms, two bathrooms, a nearby EV charging station, and garage parking.

She grabbed them off the sideboard and had just started to spread them out on the large table near the back of the library when Mackenzie called.

"Hey!" Rylee said, putting it on speakerphone. "You done for the day?"

"I wish!" Mackenzie replied. "I still have my Artificial Intelligence law class this afternoon." There was a shout in the distance, then the sound of a door closing. "So, you're ready to look at the open apartment in the East Home complex?" she asked. "How much have you told him about the apartment and your finances?"

Rylee grabbed a chair and sat down. "Not much," she admitted. "Rule number one—"

"Never discuss money," they said in unison.

Rylee sighed. "I need to sit down with him and do a simple comparison between what he's looking at and what we need," she told Mackenzie. "Then, I can tell him about the townhouse and get his buy-in."

"That might not work," Mackenzie replied. "Don't forget, he has to pay for half of everything related to that baby. If that hasn't hit home before, he's got to be feeling it now."

Rylee sighed. "He has to know that there are ways around this. Our parents are not going to let us starve!"

"Maybe."

"What do you mean, 'maybe'?" Rylee demanded. "Are you saying Sam's family is going to stand by and let our parents fill in the gaps if we don't have enough money?"

"I'm saying that the Williams family has always looked down on us *because* of our money," Mackenzie told her firmly. "Unless both families sit down and talk this out, you have no way of knowing what Sam's parents will bring to the table."

"I can't believe he's on his own for all of this," Rylee replied.

"You don't know anything for certain," Mackenzie reminded her. "All we know is that he's very concerned about his personal cash flow. It's time to talk this out."

Rylee sighed. "You're right."

"So, are we good?" Mackenzie asked. "It's just about time for me to leave for class."

"Sure," Rylee replied. "Catch up this weekend?"

"Sounds good," Mackenzie said and ended the call.

Rylee stared at her phone for a moment, then pulled up Sam's phone number. "Hey, Sam," she said when he answered. "Gotta minute? It's important."

"Sure," he replied.

"Did you take a look at the apartments that I sent you?" she asked.

"I did," Sam replied, sounding aggravated. "They're all too expensive."

"No, they're not!" Rylee shot back. "If you don't think they work for us, we can keep looking. But I need to live on the East Side."

"Oh, for heaven's sake, Rylee, we can't live on the East Side!" Sam yelled, nearly overloading her speaker. "You're already in your second trimester and we have to get moving on this. Have you even looked at the apartments I sent you?"

Rylee sighed. "Sam, please don't yell at me," Rylee said, trying to remain calm. "Of course, I looked at the listings. Not one of them has enough room or amenities we'll need when the baby is born."

"Look," Sam told her, sounding like he was at the end of his rope. "We can only afford so much per month."

Rylee rubbed the side of her face and sighed. "I know you're working on a budget for that 'financial class,'" she finally said. "But we don't have to live in actual poverty. We have options."

"Really, Rylee?" Sam growled at her. "I know you have some money of your own, but we're only allowed to get $15,000 a year from each of our parents. So, unless you're sitting on a pile of money that I don't know about, we're going to have to stay on budget."

Mackenzie was right, Rylee thought, feeling a bit nauseous. *His parents were forcing him to pay for everything on his own.*

"Well, in theory, I do have money . . . " Rylee trailed off, trying to find the balance between trying to reassure him and not giving him too much information. She did not want to bring up her income from Three Sisters. That was none of his business.

"Really." Sam's voice was flat, almost lifeless.

"Sam, it's no secret that my family put away money for me when I was a child," Rylee reminded him. "I mean, that's how it's done."

"Get to the point, Rylee."

"Under normal circumstances, I wouldn't have access to my trust fund until I graduated from Wellesley," she told him. "But I'm working with our family attorney to find a way to legally get access to the money after the baby's born." She giggled nervously, afraid she was giving Sam too much information, but still plowed ahead. "According to my financial adviser, this should constitute a 'significant life event', so he should be able to free up some money to cover expenses."

"How much?" Sam asked, curious.

"That depends on the attorney," Rylee told him. "I should have an update in a few weeks."

"Rylee, this changes nothing," Sam told her.

"Why not?" He was wrong. This changed everything.

"Because, unlike you, I don't have a trust fund to draw from," Sam growled. "We have to divide our living expenses equally between the two of us. That means we can only spend as much as I can afford. Period."

"Well, no one has to know," Rylee told him, trying to sound reassuring. "Our actual budget is no one's business."

"Oh. My. God! Rylee, haven't you been paying attention at all?" he growled.

"What do you mean?" she snarled back.

"Didn't you listen to your dad?" he ground out. "All of our documentation has to be submitted to the Court. That includes the apartment lease!"

"I know that," Rylee snapped back. "We just need to turn in some of our receipts. It's not like anyone's going to actually do the math!" Or look at comparable rentals in the area.

"Right," Sam growled. "So, if you pick out a place that costs $3,000 per month, no one's going to look at my paycheck and figure out that I can't afford my half. With my schedule, Door-Dash doesn't pay anywhere near enough!"

"It doesn't?" Rylee asked, confused. "I thought that made good money."

"For some drivers, sure," Sam shot back. "But I'm trying to get through my regular classes, take these stupid mandatory parenting classes, and squeeze in time to make myself available for deliveries during prime time. I'm not making a whole lot here."

"Well, I've been busy, too, you know," she snapped. "Pregnancy is a lot of hard work and I'm trying to get us ready for when this baby is born!"

"Rylee, unless you find something that's within our *actual* budget, one that has two bedrooms and is affordable, it's going to be a hard pass."

"I'm absolutely positive that there's a way around this," she said, appalled. Two bedrooms weren't enough!

"Rylee, you've got to meet me halfway on this," he told her. "We need to keep looking. Think about the near east side of Milwaukee, or the lower east side."

"Why not Mequon or Bayside?" she asked. "Those are much closer to home."

"Because the rents are closer to $1,500 a month, and we need to keep it under $1,000."

"But $1,000 is nothing!" she exclaimed.

"I know," he told her. "But we have other bills to cover, and this is the best we can do for now."

"Fine," Rylee took a deep breath as she tried to calm down. "But I won't settle for living there for more than a few months. I just can't!"

"Fine," Sam retorted. "We'll keep looking, okay?"

"Yes, we will," she hissed. Then, she jabbed at her phone to end the call. She stood up and walked to the windows. From here, she could see the guest house through the barren tree branches. She couldn't understand why his parents were doing this to him. It might be different if he had a real job, right? But, as a student?

She stepped back from the windows and headed back to the table. Time to open that iPad and take a closer look at Sam's numbers.

Rylee slowly walked into the mentoring meeting. She was still uncomfortable wearing short boots to cover that tracker, but this pair was a bit wider at the ankle and might not chafe as much.

"Rylee," Erin said as she caught sight of her. "You're early. Why don't you help me set up the refreshments?"

Rylee smiled. "Sure," she replied. "Give me a minute." She quickly shed her coat and hung it up on the portable coat rack near the door. Then, she joined Erin at the small table next to the door and helped her lay out the white tablecloth across it. Erin grabbed an electric kettle from her bag, plugged the base in, and excused herself to fill it from the kitchenette down the hall. Rylee set out the individual tea and coffee bags, disposable paper cups, and small paper plates.

Other members of the group started to filter in. Zara seemed to have taken Brittany, Emma, and Grace under her wings. Mia and Zoey were having an intense conversation as they giggled about baby clothes, while Lily and Charlotte were looking at a book Charlotte had brought with her. Everyone seemed to be making friends and swapping numbers, even though it had only been a few weeks.

The only one not socializing was Devi, and she looked as lost as Rylee felt.

"Water's ready, if anyone would like tea," Erin announced. "I also brought some treats from the Cookie Jar Boutique. Please help yourselves."

As a group, the women converged on the snack table, chattering as they helped themselves. Rylee joined the line that quickly formed and grabbed a chocolate chip cookie and a cup of chamomile tea. She waited until Devi had returned to her seat, then sat next to her.

"All right, ladies," Erin said. "Why don't you all have a seat and I'll begin."

Most of the group ignored Rylee as they settled down into their seats. She saw a few covert looks in her direction and glanced down at her outfit. Jeans, a light sweater, and minimal jewelry. She'd even toned down her manicure.

"Today, we're going to talk about navigating the changes in a woman's body during pregnancy," Erin told them.

There was a collective groan.

"This was covered in my high school health class."

"I don't have time for this!"

"I'm pregnant. I'm due at the end of March. What else do I need to know?!"

Erin sipped her tea, pointedly ignoring the uproar. She ate one cookie, then another, looking past them and out the front window.

The outrage slowly died down. Everyone looked at Erin to see why she hadn't tried to stop them. "The sooner you settle down, the sooner we can get started," she said into the sudden silence.

Mia and Lily sat down, looking more puzzled than outraged. Zara, however, looked pissed, her maroon head wrap accentuating the deep frown line between her eyebrows.

"I know that most of you may have heard all of this before," she told them. "What we have here is an opportunity to talk things out and share our collective knowledge. Zara, for example," Erin waved a hand in her direction, "I'm positive you have some great insights to share with those of us who have never been pregnant before."

Zara sat back and studied Erin. After a moment, she smiled. "Of course, I do," she replied. "But these young women do not need a lecture. As women, we intuitively know what our bodies are telling us."

Erin nodded. "I agree. So, why don't we start with what your body is telling you?" she gently asked.

Zara studied Erin for a moment, then nodded back. "My body is telling me that this pregnancy is different from my previous one," she confided. "I'm older, but I'm also feeling a lot more stressed than when I was pregnant with Kwame."

"Because of the divorce?" Erin asked.

"Because of how Matthew treats us," Zara told her. "He doesn't want to let us go. So, if I continue with the divorce this child could not be his."

"What other changes have you noticed in the last few weeks?" Erin asked.

"I tire easier than I used to," Zara replied. "Poor Kwame has to spend much more time with his grandmother."

"Kwame is five?" Erin asked.

Zara nodded.

Erin pursed her lips. "What about breast tenderness?"

"I breastfed Kwame until he was more than two years old," Zara proudly told the group. "My breasts don't feel more tender than when my milk came in."

"Anything else you'd like to share about the changes you're going through?" Erin asked.

Zara looked around the room. "I had gestational diabetes with my first pregnancy," she told them. "I periodically check my blood sugar just to be sure that this baby is not at risk."

"What kind of symptoms did you have?" Grace finally asked.

"I was hungrier and more thirsty than usual," Zara told her. "I thought it was because I was eating for two. I didn't think much about it until it came time for my third-trimester ultrasound. Kwame was much bigger than he should have been."

The group exchanged worried looks. "What did they do?" Mia asked, fearfully. "Diabetes runs in my family and I'm terrified I'll do something wrong."

"I had to take insulin to bring my blood sugar down," Zara told her. "But only because I'd let it go too far along. That's why it's really important to keep your doctor appointments."

"Today's notes will include information about gestational diabetes," Erin told the group. "Symptoms to watch for; questions to ask your doctor. That kind of thing."

Mia nodded, biting her lip. "Thank you," she said.

"Why don't we go around the room and get a quick check-in from everyone about how far along you are and what you are experiencing?" Erin asked. "We can talk through any areas of concern, and I can upload specific information for you to review on your portal account."

Rylee took another sip of tea. She tried to pay attention as each of them went through their personal story. In many ways, it was almost as if they were talking about puberty, except instead of prepping for breast pain because they were starting to develop or about what to expect from their first period, they were talking about strange food cravings, vivid dreams, intense mood swings, and something called 'pregnancy brain', which seemed to sporadic forgetfulness.

As they talked things out, Rylee also noticed another disturbing thing: Devi was just as much an outcast as she was. No one followed up on Devi's almost monotone description of what she was going through. Lily didn't reach out and touch Devi's hand, like she did when Charlotte was talking, even though she also sat next to Devi. Zara didn't follow up with meaningless snippets of advice. They just nodded and moved on to Rylee.

She decided to keep it as brief as possible. "I've noticed much of the same things," she said when it was her turn. "The cravings can be pretty intense, but I have a few healthy go-to snacks that I'll try first. Usually, it helps."

"What snacks?" Erin prompted.

"Cottage cheese, yogurt, nuts, and whatever fruits are in season," Rylee replied. "If that doesn't help, then I'll grab a handful of crackers and some fresh hummus."

Mia smirked. "Fresh hummus, huh?"

Rylee nodded. "We seem to go through a container every few days," she replied, trying to downplay that it was made by their personal chef. "I open one in the morning and it's completely gone the next day."

Mia looked a bit surprised. "I'll have to give that a try the next time I'm having a craving," she said.

"Thanks for sharing that, Rylee," Erin said, then looked around the room. "It's just about time to wrap up, ladies. I'll upload our notes and informational packets to the portal later today, so be sure to take a look. I'll be happy to answer any questions you might have next week."

As everyone got up to dispose of their cups and plates, Rylee followed Devi as she quietly moved to the coat rack.

"Hey, Devi," Rylee said.

Devi turned around, coat in hand. "Yes?" she asked, concern in her dark brown eyes.

"It's lunchtime and I'm starved," Rylee told her. "I'm going to give that new place around the corner a try. Care to join me?"

Devi looked down. "I don't think that's a good idea," she told Rylee quietly. "I didn't bring any money with me."

Rylee grabbed her coat and quickly put it on. "No worries," she told Devi. "It'll be my treat." She moved a bit closer. "If you'd like, we can just split a few appetizers."

Devi frowned but finally nodded in agreement. "I need to be on the road in about an hour," she said, then put on her coat.

"Let's do it!" Rylee said as she grabbed her purse in one hand and Devi's arm with her other as she led them out of the building. "I'm starving!"

Devi looked over the menu, a perplexed look on her face. "There doesn't seem to be much variety," she said. "For a restaurant that specializes in everything 'fusion,' there doesn't seem to be very much 'fused.'"

"I hear you," Rylee replied as she leaned forward. "Anything that you're in the mood for? We could ask if they could make it up fresh for you."

Devi shook her head. "No," she replied. "This will be fine."

"Are you sure?" Rylee asked. "Maybe they can substitute the Thai-spiced tofu for the sushi in the tacos."

Maybe this place wasn't such a good idea, she thought. Some of the items on the menu didn't sound very appetizing.

Devi frowned. "I think I'll go with the mango papaya Caprese, Rylee," she told her as she set the menu down. "Mango, papaya, and fresh mozzarella. Sounds interesting."

"Sounds good," she replied. "I think I'll give the Peking Duck sliders a try." She waved a hand for the waiter, who quickly came over to take their order.

While they waited, Rylee glanced around the small dining room. The cream-colored brick walls were littered with framed art from local artists, along with a smattering of enlarged historical photos and a few small sculptures. It felt cozy.

Devi glanced down at her watch. She looked uncomfortable.

"So, Devi," Rylee said, trying to break the silence. "Are you from Milwaukee?"

Devi shook her head. "I'm actually Canadian," she told Rylee.

"Really?" Rylee softly exclaimed. "How did you end up here?"

Devi looked away.

"Oh, gosh, I'm sorry," Rylee quickly said. "I didn't mean to pry."

"It's okay," Devi said, looking up to meet Rylee's eye. "I'm studying biotechnology at the University of Wisconsin-Madison."

"Oh." Rylee took a sip of water. She wasn't sure how to ask all of the questions that threatened to spill out of her mouth, like, 'How did you get stuck in Milwaukee?' Or 'Did you have to drop down to part-time status like Sam?' Finally, she said, "Biotech. That sounds interesting."

Devi laughed, shaking her head in amusement. "Yes, it does," she replied. "I met Tyler at a biohealth summit. He was nice. Friendly. Interested in hearing about what I was working on. He seemed . . . perfect."

The waiter interrupted at that moment, bringing their plates and offering refills on their drinks. "They always do, don't they?" she replied.

Devi nodded as she picked up her fork and nudged a piece of mango. "Tyler lives in Milwaukee. We started seeing each other, but it wasn't serious," she said sadly. "My parents expect me to settle down with a nice Canadian of Indian descent. As my father puts it, 'Americans need not apply.'" She shook her head.

"Does Tyler know that?" Rylee asked before she could help herself. She took a quick bite of her slider, stopping to puzzle over the strange mixture of hoisin sauce and cucumbers. Definitely did not go well with the Peking duck. She quickly swallowed. "Sorry, TMI."

"No," Devi said. "It's okay. He seemed to be okay with the idea of us not being serious. But, sometimes, he seemed to want more." She shook her head. "We spent the weekend together in Madison. A few months later, I found out that I was pregnant. I drove down to talk with Tyler about getting an abortion but I was arrested before I got to his apartment."

Rylee almost choked on her slider. She wiped at her mouth, gaping at Devi. "You were what?" she demanded.

"Arrested," Devi repeated. "One of my roommates found the home pregnancy test." She looked down at her bowl with a sigh. "I should have just gotten on a plane and headed back home. But I didn't want to answer any questions from my family."

"Oh." Rylee didn't know what to say.

"Exactly."

"So, did you have to drop out of school until after the baby's born?" Rylee asked. "Or are you attending remotely?"

Devi snorted. "My attorney convinced the judge to allow me to return to campus," she said. "I have to check in with a parole officer every time I plan to travel between Madison and Milwaukee."

Rylee blinked. "Is that because you're staying within the state?" she asked. "Sam wasn't allowed to go back to Northwestern."

"Possibly," Devi replied, spearing another slice of papaya to eat. "I haven't told my parents yet."

"Oof," Rylee breathed. "I can't imagine how hard that's going to be," she told her.

Devi nodded, glancing at her watch again.

"When do you need to get back to Madison?" Rylee asked.

Devi's phone buzzed. She flipped it over to look at the text, but quickly put it back down. "I'm sorry, Rylee," she said. "I can't stay much longer." She wiped her mouth quickly and set the napkin next to her nearly uneaten plate.

"That's okay," Rylee told her. "Can I drop you off anywhere?"

Devi shook her head. "Tyler is picking me up."

"Well, it was fun going out for lunch," Rylee told her, grabbing her wallet from her purse on the floor. "If you'll give me a minute—"

Devi stood. "I have to go," she said, with an apologetic look.

"No worries," Rylee told her, forcing a smile. "See you next week!"

Rylee stood in front of the mirror on the exam room's door, giving herself a once-over. It may have been the princess cut of the tunic she was wearing or the fabric of the skirt, but it almost looked like her baby bump was starting to peek out.

She ran a careful hand across her belly, trying to feel if it was just the shirt or if there was a definite curve to her stomach.

"Oh, my God," she breathed uncertainly. "I think I'm starting to show!"

She tried to catch Sam's eye in the mirror as he snorted, but he had his head down, studying that ever-present phone.

There was a knock on the door, followed almost immediately by the nurse. "Why don't we get a quick look at that baby?" she said, a bright smile lighting up her face.

Rylee quickly got onto the exam bed and laid back against firm plastic. The nurse grabbed a white sheet from one of the upper cabinets and laid it on Rylee's lap before pulling the skirt higher to expose her belly.

The nurse grabbed the medical gel from the warming tray, squirted a bit on her lower abdomen, then grabbed the flat-headed wand and began to roll it across her stomach.

There was a long, almost uncomfortable pause as she moved the wand from one side of Rylee's stomach to the other. Then, a small blur appeared on the screen.

"There we are!" the nurse told her with a chuckle. Rylee laughed in relief, staring intensely at the screen.

"Did you know that your baby is able to open and close their fingers and curl their toes?" she told Rylee as she rolled the wand over to the left side of her abdomen.

"Really?" Rylee breathed, then stole a glance at Sam. He was still engrossed with whatever was on his phone.

"Yup," the nurse told her. "Baby's nose and even their little fingernails are starting to form." She moved the wand higher up, then paused it. "And here's the heartbeat," she told them. Rylee craned her neck, focusing on that single spot in the middle of the screen. It flickered rapidly, the movement blending together as if it was pulsing to get her attention.

"Would you like to hear it?" she asked.

"Oh, yes," Rylee breathed.

The nurse smiled as she picked up another wand and coated it with gel. Then, she moved the wand around Rylee's belly, hunting for the heartbeat. After a long while, she pulled the wand away.

"What's wrong?" Rylee demanded. Was there something wrong with the baby?

"You're in your fifteenth week, so it might be just a bit too soon for the Doppler to find it," the woman finally told her. "Your baby is fine. We should be able to pick up the heartbeat at your next visit."

She grabbed a cloth, quickly cleaned the Doppler wand, and set it aside. Then, she grabbed the original wand, added a bit more gel, and placed it back against Rylee's belly.

Rylee pulled herself up on one elbow and glared up at the nurse. *That didn't sound right*, she thought. She could have sworn that Chloe had heard Patrick's heartbeat early in her second trimester. Was there something wrong with the baby?

Sam stirred from the far corner and held up a hand. "It's okay, Rylee," he told her, almost matter-of-factly. "You saw the heartbeat on the screen, right?"

Rylee ground her teeth. He only paid attention when he wanted to. "When will I be able to feel the baby move?" Rylee asked, hesitantly.

"Well," the nurse told her. "You should start feeling the baby move when you're in your twentieth week, so you've got a bit of time." She fiddled with a control and zoomed. "Let me get a quick measurement of the baby's neck and we'll be done."

There was a quick rap on the door and Dr. Zastrow came in. He crossed the small room, looking over the nurse's shoulder as she continued to take screenshots. Sam slouched down in his chair and buried himself in his phone again.

"Alright," Dr. Zastrow finally said. "Let's go ahead and get you cleaned up." He stepped back, and the nurse handed her a cloth to wipe her stomach. The nurse gave the wand a quick swipe of a clean cloth and quickly left the room.

Rylee sat up, slowly pulling her tunic down and placing a protective hand over her stomach.

"Let's get started," Dr. Zastrow said as he moved to his seat at the desk. "We're seeing a healthy development, Rylee, and the ultrasound confirms that you are fifteen weeks pregnant."

She nodded.

"Your risk of miscarriage will continue to go down the further along you are," the doctor continued. "Preliminary ultrasound doesn't show signs of a chromosomal disorder, but we'll be following up with a blood test to determine if you have risk."

At that, Sam stirred. "Meaning what?" he demanded.

Dr. Zastrow turned and looked at him. "Prenatal screening cannot diagnose any specific condition," he told him. "A fetus with a buildup of fluid at the base of their neck is at increased risk of having a chromosomal problem, such as Down's Syndrome."

He turned to look at her. "You need to keep in mind that we can only assess the risk, Rylee," he said in a reassuring voice. "We'll need to follow up with a blood test but, as of right now, things look very positive."

"Hang on a minute," Sam interjected. "At our court hearing, we were told that you couldn't test for this stuff until later." He thought for a moment. "I think it was called amnio?"

The doctor nodded. "Ah. Yes, amniocentesis can be performed at about fifteen weeks' pregnant to analyze fetal chromosomes for abnormalities," he replied. "We insert a needle into the mother's uterus—"

Rylee gasped. "Um, no!" Her hands automatically rubbed protectively at her small baby bump.

"—however, this is only done if we determine that there is a significant risk of genetic abnormality," he continued.

"But you'd also be able to verify paternity, right?" Sam asked, shooting a glance at Rylee.

She looked away. *How could he even think that this baby wasn't his?*

"We could," the doctor slowly replied, looking at Rylee, then back at Sam, "but given the circumstances, we'd need approval from the Court to run a paternity test if we need to proceed with amniocentesis."

Sam took a deep breath and nodded, a disappointed look settling on his face.

Dr. Zastrow looked down, clearly uncomfortable, and then cleared his throat before he began to quiz Rylee about her appetite, morning nausea, and periodic lightheadedness. It almost sounded like a repeat of Erin's endless questions about how their bodies were changing.

As they talked, she looked over to Sam. He seemed to have tuned most of it out, even though he hadn't buried his face in his phone again. Every once in a while, Dr. Zastrow would try to include Sam in the conversation, but Sam would just nod. It was as if Rylee didn't exist.

After a few more minutes, Sam pulled out his phone. He glanced at it and then put it away. "Um, I hate to interrupt, but I need to leave soon," he told them. "I have a test today. It's a third of my grade, so I can't miss it."

Dr. Zastrow stood. "That's fine," he said, giving Sam a disapproving look. He turned back to Rylee. "Please touch base with our billing department. I believe we may have gotten approval for your doula." Then, he looked back at Sam. "I'll see you again in four weeks."

He left, not quite slamming the door behind him. Sam looked at Rylee in surprise. "What did I do?" he asked.

Rylee got off the exam table and smoothed her clothing. "Doesn't matter," she finally told him with a shrug. "You're going to be late for your test." *If you even have a test today*, she thought.

Chapter Nine

Rylee looked out the car window, glaring at the rundown, three-story place that was next on Sam's list of potential apartments. The old house had started as a simple single-family unit. At some point, the owner had broken it up into two small apartments.

The siding was a faded gray, with brown brick, window casings, and door frames. A small balcony overlooked the front doors. Dead plants wilted in pots lining one side of the steps leading in.

She still couldn't believe Sam had gone through and eliminated all of her candidates from the potential list of apartments. Even the single bedroom with a large den! Somehow it kept coming back to money.

Sam was staring at her from the sidewalk. Rylee sighed and slowly got out of the car, bracing herself for what was to come. There was no way this place was going to work.

She followed Sam up the slightly uneven wooden steps to the front doors. He knocked on the right door and a woman let them in.

"Sam, right?" she asked.

Sam nodded. "We're here about the apartment."

She opened the screen door. "Come on in," she said with a smile. She waited until they were both in the small entry, then gestured up the stairs. "This way."

Rylee grabbed the handrail and dutifully trailed after the pair as they quickly climbed the old wooden stairs to a small living room. A two-seat couch hugged the space directly under the front windows, with a recliner pushed into the far corner. A dozen or so boxes were piled up in front of a small entertainment center on the far wall.

The property manager walked across the room and into the small kitchen. It had two different styles of cabinets on either side of the wall. A kitchen sink was tucked into one corner, almost an afterthought.

"This place is about as big as my bedroom," Rylee muttered as they followed the apartment manager to the second floor. "I can't believe you're suggesting that we live in such a dump!" she hissed.

Sam shot her a dirty look over his shoulder. "Well, if you hadn't spent so much on maternity clothes, and your urgent *spa time*, we might have been able to afford more!" Sam retorted. "We need to save some money!"

"Well, excuse me for being pregnant and needing deep tissue massages!" Rylee shot back. "This baby of yours is starting to push my back out of place and I can't take anything for the pain! Besides, if we're running out of money, maybe you should, you know, work more hours!"

"Yeah, that would work, wouldn't it, Rylee?" Sam growled. "Maybe I should just drop out of school so that I can give you money for more massages! Besides, why don't you use your own money?"

"Because you and my father have made it *very apparent* that I have to turn *every single receipt* into the Court, Sam!" she snarled at him. "Which means my parents can't cover my bills anymore. It's not like I can walk into any business, and they'd just hire me!"

Rylee followed him into the bathroom. *It was no bigger than a closet*, Rylee thought. How could he expect them to live like this?

Sam turned around to look at her. "Look," he said, lowering his voice. "We really need to get a place, and this one will do until we find something better. It's only $950 a month."

Rylee looked over at the pedestal sink, giving it a critical eye before turning to him. "I don't like this. There's no room for my make-up or anything."

"We can get a small cabinet or some shelves or something," he replied. "There's plenty of room against that wall." She opened her mouth to protest, but he overrode her. "As it is, this place doesn't become available until January 1st. We don't have a lot of options and are running out of time."

She glared at him. She'd given him a list of acceptable apartments, including the three-bedroom at the East Home Complex. He'd turned every single one of them down.

She sighed. "Point," she finally replied. "I just need this to be over."

"You and me, both," Sam said with a sigh.

Rylee left the bathroom to check out the bedrooms. Sam followed her. They were approximately the same size, with tiny closets and windows on two sides of the room. The room in the back had more of an airy feeling, despite its size. She could see the tops of the trees in the backyard.

She stood with her back to the window, looking out into the hallway. *It wasn't fair*, she thought. Mackenzie had cut the rent to only $1,500.

The apartment manager poked her head into the room. "Would you like to check out the backyard?" she asked, a wry smile playing on her lips. No doubt she heard the argument.

"Sure," Sam said as he walked out of the other bedroom. He headed down the stairs after her, and Rylee carefully followed them.

"There's only room for one car in the garage," she told them. Street parking was always an option, but Rylee knew it would become almost impossible to find, given winter parking restrictions. Plus, she doubted the garage had an EV hookup.

Sam explored the small yard. An ancient grill sat outside of the garage, missing the propane tank that should have been nestled underneath the burners. An old picnic table had been placed near the back steps, the worn brown paint peeling from exposure. A rusted fire bowl and a few folding lawn chairs were propped up against the side of the house.

"I'll leave the two of you alone to decide," the manager told them. "I'll be upstairs if you need me."

Sam nodded and took a seat at the old picnic table. She sighed, but after a moment, she carefully sat down across from him. Ancient food stains had soaked into the unprotected wood. She grimaced, but finally found a place for her hands.

Sam reached over the table for her hand. Rylee briefly hesitated, then gently put her hand in his. He absently rubbed his thumb against the back of her hand a few times, studying their hands. It reminded her of better times. When they didn't have to yell at each other to make their point.

Sam looked up, a sad expression on his face. "This is the least expensive place we've seen, Rylee," he told her. "We need to pick a place so we can check it off the list."

Rylee stared at him. She'd already told him she couldn't live poor. What more was there to say? That she was terrified of living in such a bad neighborhood? That she felt like she was giving up everything she had just to have this baby?

He shook his head. "It's only temporary until we can find a place we can afford," he told her.

Rylee sighed, leaning forward to stare at the worn table beneath their hands. She wasn't going to win this one. "Okay," she finally said. "We can take this place for now as long as we can keep looking."

Sam nodded once. He stood up, pulling out his wallet. He looked down at her and she slowly got to her feet. She wasn't sure how long it would take the property manager to run their application and credit check, but she was not looking forward to the coming months.

A week later, Rylee wandered around the first floor of the Birthing Center, completely lost. She'd parked in a nearby parking structure, only to discover the entrance was for another medical building on the campus. So, she'd found her way outside, entered a side door, and found herself wandering the hallways.

Eventually, a nurse took pity on her and directed her to the front desk to check in. She sat down on a nearby couch and checked the time. She sighed. Ten minutes late. Hopefully, she wouldn't have to reschedule. She was meeting Sam after lunch.

"Rylee Williams?"

Rylee turned around. An older woman, with short blond hair and an easy smile, stood near the front desk. She nodded and went to meet her.

"I'm Rylee," she said. "Are you Diana?"

"I am," Diana said. "Why don't we go to my office so we can talk?"

Rylee nodded. "Of course."

She followed Diana down a brightly lit corridor. Large windows lined one side of the hallway, allowing natural light to filter in. The soft, muted tones of pale blue and pink on the walls blended with the warm, neutral carpet.

Diana opened the door to an office on the right. There was no desk, just a few comfortable seats around a small table.

"Why don't you have a seat?" Diana asked. She picked up the tablet from the table and settled it on her lap.

Rylee sat, looking around. The far wall was a floor-to-ceiling window, with a snow-covered shrub hugging the bottom quarter of the view. The wall to her right held an enormous whiteboard, with diagrams and pages magnetically pinned at random intervals. It was a calm type of chaos.

"According to the information you uploaded on MyChart, you're seventeen weeks pregnant," Diana told her as she rapidly scanned the site on her tablet. "That means your due date is April 22nd, give or take a few weeks." She crinkled her nose in amusement.

"What do you mean?" Rylee asked.

"This is your first pregnancy, right?" Diana asked. Rylee nodded. "First pregnancies can take a bit longer. When I'm scheduling first-time mothers, I always create a four-week window."

Rylee gasped. "Four weeks?!"

Diana laughed. "Two weeks on either side of the due date," she told Rylee. "Some babies are early. Some are late. And some," she said as she reached over to place her hand on Rylee's, "some are right on time!"

Rylee smiled in return.

"Now, before we get started on discussing your birth plan, I'm going to need to ask you a few questions," Diana told her with a warm smile. "A doula is part mentor, part birthing instructor. But, I'm much more than that, Rylee. I provide my clients with both emotional and physical support, not only during the actual labor, but also before and after their baby is born. This means I need to get a bit deeper into your life than you might be comfortable with." She paused, searching Rylee's face for a moment. "Anything you tell me will be held in the highest confidentiality."

"What do you need to know?" Rylee asked, a bit perplexed. "Everything should be in my medical file."

Diana sighed. "I'm somewhat familiar with the WIFE program," she told Rylee, her quiet voice and soft expression putting Rylee more at ease than her actual words. "I have a few questions about how involved your partner is."

"Oh," Rylee murmured. She took a deep breath and let it out. "What do you need to know?"

Diana smiled. "Thank you for trusting me," she said. "First, your partner's name is Sam, right?"

Rylee nodded.

"How involved is he with your preparations?" Diana asked. "I know he's required to go to all doctor appointments and the birthing classes, but has he been actively engaged?"

Rylee looked away. She shook her head sadly. "He's taken me shopping a few times, and we finally found a temporary apartment to live in until the baby's born, but otherwise . . . " Her voice trailed off.

"That happens sometimes," Diana told her. "Either way, we'll work through this together. Sound like a plan?"

Rylee nodded.

"Good!" Diana slapped both hands against her lap, then stood. "Let me grab a few things and we'll get started on your birth plan, which is subject to change, based on what *you* need. Nobody else!"

Rylee leaned back in her chair, watching as Diana pulled a few pieces of paper off the whiteboard for her. She'd already taken the Preparing for Labor course, but it was just a basic overview and she had so many questions.

Diana sat back down and passed Rylee the tablet. *Time to get to work*, she thought.

Rylee pulled yet another maternity top out of the rack, shook her head at the poor-quality fabric, and quickly put it back. She needed to plug a few holes in this 'capsule wardrobe' she was supposed to be wearing for the next few months, but this was ridiculous. It didn't matter that the store was having a 'blowout' sale. What mattered was finding something that wouldn't fall apart the first time she had it washed.

She moved to the next overstuffed rack. Sam slowly followed, holding the few items that had made it to the 'maybe' list. He was clearly irritated, but too bad. He'd complained so much about how much she was spending. Let him see the effort that she was putting into saving money.

A maroon dress caught her eye. Long-sleeved. Boiled wool. That might work for this year's Advent by Candlelight. She checked the label. Fifty percent off. She handed it over to Sam and continued moving down the aisle.

Sam cleared his throat, moving closer. "Did you hear that Tyler and Devi have decided to put their baby up for adoption? Makes me wonder—"

"Stop it, Sam," she snapped. "Adoption is not on the table and never will be!"

"Why not?" he demanded. "Don't you want to get your life back when this is over?"

She stopped and pulled a navy two-piece dress out. She studied it for a moment before putting it back. Not long enough to hide the tracker.

"I do, Sam," she conceded. "But giving this child up for adoption is not an option."

Sam frowned. For a moment, he looked like a child who had been told he couldn't have another slice of pie for dessert. "Can you at least tell me why?" he demanded.

Rylee gave him a long look before she moved deeper into the store. "This baby is a miracle," she told him. "An actual gift from God. I shouldn't have been able to get pregnant and I am not giving up this baby." She paused to pull a few sweaters out of the shelves against the far wall.

"Why couldn't you get pregnant?" he asked, ducking around the shelves so that he could look directly at Rylee.

She sighed. This was not the right place to have this discussion, but she didn't think he'd be satisfied with her brushing him off. "Because I have fibroids and my ovaries don't really work," she finally told him. She handed one of the sweaters to him. "Same as Chloe. Which means this may be my only chance of becoming a mom. I have to take it, whether I'm ready or not."

"What about me?" he growled at her. "I'm not ready for any of this shit!"

"Neither am I, obviously," she snapped, throwing another sweater in his direction. "But we have to make this work."

Sam caught the sweater and glared at her. "How?" he demanded. "I've given up tennis. My scholarships. I'm not going to graduate on time. I even got a side job to help pay for all of this. It's not enough, Rylee. How are we going to make this work?"

Rylee grabbed the pile of clothes and glared up at him. "We will find a way," she snapped. "Just because you've given up doesn't mean that I will!" And, with that, she fled to the changing rooms.

She locked herself into the first open room, then sat, clothing falling to the floor at her feet. She covered her face with her hands as hot tears threatened to flow. *Stop it!* she told herself. *Never, ever, let them see you cry!*

After a long moment, she fumbled for her purse and pulled out a tissue. Then, she studied her face in the mirror as she carefully blotted away the evidence. Blotchy eyes. Smeared makeup. Great. She pulled her emergency gear out of her purse and got to work fixing her face.

She didn't understand why Devi had agreed to give up her baby for adoption. She'd never mentioned it at the group meetings. Was she being forced to do this so that she could stay and finish her master's degree? Was this any of her business?

Possibly not. She put her makeup away and looked down at the pile of clothes on the floor. She didn't care if this stuff was on sale—time to go home.

That night, Rylee stared at the chessboard, plotting her opening move. Her mom had moved her pawn two paces ahead, directly in front of the king. Should she mirror that or advance her rook's pawn?

Her phone chimed. She looked down. A text from Devi.

She quickly moved the rook's pawn forward, then picked up her phone to read the message. After Sam had dropped her off, she'd sent a quick text to Devi just to see how she was doing. She hadn't expected a response.

Not good. Can we meet for coffee?

Sure, Rylee replied. *Before the group meeting or after?*

There was a long pause, then, *Can you meet me at Amy's Farmington Inn? Looks like it's just under 40 miles from the Milwaukee courthouse.*

Rylee stared at the text. Meet in the middle of nowhere?

She pulled up her phone's browser. Looked like that restaurant was 39 miles from the courthouse, right off the freeway.

"Everything okay?" her mom asked.

Rylee looked up from her phone. "Just one of my friends."

"We can take a break if you'd like to talk to her," her mom told her.

"Just a sec," Rylee responded. *Sure,* she typed back. *Is that too far away for you?*

No. Can you meet me there tomorrow?

She thought about it. Tomorrow was Friday. That was the day the boys had their mentoring meeting. *Lunch? Say noon-ish?* she quickly typed.

There was a long pause. *That works. See you then!*

Rylee looked up the address and saved it to her phone. Then, she sat back and looked at the chessboard again. What was so urgent that Devi needed to meet with her in farm country?

Rylee pulled into the parking lot, relieved she'd made it in one piece. The drive from Milwaukee was uneventful but scary all the same. Farmington wasn't immediately off of the freeway, so she'd had to get off at the Concord exit and take the back roads in. All she could do was closely watch her trip odometer and pray she didn't accidentally go over the fifty-mile limit from the courthouse.

She scanned the parking lot. Her Lucid Air looked so out of place among the gas-powered pickup trucks and the car with the rusted side panel. She spotted a newer hybrid parked around the back of the restaurant and knew she was in the right place.

She parked her car next to Devi's and headed inside. It looked like it had started as an old farmhouse, two stories with an outdoor seating area under a large awning. An impressive front porch with three steps.

Rylee pushed open the main door and paused to let her eyes adjust after the bright sunlight. A bar was set up to her left, with restaurant seating to her right.

"Be right with you," a waitress called over as she walked across the room with a tray of food from the kitchen.

Rylee looked around. Devi waved at her from a booth in the far corner.

"I see my party," she told the waitress. Then, she walked over to the booth and slid in across from Devi. "Sorry I'm late," she said, pushing her purse onto the seat.

Devi took a sip from her water glass, nodding. "I was afraid you weren't able to make it," she said nervously.

"I've been looking forward to it," Rylee responded. "I just got turned around a bit."

"Hello," the waitress said, laying down menus in front of them. "First time?" They both nodded, ruefully making eye contact with each other.

"Great!" the waitress said. "I always recommend our specialty burgers but, if you're looking for something a bit different, take a look at our char-grilled sandwiches. All sandwiches come with chips and a pickle, but if you're interested in fries, I'd recommend our sour cream and chive fries." She pointed them out on Devi's menu. "Can I get you anything to drink?"

"Coffee, please, decaf," Devi told her.

Rylee nodded. "Same."

"Sounds good," the waitress replied. "I'll give you a few minutes to decide," she told them. There was the sound of a bell ringing, and she hurried off to pick up another customer's order.

Devi smiled, looking down at her menu. "I guess I am a bit hungry," she sheepishly admitted. "How do you feel about cheese pizza?"

Rylee scanned the menu. As interesting as the portobello mushrooms sounded, she suspected most of the appetizers were deep-fried and she didn't think she could stomach that right now. "Sounds good to me!" she said.

She gestured, and Devi gave her the menu. She put them together and set them on the side of the table.

"So," she asked. "How're you doing?" That sounded lame, but she couldn't think of anything else to say.

Devi gave a sad smile. "I'm as okay as I can be under the circumstances," she replied. "And you?"

Rylee chuckled. "Same."

Devi looked over Rylee's shoulder, studying the restaurant. "I don't talk about the baby with anyone else," she confided. "I still haven't told my parents."

"You haven't?" Rylee asked, amazed. Devi was over seven months pregnant!

Devi slowly shook her head. "I couldn't do it. I tried, but . . . I just can't get the words out." She swallowed, looking frightened. "I don't know if I can ever tell them."

Rylee reached out and briefly put her hand on Devi's. "I'm so sorry," she told her. "Sometimes I forget that your parents are back in Ontario."

The waitress stopped at their table, coffee cups in hand. She poured them some freshly brewed coffee, the slight scent of toasted nuts and a hint of caramelized sugar lingering in the air.

"How much do your parents know?" Rylee asked. Then, she stared at Devi in horror. "TMI," she immediately told Devi. "I'm sorry. None of my business!"

Devi smiled. "No, it's okay," she reassured her. "They know that I've met someone they won't approve of."

"Sounds complicated," Rylee said, wrinkling her nose.

Devi nodded. "I'd hoped to avoid husband hunting until after graduation." She looked down. "I'm not sure how I'm going to get through this while holding down a full academic schedule and working on my thesis."

All Rylee could do was nod in sympathy. *Something would have to give*, she thought. She'd watched Chloe struggle to stay on top of her responsibilities as COO while she was pregnant. She couldn't imagine being pregnant, taking a full class load, and traveling to Milwaukee every week for the mentoring meetings.

Devi looked up. "Ah, the food's here."

The waitress set down a dented pizza pan in front of them and then gave them small plates. "Anything else I can get you, ladies?" she asked. They both shook their heads. "Okay, then. Bon appetite!" she said, then walked away.

Rylee picked up a slice of pizza, the cheese stretching as it struggled to retain its place on the pan. The crust was a bit limp but had a homemade texture.

"It feels good to get out of the house," Rylee commented between bites. "We should do this more often!"

Devi smiled. "I'd like that."

Rylee put her slice down and pulled her phone out of her purse. "What do you say about scheduling something?" she asked. "If we don't get in trouble for leaving our safety zone, that is!"

"Or," Devi said, that smile turning sad. "We could always set up a video call."

"Done!" Rylee replied.

Chapter Ten

Rylee ducked into the butler's pantry. She knew she'd taken out the gravy boat, but she couldn't remember where she'd put it down. She'd already checked the dining room, the kitchen, and the china cabinet, just to be sure. They weren't kidding about 'baby brain'.

There it was, right behind the serving bowls! She piled them all together and hurried back into the kitchen. It had been quite the morning already. Mom insisted on cooking everything from scratch, even though their personal chef had repeatedly offered to come in for a few hours to assist. Thanksgiving was her holiday; the one day that everyone converged on the family compound.

Everything had to be perfect. Mom was up at the crack of dawn, so the turkey got into the oven early. Rylee and Mackenzie started working before breakfast, peeling an entire bag of yams, followed by a bag of Yukon potatoes, and then, they moved to prepping green beans for the casserole and chopping up apples for the holiday pies.

"Chloe's here," Mom exclaimed, as she bustled back into the kitchen, frantically looking over the preparations. Any minute Nana was going to poke her head in, and every single time, Mom took it personally.

"Make way!" Chloe yelled, just a few steps behind their mom. "We have pie crusts that are ready for filling, and I made a small pecan pie last night with the leftover dough." She carefully placed the box with the crusts on the island countertop, smiling with relief. "Be right back," she told them. "I need to get Patrick settled."

Rylee looked over at Mackenzie. "She's going to be useless today," she muttered. "Baby's first Thanksgiving."

Mackenzie nodded. "Okay, I'm ready to move on to the stuffing," she announced.

Mom pulled out a mixing bowl and placed it on the kitchen table. "Let's get those apples in the refrigerator for now," she told them. "Rylee, there's some baby spinach and kale under the counter. Get that chopped up and added to the salad."

Rylee nodded.

"Ashley, darling," Nana said, sweeping into the kitchen with a practiced step. "Do you need any help?" Rylee bent her head to hide her smile. That silk Carolina Herrera suit was out of place in any kitchen.

"Of course not, Mother," Mom fired back, forcing a smile on her face as she wiped a cheek against her shoulder. "We're good."

Nana casually looked over the preparations, then brushed an elegantly manicured hand across her carefully styled silver hair. "I'll play hostess, then," she told them, looking faintly disappointed. "Will Ryan be joining us, Mackenzie?" she asked.

Mackenzie looked up from her mixing bowl. "He's here, Nana," she replied. "Let me introduce you." She dusted off her hands on her apron.

"Excellent," Nana replied. "I'm looking forward to meeting him." Then she turned to Rylee. "And Sam? Will he be joining us?"

"Um, no, Nana," Rylee replied. "He, uh—" He wasn't invited, but Rylee couldn't seem to make the words get past her lips as she glanced at her mom.

"The Maxwell family has their *own* family gathering planned, Mother," her mom told her, that fake smile fading just a bit.

"Ah," Nana responded with a slight frown. "Another time, perhaps." Her tone made it clear that she expected Sam to attend Christmas dinner.

There was a muted burst of baby outrage. Chloe almost ran into the kitchen, a frantic look on her face. "Binky," she told them. "Has anyone seen Patrick's binky?"

"Oh, dear," Nana said, already looking around the floor. Patrick was very specific when it came to his pacifiers. Only his blue one would appease him.

Rylee moved to the other side of the island and started looking around the box that the pie crusts had been in. Nothing. She carefully retraced Chloe's steps to the back entrance. Nothing on the floor. She found their winter coats in the mudroom closet. Patrick's blue binky was still attached to his jacket.

"Found it!" she yelled over her shoulder. She quickly made her way back to the kitchen, but Chloe had already gone back into the family room as she tried, unsuccessfully, to calm poor Patrick down.

She rinsed the pacifier and then found a clean towel to dry it. "I'll be right back," she told everyone. Nana nodded and followed her out of the kitchen.

They walked down the tiled hallway to the main family room. It was a bit cozy, with most of the family gathered. Chloe was at the epicenter of the storm, little Patrick refusing all attempts at being comforted. He was screaming, little fists balled up as he screamed.

"Here you go," Rylee said, popping his binky into his mouth.

Patrick froze, eyes opening as he recognized the binky. Both of his fists came up and claimed the pacifier, and he glared at her as if she were the cause of his outrage.

Chloe gaped at Rylee, then pulled the binky out of Patrick's mouth, sparking fresh outrage. She popped it in her mouth, sucking hard at it before putting it back in Patrick's mouth. Then, she rubbed his back, trying to soothe him.

"It was fine, Chloe," Rylee told her. "I rinsed it off and wiped it with a clean towel. It was still pinned to his coat."

Chloe rocked back and forth on her hips, glaring at Rylee.

"Okay . . ." Rylee said, not quite understanding what the problem was. Patrick had his binky, right?

"I wish that we were going to Belize after Christmas," she heard Mackenzie tell their grandfather. "I need a bit of a break."

Rylee didn't quite hear what Papa said in return, but Mackenzie's boyfriend, Ryan, spoke up. "We can go by ourselves, Kenzie," he said. "Just the two of us."

"Mackenzie," her father said, a firm tone to his voice. "As much as we always look forward to our annual Christmas vacation, this year we need to pull together as a family for Rylee." He paused, visually sweeping the room with a look that was meant to put to rest any argument. "If you need to take a break, I'm sure you can find something closer to home."

Rylee cringed and quietly made her way out to the hallway. She almost made it back to the kitchen before she heard Chloe coming up behind her. Patrick was making singing noises around his binky. She turned around.

"You know, Rylee," she said in that quiet, vengeful tone that only a sister could master. "Poor Patrick may not have a little brother or sister for a while, thanks to you."

Rylee turned back, looking at Chloe, confused. "How is that my fault?" she demanded.

"You got pregnant without any help," Chloe hissed. "So, Alexander thinks that we should try to have another baby the old-fashioned way."

Rylee slowly blinked at Chloe. "Is this the part where I'm supposed to apologize for being pregnant?" she ground out, trying to keep her voice down as she leaned forward a bit. "Yes, I had sex with Sam," she stated, one hand clasping her baby bump protectively. "Yes, it *bothers me* that we can't have a normal Christmas vacation because *the state* decided to put me under house arrest for the *crime* of getting pregnant!"

She rubbed at her stomach, feeling a strange fluttering sensation low in her abdomen as the baby started kicking. "I don't understand why you're angry with me," she told Chloe, feeling hot tears threatening to spill down her cheeks. "Getting pregnant is not a competition event!"

With that, Rylee fled back into the mudroom. She huddled on the bench, trying to swallow the sobs that threatened to escape her fragile control.

After a long moment, she looked down at her baby bump. "It's going to be okay, little one," she told the baby as her right hand circled her belly in a long, quiet movement. "Auntie Chloe is just being her normal bitchy self today."

She looked out the window across from the bench. Any sympathy she'd felt for Chloe's long struggle with infertility had just evaporated. In time, she might be able to forgive Chloe, if only because it was the right thing to do, but she would never forget that the very first time she felt her baby kick was in response to Chloe's temper tantrum.

Rylee settled back against the car seat, trying to find a more comfortable spot as Sam drove them to the apartment. She still couldn't believe she'd agreed to this. All because she was trying to help Sam and his worry about money.

As always, Sam completely ignored her. She found herself trying to fill the void. "I love my doula," she told him, trying to find a bit of enthusiasm as she went through the list of things that she'd been working on the last few weeks. "Diana is also a lactation specialist, so she'll be able to help if the baby has any problems latching on."

Sam grunted, scanning the road ahead. Parking was at a premium in this part of the city, so the cars that crowded either side of the street made navigating the narrow streets especially treacherous after the recent snowfall.

Rylee sighed. "I really wish we'd kept looking," she told him, hearing the whine in her voice but unable to help herself. "I have no idea how I'm going to get up and down those stairs every day. I'm in my twenty-fifth week, you know!"

Sam pulled into the alley behind the house. He parked the car next to the garage so that he had a clear path directly into the backyard. Then, he got out, popped open the trunk, and grabbed a box, completely ignoring Rylee as she struggled to get out of the car by herself.

She carefully walked over to the chain-link fence, watching him stomp his way through the low drift of snow. He used his elbow to push aside some of the snow that covered the picnic table, then set the box on the table.

He turned around and looked over at her. "Aren't you going to help?" he asked.

She frowned, looking from him to the box and back. "You know that I'm not supposed to lift anything heavy!" she reminded him.

"Good thing these are small boxes and weigh less than five pounds!" he told her. "Wouldn't want you to strain anything."

Asshole! "Fine, I'll help!" She slowly moved around the car. It felt like the bottom layer of slush had frozen solid. "But if I fall, it's your fault!"

Sam stomped his way back to the car, glaring at her as if it was her fault they had snow on New Year's Day. "Well, maybe you should have told me before you stopped taking your birth control pills so that I could've gloved up!" he snapped. He looked over the pile of boxes in the trunk that were waiting to be taken in.

Rylee moved past him and opened the backseat door. She grabbed a few shoe boxes from the top of the pile. Babolat, of course. Wimbledon Whites.

She stood, looking over at him. "Sam, we've already gone over this," she told him as patiently as she could. "I have a medical condition. I wasn't supposed to be able to get pregnant without help."

"Bullshit!" Sam snapped at her. Rylee jumped, startled by his sudden outburst. "Obviously, you could—and did!—get pregnant!" He stalked around the back of the car to glare at her.

She held the shoe boxes tightly against her chest. "Don't you remember the problems that Chloe had getting pregnant?" she asked him, sharply.

He clenched his eyes shut for a second. "Why would I?" he demanded, his eyes snapping open.

"Because she's my sister, Sam!" Rylee pushed away from the car, glaring back at him. "She had to go through IVF and even that wasn't easy!"

Sam clenched his hands into fists. "What does that have to do with you?" he growled.

Seriously? "Every single woman in my family has struggled to get pregnant, Sam!" she yelled, glaring up at him. "Did you ever wonder why there is a four-year gap between Chloe and Mackenzie and a three-year gap between Mackenzie and me? No? Well, apparently my parents had problems having kids, too!"

Sam stared at her, puzzled. "So?"

Was basic biology beyond him? Rylee thought, feeling her rage bubbling up. "So, why should I take pills every single day that mess me up, when I only have my period two or three times a year because I can't ovulate!" she yelled at him.

"Don't ovulate, huh?" Sam laughed, shaking his head at her. "Seems like you managed to squeeze an egg out, didn't you?" he growled. "You should have told me you had stopped taking the Pill. I could have picked up a box of condoms and we wouldn't be here!"

That was it. Rylee found herself sliding back into the car, perching on the very edge of the backseat as the sobs she'd been holding in finally let loose. She let the boxes of shoes fall to the muddy asphalt, not caring if she ruined his tournament shoes.

She heard Sam move around the car and pull another box from the trunk. "When you're done, I'll be upstairs," he muttered in her direction. Then, he walked away, leaving her alone in the cold.

After a long time, Rylee slowly pulled herself together. She could hear traffic close by and the sounds of people out shoveling the slushy ice from in front of their garages. She rummaged around Sam's car until she found the tissue box that she'd stashed during allergy season. She took a few minutes to compose herself, then gathered up Sam's tennis shoes and carefully walked across the yard to let herself in.

She slowly climbed the steep stairs, feeling the strain in her lower back as she moved. She paused at the landing to slip her boots off and watched the muddy slush drip to the floor as she set them down. *There was room for a small bench,* she thought, *and maybe a boot tray.*

She slowly opened the back door, looking for Sam, before stepping into the kitchen. He was putting dishes into the cabinet near the stove. He glanced over, then went back to ignoring her.

The pungent smear of paint hung in the air. Rylee found herself breathing shallowly as the scent assaulted her, making her feel trapped in the tiny space.

She dropped the shoe boxes near the closet, quickly crossing the room to open the front windows. She took a few deep breaths of cold air as she steadied herself against the window frame.

"What are you doing?" Sam snarled, storming into the living room. "It's thirty degrees out there!"

"Airing this place out," she replied. She was amazed he couldn't smell it. "Paint fumes are bad for the baby. It's bad enough we already had some furniture delivered, so everything picks up that horrible smell." She looked from him to the couch and back, challenging him to say something.

He only glared at her, so she walked past him and into the kitchen. She opened that window, as well, then looked at the back door. No, letting it out to the hallway would just trap the fumes.

She saw him move to the thermostat and turn off the heat. *Of course, he did*, she thought as he slowly walked back into the kitchen. He grabbed another box off of the floor and moved it to the counter next to the stove.

"You going to help or what?" he asked snidely.

"Sure," she sniped back. She stepped past him and started to unpack the cups and assorted silverware. "I can't believe you're okay with the smell."

"It's just paint, Rylee," he told her, scolding her as if she was a child. "Give it a few days and it will be fine. Besides, we don't have to officially move in for a few weeks. All we have to do is get it ready for inspection."

He grabbed his empty box and placed it next to the back door. Then, he looked over the appliances with a wary eye, almost as if he shared her concern about how ancient everything was. He abruptly turned around, picked up the empty boxes off the floor, and headed back outside.

She watched him go, feeling empty. The kitchen layout was strange. The small kitchen sink was up against the living room wall, with barely enough room on the counter for an equally small dish drying rack.

She stood in front of the sink and took a few steps back, almost bumping into the side of the stove where it stood up against the wall next to the small pantry. The original kitchen cabinets were across from the stove, with the refrigerator directly to the right. There was room for a two-person table in the far corner. It felt like a prison.

Rylee walked back into the living room and stood looking at the busy street below. So much traffic. It was going to be impossible to get much sleep here.

She pulled out her phone and found Kathryn's number. She just needed to talk to someone, anyone, who might understand what she was going through.

"Hey, Rylee!" Kathryn said. "How's moving day?"

She heard the back door creak slightly as Sam came back in. He tossed a few boxes on the counter.

"Not so good," Rylee told her. "I don't like this place very much, Kathryn. It's such a dump. The carpet is old. It smells, and it's so small! I just want to go home!"

"I'm sorry," Kathryn replied. "But it's not like you have to live there very long, right?"

Sam tore open one of the boxes and began to loudly shove things into the cabinets. "They must have just painted and the fumes are almost overwhelming," Rylee found herself complaining as she glared into the kitchen.

"That's bad for the baby, right?" Kathryn asked.

"No, Sam says it's fine," she whimpered.

"What?"

"Yeah, I know. He doesn't understand what it's like to have to climb two flights of stairs just to get to the bedroom with a baby growing inside of you!" She paused for a moment. "I gotta let you go. It's freezing in here and I need to turn the furnace back on."

"Okay," Kathryn said. "Talk to you later."

Rylee put her cell phone down on the windowsill and started across the room to the thermostat, but Sam headed her off. "Close the windows first, Rylee."

"It's cold in here, Sam," she said, stating the obvious.

"That's because you had to open up all of the windows," he told her. "It's winter, for chrissake!"

The baby started moving, kicking at her lower abdomen insistently. Rylee slid a protective hand over the intermittent taps, trying to calm them both down. "But it still smells in here!"

He looked down at her hand, frowning as if she was reminding him why they were stuck there. "If you're worried about the baby, go home," he told her. "I can finish unpacking and close things up before I leave."

"But you drove us here," she protested.

"So, call Kathryn back," he shot back, grimacing. "Call your mom. Hell, call an Uber if you want to." He turned to head back into the kitchen. "Or you can help me put things away so we can get going sooner."

"Fine. I'll help," she told him. "Those back stairs are pretty steep, though. If I break an ankle, it will be your fault!"

The delivery crew arrived early, even though Rylee had specifically told the sales manager she couldn't be there before lunch. That meant cutting her exercise class short and racing to the apartment so they didn't force her to reschedule. Irritating, yes, but necessary because the housing inspection was coming up.

She carefully navigated the small alley and parked her car in the garage. Then, she headed to the front yard, where the crew had already started staging the small amount of furniture her tiny budget had allowed: a full-size bed frame, a dresser, a nightstand, and a bistro table with two chairs that just *might* fit in the kitchen. She'd carefully measured and remeasured the rooms, but there was no way to know until they brought the furniture in.

She looked over the group of men to find the foreman. One of them, a tall African-American, had a clipboard. It must be him.

She walked over, trying to find a pleasant smile for him. "Hi," she said, "I'm Rylee Williams. You must be here to deliver my furniture."

He nodded. "Sorry we're a bit early, but today's a light day." He looked up at the sky. A tiny snowflake swirled by.

"I understand," she reassured him. "Let me take you up."

She led him up the steps to the porch, then opened the ancient screen door to unlock the door to their apartment. They went up the steep stairs and into the living room.

"The stairs to the bedrooms are right around the corner," she said, pointing to the far side of the living room. She led him up the second set of stairs, holding on to the railing as she pushed herself upward.

The stairs opened up to a short hallway. "The main bedroom is to the left," she said. They slowly walked down the hallway, the sound of their movement echoing against the antique hardwood floors.

Rylee pushed open the door, looking over the small room. One wide window, framed by two narrow windows on either side, overlooked the busy road below. The door next to the windows led to a tiny closet. The mattress and boxspring were propped up against the far wall.

"The dresser should go next to the closet," she told him as she walked to the left side of the room. She peered into the open closet door, then firmly closed it. She'd moved about two weeks' worth of clothes and it seemed to overwhelm the small space.

He nodded. "Small room," he told her. "But we can make it all fit."

She nodded back. "I'll be in the kitchen if you need me."

Rylee fled down the stairs as quickly as she could, feeling just a bit overwhelmed by the feeling that the apartment was slowly starting to claim her. She made her way to the kitchen and pulled her iPad out of her bag. She set it on the countertop next to the stove so she could keep an eye on the movers as she worked.

She needed to understand why Sam was so stressed out about how much money they were spending. She glanced around the living room but didn't see a router.

Didn't matter. She unlocked her phone and got to work setting up a mobile hotspot. Then she hunted through her emails until she found the one that gave her access to the budget he'd created with the financial advisor, pulled it up, and started looking.

The crew brought in the dresser, carefully moving through the living room. She ignored them as she scanned through the simple spreadsheet. Each tab was a separate month and she could see his budget for rent, utilities, groceries, gas for his car, and estimated insurance costs.

Rylee traced her finger along the outside of the iPad, studying the numbers. This budget didn't make any sense. Where was he tracking the actual expenses so that they could validate their over-under? Seriously, wasn't that Budget 101?

She rolled her eyes and started searching through the folder to find the electronic receipts. Then, she updated the January sheet with everything she could find that qualified as 'pregnancy-related' expenses, added a few formulas so it could auto-calculate the account balance, and added a description field so they could quickly sum up each category.

As she worked, she found receipts for all kinds of things, including his online gaming habit. In the last few weeks, he'd bought two new titles, some avatar 'weapon enhancements,' and paid a premium subscription fee for something called 'Cosmic Battlegrounds'. All of that added up to over a hundred and fifty dollars.

Rylee thought about all of the complaints she'd fielded over the last few months. About how much money she was wasting while he spent money on his toys. She even found a receipt for something called a 'motion controller' that promised to provide the user with a more immersive experience for the low cost of three hundred dollars.

When she was done, she realized they had spent over $5,000 of the money their parents had deposited in the joint account to help them get started. No wonder Sam was freaking out.

"Where would you like the kitchen table?" one of the workers asked.

She pointed to the far corner of the kitchen. "Let's see if it fits there," she told him. She watched as they brought the small table in, followed by the two chairs.

It fit, but just barely. It would have to do.

She looked into the living room. Maybe her mom was right, and she should have her cleaning service stop by weekly to help out. Temporarily adding the apartment wouldn't cost much more than what Mom was paying now and it wouldn't need to be reported to the Court if it was tacked on to her parent's current account.

In the meantime, they had time to rework this budget into something more reasonable. She picked up the phone and iPad and had a seat while she waited for them to bring in the bed frame. The first step was to reach out to the accounting firm her family used to ensure they had an accurate 'poor people' budget to work with. Then, she had to figure out a way to report only items to the Court that fell within that budget until they went their separate ways.

Chapter Eleven

Rylee sat down on the yoga room floor, a bit apprehensive. Today's class was all about preparing for labor and so far, everything she'd read about it had terrified her.

Sam sat down beside her. He'd graduated from his usual Wimbledon Whites into a much more down-to-earth wardrobe: a dark green sweatshirt, worn jeans, and loafers. It made her feel just a bit more relaxed. Maybe he was ready to focus on the baby.

"Good morning." The instructor, a buff, blond woman, who had probably never been pregnant before in her life, smiled as she looked over the group. "I'm Jane and I'll be your instructor for this session."

She paused, looking over the small group. "We'll get started in just a few minutes," she told them. "In the meantime, why don't you pair up?"

There was a bit of shuffling while the guys moved to sit behind their partners. Rylee looked over to Sam. Should she move? Was he going to?

He sighed and moved behind Rylee, copying the other participants so that she was seated between his legs and able to lean up against his warmth. He leaned back on his hands, almost like he was avoiding even touching her.

As the last couple straggled in, Jane waved them to have a seat. "Today, we're going to work on breathing," she told them. "I know you're thinking, 'why do I need to work on breathing? I do that every day, right?'"

The class laughed.

"We're going to learn three different breathing techniques today," she told them, as she settled down on the floor in front of them. "One is for active labor. One is for transition, which can be the most painful part of labor. And the last one you'll use is when you're ready to push."

One of the women raised a hand, nervously biting her lip.

Jane leaned forward to read her name tag. "Yes, Julia?" she asked.

"Should we be practicing that last one?" Julia asked. She sounded a bit panicked to Rylee. "I mean, I have six more weeks to go and don't want to go into preterm labor!"

"Good question," Jane responded, cocking her head with concern. "Each of these exercises are designed to help you relax and work with your body when it's actually needed. It's perfectly safe to practice these in advance. In fact, we encourage it!"

She looked over the group. "Let's start this exercise with your hands on your belly," she told them. "This will help to remind you to breathe deeply into your diaphragm. You should feel your hand move as you breathe in and your belly expands.

"Breathe in, ladies. Slowly let your breath expand beneath your hands." Rylee shifted position, slowly breathing in as deeply as she could. "Pause for a moment. Now, slowly release that breath. Good!"

Rylee slowly let her breath out. This was similar to the breathing exercises she did for her yoga class, and she found herself moving her hands in a slow, circular motion along the sides of her belly.

"Now remember, when you are in active labor, that space you're breathing from is where your baby is, so that's where you need to focus your energies," the instructor told them. "Let's try that again, ladies. We're going to focus on breathing in for four to six seconds. Slow and steady. Fill that tummy like it is a balloon and make sure you are breathing only as deep as is comfortable for you."

Rylee closed her eyes and found herself relaxing back into Sam. She felt herself inhaling deeply, slowly filling her lungs with air. Exactly what she needed.

"Hold for just a moment," Jane told them. "Now, quietly exhale through your mouth." Rylee could hear the quiet exhalations around her and opened her mouth slightly to join them.

"This time, we're going to count it out. I need everyone to breathe with me, even you, dads! Expand that tummy as you inhale. Relax and breathe in one, two, three, four. Pause. Now exhale, breathing out all of that tension. And again . . . "

Behind her, Sam seemed to make a half-hearted attempt to follow the breathing exercise. She felt him take a shallow breath. His stomach barely moved behind her back.

"We do this four times in a row because this will help you focus during your contractions, which last anywhere from forty-five to sixty seconds during active labor," Jane told them. "Once you are in transition, your contractions may last up to ninety seconds long and come about every two minutes. Breathing through them is very important as it will help your body relax and help the baby move down into the birth canal."

Rylee squirmed a bit, trying to find a comfortable spot on the cushion. Her butt accidentally brushed up against Sam. Almost immediately, he moved away from her and she found herself leaning away from the minimal amount of support he'd been providing.

"Our next breathwork is to help you resist the urge to push before you're completely dilated," Jane told them. "These breaths are two short, shallow breaths."

She demonstrated, breathing in two short breaths through her mouth, followed by two sharp pants. There was a slight whistle, almost like she was sucking air in through a straw and then panting it out in two hard exhales.

Jane smiled. "Now, it may sound like you're hyperventilating," she told them. "But you're taking two purposeful and shallow breaths, followed by two purposeful breaths out. Let's give it a try, everyone."

Rylee pursed her lips and followed suit, drawing in two rapid but shallow breaths. Then, she panted them out, feeling her stomach muscles sharply contract as she pushed them out.

"Let's do that again, everyone," the instructor said, leading them through it one last time.

"Great job, everyone!" Jane said. "Our last exercise is breathing for the final stage of labor: the big push." The group laughed and she smiled. "Here's the thing: most women instinctively hold their breath while they try to push. But that may actually cause vaginal tears."

Rylee forced herself to lean back against Sam. She needed his support for this.

"We're going to start by breathing in deeply and comfortably," Jane said. "Expand your belly as you did in our first exercise. As you exhale, groan in the back of your throat as you tighten your abs. If it helps, try to envision that groan extending all the way down into your uterus, relaxing the birth canal to help your baby come into this world."

"Let's give it a try, shall we?" she said. "Breathe in . . . now exhale . . . "

Rylee breathed out a low groan, feeling Sam chuckle against her. She took another deep breath and groaned a bit louder, her anger giving it a bit more energy.

"Great job!" Jane exclaimed, smiling as if they'd done something amazing. "Just remember to tighten those abs and relax as you push all of that energy down and breathe that baby out!

"Last thing, ladies. Don't be afraid to practice this while you're sitting on the toilet." She grinned. "I know it sounds silly, but for those of you who have never given birth, pooping is the closest sensation to giving birth."

Rylee rolled her eyes. *Really? Is that really the last takeaway they needed to hear before their lunch break? Pooping is like giving birth?*

She couldn't wait until this session was over. Now, every single time she was in the bathroom, she'd have to worry about Sam making fun of her.

Rylee stood outside the classroom, watching Sam walk to his course on partner empathy. *Good luck*, she thought sourly. She highly doubted Sam was capable of even a small amount of understanding or sympathy after the way he'd acted this morning.

"Hey, Rylee!" a voice chirped from behind her. She turned and saw Mia wave as she strolled down the hallway, a relaxed look on her face.

"Hey, Mia!" She looked around but didn't see Zoey in the group of women crowded in the small room. "Where's your partner-in-crime?" she asked as Mia joined her, curious. They had become so close it was almost like they were sisters.

Mia giggled. "She took an earlier class," she told Rylee. "We got our schedules mixed up!"

The two of them walked in together and found a seat in the circle of chairs. Rylee didn't recognize many of the faces but was happy to have another person she knew there.

"Good afternoon, ladies," an older woman said as she walked into the room. Her red hair was drawn up into an intricate bun, echoing her elegant floral dress. "I'm Dawn Emerson, an esthetician. Today, I'm going to teach you the art of self-care."

"Self-care?" one of the women said, frowning. "My self-care routine has been reduced from 'coffee, coffee, coffee, sleep' to 'decaf, decaf, try to focus, couch, and sleep.'"

"Yes, I know," Dawn told them, her wry tone cutting through the chuckles. "Pregnancy can be especially challenging." She looked around the room. "Each of us learned early in life how to take care of ourselves. Wash our faces. Brush our hair. Some of us even were lucky enough to have a mom or older sister who helped us learn the basics of make-up and nails." She looked around the room expectantly. "But, how many of us actually know how to take care of ourselves?"

Rylee looked around the room, frowning. Of course, she knew how to take care of herself. Why wouldn't she?

Dawn picked up a large cloth bag from the floor next to her and set it down on the table at the front of the room. "Self-care is more than getting enough sleep or remembering to stay hydrated," she said. "It's about learning to put yourself first. After all, you're doing all the heavy lifting these days!

"Today, I'm going to give you some insights that will help you embrace the changes your body is going through," Dawn continued. She pulled a small bottle out of the bag and set it on the table. "We'll start with what to look for in pregnancy-safe skincare products."

More bottles followed as Dawn carefully lined them up along the front of the table. "We're also going to walk through how to pamper those sore and swollen feet, talk about pregnancy-safe essential oils to help you relax, and even talk about treating yourself to an occasional DIY spa day," she told them, a broad smile on her face.

Rylee looked at her, confused. So, self-care was all about going in for a spa treatment? That didn't seem right.

Dawn let the confused buzz build for a moment, then gestured to the back of the room. "If you'll grab a bag, we can get started," she told them. "All of the products, including a variety of soaps, moisturizers, shampoo, conditioner, face and body masks, scrubs, foot wraps, bath treatments, and the essential oil starter kit are courtesy of Pampered Moments, one of the sponsors of this course."

There was a pause, and then everyone seemed to stand up at once to converge on the back table. Rylee hefted her bag up with both hands, trying to get an idea of how much was in the bag. Mostly sample sizes, but it felt like a generous number of products were stuffed into the bag. She'd never heard of the company before but, based on the excitement around her, it might be something to look into.

"Before I introduce you to each product, I want to take a moment to remind you of something very important," Dawn told them as the group settled back into their seats. "Listen to your body."

Mia giggled at Rylee. "Listen to your body," she whispered. "Is that all?"

"It may sound like a simple thing to do," Dawn told them. "But how much of your day is spent ignoring the pain in your feet or lower back? How many times do you stop and say that you need a bit of a rest?"

Rylee cautiously looked around the room. Most of the women seemed to agree, so she nodded as well. Most of what she knew about pregnancy came from Chloe.

"My job doesn't let me take time off," a woman told the group. "If I don't work, I don't get paid. And if I don't get paid, I don't eat."

Dawn nodded. "One of the topics we're going to explore this afternoon is the idea of 'micro-scheduling' around a busy day," she told them. "Small changes to your daily routine can have a significant impact."

"Like what?" the woman asked.

"Why don't we start by going through each of the samples, and then we can review how to best incorporate micro-scheduling into your daily life. "Dawn told them with a smile. "We will cover micro-scheduling a bit later."

As they went through the samples, Rylee found herself drawn into the larger discussion. At twenty-nine weeks, she found it reassuring that there were simple things to do about her back pain, the swelling in her hands and feet, and being so tired that she had started taking afternoon naps.

As the class wound down, Mia was excited to give the DIY home spa idea a try. "I don't have a lot of time to myself," she confided to Rylee, "but this looks like fun!" She fanned a few of the sample recipe cards out. "I never would have thought of creating a homemade face mask from turmeric, lemon juice, and honey, but if it helps with those dark patches on my face, I'm all for it!"

Rylee quickly stashed the cards into her bag. They looked to be fairly simple to make, and she knew she could grab the ingredients from home. This wasn't just for women who couldn't afford to go to a spa. Dawn had told them that creating these items was another form of self-care. A way of taking care of oneself, without the need to rely on other people.

"I've included my card, along with our company's website," Dawn told them as they were wrapping up. "All participants here today automatically receive free shipping."

Rylee hid her smile as she packed everything back into the bag and grabbed her stuff. Give away free samples with free shipping and you might have a customer for life.

Mia and Rylee walked out into the hallway. She saw Sam a moment before he saw her. He was wearing an enormous black pregnancy vest, complete with large breasts and a baby bump that was bigger than hers. Mia giggled and pointed, setting the rest of the group into a fit of laughter as they converged on the poor guys.

"Oh, my God!" she squealed as she closed the distance between them. She just couldn't help herself. "They didn't tell us that we'd be twins for the day!"

Sam scrubbed at his face, looking like he'd just swallowed glass. "Rylee, just leave it be for once," he growled at her.

"But it's awesome you get to feel what I'm going through, even if it doesn't include the heartburn and cravings!" she told him. She couldn't help but gloat at his discomfort. "Speaking of which . . ." she trailed off suggestively, tracing a delicate finger across her belly.

"No," Sam snapped at her. "I'm not taking you out for custard. Not today. We're going back to the apartment and I'm going to get some homework done and watch a little TV. Period."

Rylee opened her mouth to protest. After all, they could just go through the drive-thru.

"For once in your life, can you think about someone else for a change?" he snapped at her.

Rylee looked up at him, matching him glare for glare. "I am thinking about someone else, Sam," she told him. "I'm thinking about your baby. You know, the one that I'm currently carrying?"

Sam turned away, shaking his head as he gingerly walked down the hallway to the stairs. "Dammit," he swore under his breath. "Bathroom first. Then, we're going back to the apartment."

As he headed down the hallway, closely followed by several other guys, Rylee couldn't help but laugh. They looked so silly.

Later that night, Rylee loaded the dishwasher, trying to find the right way to broach the subject of hiring a nanny. Her mom had reminded her—repeatedly—that she needed to set up the interviews as soon as possible so they could have a signed contract before the baby was born. It took time to work through the interview process, conduct a decent background and criminal background check, and set up payroll.

There were only ten weeks left until her delivery date. Time to quit stalling and have an open conversation with Sam.

She slowly walked into the family room, trying to gauge his mood. Sam was sitting in the middle of the couch, drooping against the futon as he stared at the tiny TV he'd brought from home. Some war movie was playing. He looked exhausted.

He looked up at her, briefly frowning as she walked in front of the TV, then went back to ignoring her. Rylee carefully eased herself into the rocking chair next to the living room windows. She moved her right hand across her belly, feeling the baby kick.

"We need to talk, Sam," she told him.

"I don't have anything to say, Rylee," he told her. "I'm tired and I just need to relax for a bit." He squirmed his shoulders against the futon as he tried to find a comfortable position, his forearms resting on his belly.

Allison started jabbing at her, almost as if she was upset at Sam's tone of voice. "Oh, she's really moving around in there. I think we might have a future gymnast on our hands!" Rylee exclaimed. She found herself rubbing both sides of her belly in an almost rhythmic figure-eight gesture that sometimes seemed to help.

She looked over, waiting for Sam to respond, but he refused to even look in her direction. Apparently, an alien war movie was more important than his own child.

She sighed, shaking her head in frustration. "My mom helped me work through the list of potential nannies so we can set up a few interviews for next week. I really need your help deciding—"

Sam turned to glare at her, struggling to sit upright. "What?" he barked.

"Well, you know. A nanny," Rylee replied, perplexed. She'd mentioned it once or twice, she was sure of it. "We're going to need some help when the baby's born," she reminded him. "I mean, we could go with an au pair, if you'd like, but then we'd still need an extra bedroom."

Sam threw the remote control, startling her. It arced off of the coffee table and came to rest under the bookshelf. "A nanny," he growled at her. "What makes you think we can afford a fucking nanny?"

Rylee closed her eyes as she continued to rub against her belly, trying to help the baby calm down. "There, there, Allison," she softly crooned. "I know Daddy's yelling, but that's just how he is." She shifted her weight so she could put her feet up on the footstool, coolly looking at Sam.

"My attorney says it looks like I'll have access to my money once the baby comes; that way I can pay for things, Sam," she finally told him quietly. "We're going to be fine, just like I told you."

"What the hell, Rylee!" Sam yelped at her, outraged. "We already talked about this. You know the rules. I have to be able to provide half of our budget. I can't afford a nanny. You know that. I'm barely hanging on as it is!"

She nodded but refused to back down. "You worry too much," she told him. "Everything is open for negotiation, including the budget that needs to be approved by the Court. Things might be a bit tight until I'm allowed to liquidate a few things." She paused, choosing her next words carefully. "Besides, there's no way we can continue to live here after the baby's born. I start at Wellesley this fall and you know that means we'll have to relocate to Massachusetts."

Sam clenched his eyes shut. "What?" He threw the question at her as if it was a weapon. "There's no way we're moving to Massachusetts," he told her. "We can't afford it."

"Sure, we can," she replied. "You'll have to change schools, but we can figure that out later. I've already started apartment hunting near the campus. There are a number of great condos within driving distance." She paused, looking down at Allison. "I'm still not happy that I won't be able to live on campus for my first year. That's where all the fun is!"

Sam groaned in response, mashing his fists into the cushion.

She studied his face, trying to understand what his exact concern was. "We'll need a four-bedroom unit, obviously, because the nanny, or au pair, if you prefer, will need her own room," she told him. "Babies can be so messy, you know? My mom has her service stopping by to help around the place now, but after we move—"

Sam slapped the cushion next to him. "We're not moving cross-country, Rylee! Period," he growled. "As it is, I'm going to have to take a few classes this summer to catch up, and we need to stay close to home for now."

"Why?" she demanded, matching his anger. "Neither of our parents are allowed to help much after the baby's born! There's nothing that ties us to this state, Sam."

Sam scrubbed at his face, then dropped his hands to his lap. "Rylee, I am not moving out east. I don't make enough money to pay half of a nanny's salary, and I've been told—repeatedly—that there's no wiggle room in the way the law is written. We each have to pay for half of that baby's expenses!"

Rylee shook her head. "Sam. Stop," she replied, trying to find the right words to help. "My lawyer has already drafted the financial means document that will outline to the Court what needs to be done for us to move. Once the guardian ad litem signs off on it, we're all set."

"What? Why did you do this?" he yelled at her. "I have rights, you know!"

So do I, Rylee thought. "Because I can't live poor, Sam," she quietly told him, looking at her hands. "I just can't. We deserve better." She looked up. "So, I'll pay for the nanny until you've graduated. You can pay for the next few years until we're even. Or, if you can't afford it right out of college, then you can just pay Allison's tuition for a few years. After I graduate, we can move to New York, and there are some really great private schools—"

"I'm not moving to New York, Rylee!" he told her, his voice flat. "Period."

"Well, I am!" Rylee snapped at him, struggling to stand up. She wobbled for a moment, arms wide until she found her balance. "Every opportunity is waiting for me to make this move. Don't forget, you're the one who got me pregnant, Sam. You're the one with the super swimmers and didn't wear a condom!"

Sam started to respond, but she overrode him. "I'm not your mom!" she yelled at him. "I will never be a stay-at-home mom. I *will* have a decent place to live, and I *will* hire a nanny to take care of your baby until I'm *actually* ready to become a mother, and there's nothing you can do to stop me!"

"You were supposed to be on the fucking Pill, Rylee!" he snapped at her.

"You know why I stopped taking the Pill," she hissed at him. "How many times do I have to tell you that I wasn't supposed to be able to get pregnant without medical intervention."

"Bullshit!" he growled.

"So, what, you're a gynecologist now?" she demanded. "You know everything about how women's bodies work?"

Sam slowly stood, swaying as he tried to maintain his balance. "I'm out of here," he told her. "I can't deal with you right now!"

He grabbed his coat and was out the door before she could respond. *And they say women are overly emotional*, she thought as she settled back into the rocking chair.

"Daddy will come around, sweetness," she told Allison. "He's going to need a bit more time to really understand just how much work a baby is!"

Rylee slowly walked toward the mall entrance, delighting in that rather strange feeling in her right ankle. The ankle monitor had been removed at their mentoring meeting. It had been an unexpected but delightful surprise.

The crisp February air felt shocking against her skin. She glanced at Devi. "What stores would you like to hit up first?" she asked.

"I'm not sure," Devi told her with a laugh. "But our first stop must be the restrooms!"

Rylee nodded her head in agreement. Allison seemed to take pleasure in kicking her bladder these days. She led Devi to the closest restroom and then took her to a nearby drink bar to grab some hot chocolate.

"I can't believe Erin didn't tell us that the trackers were going to be removed today," Devi told her. "For a minute, I thought the officers were there to arrest someone!"

"I know!" Rylee breathed. "They looked so angry; you know?" She stopped to look at the dresses in one of the shop windows. "I'm just glad they did. That band was starting to cut into my skin from the swelling."

"I guess we're no longer considered to be flight risks," Devi told her.

Rylee nodded, gesturing for her to continue walking. "Have you considered going home now?" she asked, deliberately not looking at Devi. "Have the baby in Canada rather than the US?"

Devi sighed, shaking her head sadly. "I can't," she told her. "If I leave, I risk losing my student visa because staying in the state is a condition of my release."

"What?" Rylee was flabbergasted.

Devi stopped and looked at her. "This baby is a ward of the state. If I leave Wisconsin, I'm breaking state law. I was told a warrant for my arrest would be issued and the state would pursue an extradition order to bring me back." She looked away and started walking again. "Besides, Tyler has made it clear that adoption is the only path forward."

Rylee didn't know what to say. They made a circuit through the far end of the mall, quietly keeping each other company as they moved from store to store.

"I'm feeling a bit nibbly," Rylee told her as they passed the Thai restaurant. "Care to split a few appetizers with me?"

Devi smiled. "Sure."

They entered the restaurant. It was a bit darker than the mall and she knew it would take a while for her eyes to adjust. The hostess showed them to their booth.

Rylee shrugged off her coat and stuffed it onto the seat. She was just about to slide in when she noticed an old bruise on Devi's wrist before she pulled her sleeve down to cover it.

"Are you okay?" she asked as Devi pushed her coat into the booth and sat down.

"Sure," Devi said, picking up the menu the hostess had left for them. "Why?"

Rylee slid into the booth. She leaned forward to look at Devi. "You've got a bruise on your wrist," she told her.

Devi gave a slight shrug. "It's fine," she told her.

"Devi?"

She looked up. The look in her eyes made Rylee's stomach tighten.

"What happened?" she asked.

Devi sighed and put the menu down. "Tyler has a bit of a temper," she admitted. "It was an accident. He apologized. It's fine."

"Are you sure?" Rylee asked. "We could call someone."

"The police?" Devi snorted. "Why? So, they could file a complaint about the man that I was forced to live with between semesters and make him even angrier? Spring break is coming up. No thanks, Rylee." She picked up her menu again. "The crispy tofu looks interesting," she commented.

Rylee looked down at her menu. "Sounds good," she replied. "Um, how do you feel about some sticky rice, too?"

Devi nodded, then dropped her menu to the table. She looked out into the dining room, lost in thought.

Under normal circumstances, Rylee might have gone to her parents with this. Things were strained at home, but she was certain they would be able to help. Devi was right, though. If Tyler's temper was bad enough for him to hit Devi or throw things at her, bringing the police into the picture might only make things worse.

Their waitress came to take their order, and they moved on to a different subject.

Chapter Twelve

Rylee carefully navigated her way down the front stairs from the apartment. She still couldn't believe that Sam hadn't come home after his mentoring meeting on Friday night. Even if he was staying with his parents, the least he could have done was swing by to pick her up for Sunday worship service.

She walked down the steps, feeling every bit of the thirty-one weeks of her pregnancy. She was grateful the other tenant had heavily salted the front walk. The last thing she needed was to land in the slushy snowbanks that lined the steps.

Sam hadn't responded to any of her texts all weekend. At first, she thought maybe he had been at a party with his friend Lucas. Yes, he wasn't allowed to drink, but she knew Sam. Offer that man a beer and he'd slam a few just to prove that he could.

The Uber driver rolled down the passenger side window to get a good look at her before he scrambled out of the car to open the backseat door. Rylee carefully minced through the compacted snow that coated the parkway. He held out his hand to help steady her, and she settled into the backseat with a sigh.

When Sam hadn't come back to the apartment Friday night, Rylee had felt more rage than fear. How dare he completely ignore her? What if she went into preterm labor?

She stared out the window, not quite seeing the colorless landscape as they drove to Mequon. The dirty snow seemed to reflect her somber mood. If Sam had truly abandoned her, the Court would find out in due time. He'd face serious jail time for pulling this stunt, and then what?

They pulled up in front of Eternal Springs and joined the long line of cars dropping off passengers. She thought about directing the driver to the side entrance for a moment. *No,* she thought. *Sam may have abandoned her, but she wasn't going to hide. Let the entire fellowship see it for themselves.*

She waited until the car was directly in front of the entrance before opening the door. She struggled to get out but waved off the driver's offer to help. Her mom stood just inside the open doors as she walked into the church's crowded narthex.

Her mom hugged her. "Worship is just about to start," she said as she guided Rylee into the sanctuary. "What happened to Sam? Why didn't you call me?"

Rylee shook her head. "Not now, Mom," she said as they entered the sanctuary. "It's fine."

She slowed her pace as they walked along the back to the farthest aisle on the right. The family was already seated in the first pew on the far corner of the altar. The longer row accommodated the entire family, even with the excessively large diaper bag Chloe insisted on bringing with them when they were in town.

She took her seat at the far end of the pew and tried to clear her mind. It was the first Sunday of Lent. Time to set aside her own life with all of its stumbles and focus on the love, forgiveness, and salvation God freely gave all of His children, even one as selfish and childish, as Sam.

Pastor Chapman brought her back to the service with the opening prayer. "Lord God, You call us to work in your kingdom and leave no one standing idle," the pastor said, smiling at the fellowship before him. "Help us to order our lives by your wisdom and to serve you in willing obedience; through Jesus Christ, your Son, our Lord, who lives and reigns with you, and the Holy Spirit, one God, now and forever. Amen."

"Amen," Rylee breathed, feeling the muscles in her lower back loosen up a bit. That irritated sciatic nerve had settled down to a dull ache since the massage therapist worked her magic.

By the time worship service was over, Rylee felt more at peace with herself than she had in days. A small number had moved to the fellowship hall for coffee, but most of the families with children had already left.

Rylee scanned the small crowd for the Maxwells. This was where Wendy Maxwell held court among her friends. A place where she handed out assignments and accolades with ease and dexterity. A place where the Williams family was welcomed, but only to a point.

Rylee slowly made her way to the kitchen, ignoring the blatant stares. "Mrs. Maxwell?" she asked as she opened the door. "Do you have a minute?"

Wendy Maxwell was standing on a step stool, pulling down another container of coffee from the top cabinet. She froze, shoulders tensing, then closed the cabinet door before looking over. "Yes?" she asked, her dark red hair framing her face.

Rylee closed the door behind her and stood in front of it, warily. "I haven't seen Sam in a few days," she cautiously told her. "He's not answering my texts, either."

Mrs. Maxwell placed the canister of ground coffee on the counter and carefully stepped down. She slowly folded the stool up and stored it next to the counter. "He's fine," she told Rylee as she turned, her hazel eyes flashing with anger even as she tried to smile. "No need to worry."

Rylee frowned. "Then why hasn't he answered my texts?" she asked. "I don't remember seeing him at worship today."

"Where he is and what he is doing is of no concern to you," Mrs. Maxwell snapped at her. She grabbed the coffee and moved across the room to stand directly in front of Rylee. "Now, if you'll excuse me, I have coffee to make."

Rylee stepped aside and Mrs. Maxwell almost bolted from the kitchen. She stood there for a long moment, surprised. Obviously, the Maxwells knew where Sam was and what he was doing. Somehow, they were fine with him blowing off his responsibilities.

She took a deep breath, one hand automatically going to her stomach. "It's okay, sweetness," she told the baby. "If your daddy's not back to the apartment by tomorrow, I will have a long talk with Erin. If he gets a free pass, we're moving back home!"

That evening, Rylee spent some time picking up around the apartment. The cleaning service would be stopping by while she was at her mentoring circle tomorrow and she was always uneasy leaving the place messy. The service had enough to do without being forced to load the dishwasher and sweep the first floor for Sam's dirty clothes!

She spotted yet another pair of jeans on the floor next to the couch and slowly squatted down to pick them up, using one hand against the wall to steady herself. Then, she opened the living room closet and dropped them into the basket on the floor. Sam had shoved a four-drawer dresser inside, leaving just enough room to hang up their winter coats.

Frustrated, Rylee walked to the kitchen and grabbed her phone from the counter next to the stove. She pulled up Kathryn's number from her favorites. *Gotta minute?* she texted.

She barely had time to tuck her phone into her back pocket before it rang.

"Hey, Rylee," Kathryn said. "What's up?"

"Sam's still missing," she told Kathryn, scanning the kitchen for her earbuds. "Either his mom doesn't know where he is or he's hiding out at home. Either way, I'm still stuck cleaning up his mess so that the cleaning service can come over tomorrow."

"He's still not home?" Kathryn responded. "I thought that wasn't optional."

She spotted her earbuds on the counter and scooped them up. "Well, apparently it is," Rylee groused, popping the earbuds in. "I need to clean up around here before I call an Uber to haul my laundry back to the house to have it washed." She tucked her phone into her back pocket and slowly walked up the stairs to the second floor. "And if Sam thinks I'm doing his laundry, he's got another thing coming!"

Kathryn laughed. "You've only got to deal with this for a few more months, Rylee," she reassured her. "Come August, you're moving across the country!"

Rylee entered her bedroom. She pulled the small laundry basket from the closet floor and put it on the bed to sort. "Yeah, well, it can't happen soon enough!" she told her. "I'm really getting tired of trying to pick up after him. There's only so much room for our stuff."

"I don't remember if you told me," Kathryn said. "But some apartments have laundry facilities in the basement. Might be worth taking stuff downstairs instead of trying to haul it home or over to my place."

Rylee stopped to think. "Maybe," she mused. "I think so." She vaguely remembered something about a coin-operated washer and drier in the basement, but dismissed it because it seemed to be a waste of money.

"Well, check it out," Kathryn said encouragingly. "Worst-case scenario is you still end up calling an Uber, right? Best case is that you can get your laundry done tonight and have time to relax."

"That assumes we have laundry soap," Rylee reminded her. "I have no idea what Sam's been doing with his own clothes."

"You've got this, Rylee," Kathryn said. "Whoops! Hannah's calling. Gotta run!"

"Bye," Rylee said, but the call had already dropped. She stood there for a moment, then went to find her purse. If the machine didn't take her debit card, she'd have to hope she could find enough change to get at least one load done.

She only found a few bills in her wallet, so she started hunting around the living room. She could have sworn Sam had a jar of change in his desk. She started opening drawers. Found it! Not only was there loose change, but half of a roll of quarters.

She looked around. Somehow, she doubted that Sam's mom was taking care of his laundry. She walked over to the living room closet, pulled the laundry basket out, and found a small container of liquid soap and a few drier sheets under his clothes.

Rylee made her way across the living room and into the kitchen, grabbed her keys from the counter, and headed out the back door. She carefully locked the door behind her before hesitantly making her way down the stairs and into the dank basement.

The washing machine looked ancient. There was a coin slot that took four quarters. The dryer took two. So, a dollar and a half per load. Good thing she only had two!

She climbed the back stairs, pausing at the door. She peered out into the early twilight. It might only be just after 5 p.m., but it was already getting dark. And still no sign of Sam.

She sighed and turned away. Another night of worry.

She made her way back up to the second floor and grabbed her laundry basket. Then, she slowly made her way back down the stairs, the musty smell of the basement making her worry about mold.

She set the basket on the counter next to the washing machine. She quickly sorted the clothes, throwing the white clothes into the washer and the dark clothes onto the counter. She studied the ancient machine for a moment, then carefully poured the laundry soap over the clothes. *Looks easy enough,* she thought. *Cold wash, cold rinse.*

She put the quarters into the slots at the top of the washer, listened to the sound of the money dropping into the container beneath, and the washer started to fill with water.

She closed the lid with a smile. Her biggest concern was getting the clothes out of the bottom of the washing machine, but they had a pair of kitchen tongs that might work. Next step: find something in the fridge to heat up for dinner.

"As you know, once you've given birth, you'll be moving to the postpartum support program," Erin told the group. "You'll meet every week, starting when your baby is a month old, but the day and time will depend on the location. Our goal is to give you a neighborhood-based location and support plan."

Rylee glanced out the window, only half-listening. A few snowflakes fluttered by. Maybe it was going to snow again.

Erin gave Brittany a pile of half-inch binders to pass out, then directly handed Devi a folder. "Much of this won't apply to you, Devi, dear," she told her. "But there's still time for you and Tyler to change your mind, so I'm required to give you both of these."

Devi jerked her chin sharply, looking down as she took the folder. "I understand," she muttered.

"Zara, I added some additional resources that you might find helpful," Erin said. "I believe you may be familiar with Milwaukee Public School's Early Childhood Education Program, but I've also included some respite care services that may be able to assist during this child first few months of life."

Lily leaned to the side, resting the binder against her chair leg. "Isn't that for children with disabilities?" she asked, curious.

"In most cases, yes," Erin replied. "However, we've found that providing at-risk couples with support in those first few months can improve family stability, even when couples choose to later separate."

"How is this different from getting a babysitter?" Grace asked.

Erin smiled as she sat back down in the circle. "A babysitter doesn't typically have training in early childhood development to provide new parents guidance or can spot a developmental problem early on," she told them. "I've also included information on the area food assistance, legal aid, and childcare assistance programs."

"What if you have a remote job?" Charlotte asked. "Liam works from home, but I will need to travel once Ely is born. Can we get help with childcare?"

"Eligibility is typically determined by the Federal Poverty Level," Erin told her. She opened her binder and walked the group through the available childcare assistance programs. Then, she pulled out the copay schedule to review with the group.

Rylee found herself looking around the room. None of this applied to her. Even if she lost the fight with Sam over the nanny, they'd still be over the income threshold because of her current assets.

She heard Devi sniffling next to her. She turned and saw tears slowly dripping down Devi's cheeks.

"What is it, Devi?" Rylee whispered, putting an arm around her.

"I—I can't," Devi stuttered. "I just can't!"

Erin stopped the conversation and came over to Devi. She knelt in front of her and took one of Devi's hands. "What's wrong, dear?" she asked gently.

Devi burst into tears. Rylee pulled her into an awkward hug, looking at Erin for help. If Tyler had hurt Devi again, she'd call the police, so help her God!

"Why don't we clear the room," Zara told the group. She stood up and started to herd the other women out into the hallway. Rylee met her eyes and gave a shake of her head. She wasn't going to let go of Devi unless she pulled away first.

"Devi," Erin said softly. "Can you tell me what's going on? I can help."

Devi clung to Rylee even tighter. "No, you can't," she softly wailed. "I don't want to give up my baby. Ty—Tyler told me that

I don't have a choice. It's either adoption and I get to keep my student visa or they'll take my baby away and deport me back to Canada!"

Rylee cringed, staring at Erin. That couldn't be legal.

Erin rocked back on her heels, frowning in concern. "That's not true, Devi," she told her. "I'm not sure where Tyler got his information, but Wisconsin state policy is very clear: we will do anything to keep families together."

"Even if I want to take the baby home after she's born?" Devi asked, pulling away from Rylee. "She'll be an American citizen. I'm not." She bit her lip, tears continuing to stream down her face.

Rylee got up and grabbed the box of tissues from the tea table. She handed the box to Devi and sat back down next to her. Devi grabbed a handful and wiped at her face, fingers trembling with anxiety.

"Devi, honey, that doesn't matter," Erin told her, "There's probably a lot of paperwork that will need to be done, but I'm sure we can find someone at the Canadian Embassy to give us the correct information."

She stood, reaching out to help Devi up from her chair. Rylee stood as well, not sure what to do next.

Erin turned to her. "Will you let the group know they can go home, Rylee?" she asked. "Devi and I are going to head up to my office. We have a few calls to make."

Rylee nodded and grabbed her stuff. She headed out to the hallway, brushing past Zoey and Lily, who had been standing close to the door to see if they could hear anything. Zara had gathered most of the girls around her on the opposite side of the lobby, and Rylee headed in her direction.

"Erin says that we can leave," she told Zara. "She needs to focus on helping Devi."

Zara nodded, her mouth pursed in anger. "What did Tyler do to her?" she asked Rylee.

Rylee looked up at the ceiling for a moment. "I don't have a good answer, Zara," she replied after a moment. "It's a mess." It wasn't her place to tell Devi's story. If she wanted to share it, that was Devi's decision.

She knew one thing for sure. Tyler was a manipulative asshole, and she hoped Erin would nail him to the wall.

"He's still not back?" Rylee's mom asked her. For the first time, she sounded worried.

"No," Rylee told her, pacing the small living room in bitter frustration. She shifted her phone from her right hand to her left, rubbing the side of her belly where Allison was furiously kicking at her. "I don't know if I should call the police or his parents." She stopped by the window, leaning her forehead against the cool glass.

Ashley sighed in irritation. "Are you sure you don't know where he is?" she asked. "Did you call any of his friends? What about his mentor?"

"No, I don't know where he is, Mom," she complained. "No text, no call. Nothing. It's been three days. I'm really worried!"

Her mom started to say something, but she heard a noise in the kitchen. She turned around and saw Sam standing at the back door, frozen, standing next to the back door.

"Oh, he's home!" Rylee squealed. "Gotta go, Mom!" She pushed herself away from the window and made her way across the dining room and into the kitchen.

"Where were you?" she angrily demanded. *He had better not have crashed at his parents' house*, she thought.

Sam stopped to pick up his keys from the floor. He put them into his coat pocket, then walked around her to the refrigerator. He reached in to grab a soda. "Does it matter?" he asked, coolly.

"Of course, it matters!"

"Why?"

Seriously? she thought, feeling Allison start to kick again. She wanted to scream at him. *I can't do this alone!*

But that would be the wrong thing to say. She tried to find the right words. "Because we missed you!" she finally replied, rubbing a hand around her belly in a slow motion to help Allison settle down. "You're an important part of this, Sam."

"Really, Rylee?" Sam popped open the soda as he turned to glare at her. "Did you know that someone in your family is telling people at church that I bullied you into getting pregnant!"

Rylee's mouth fell open. "Sam, you know that's not true—"

"Really, Rylee?" he snapped at her. "From what I hear, it was your mom who started that rumor!"

Rylee blinked, confused. "My mom?!" she cried. "Whoever told you that is lying!" There was no way Mom had anything to do with the rumor mill. She hated it.

He gave her a condescending grin. "Not according to the woman who confronted Wendy!" he responded coldly. "Look, half of the rumor mill says you got pregnant on purpose so that we couldn't break up. The other half says I got you pregnant so that you would have to stay with me!"

Allison stilled under her hands, almost as if she was hiding. "And you think I had something to do with it?" she demanded.

She could feel the tears building and closed her eyes to try to stop them.

Sam sucked down the soda, almost gulping it down, like a man who had been denied water for days. He wiped his mouth with the back of his hand and looked at her. "That's the thing, Rylee. I have no idea."

Wow. "Sam, I had nothing—"

"I don't believe you, Rylee," he told her. He stared at her for a long minute, almost daring her to change his mind. Then, he turned away, leaning against the counter, and stared at the cabinet. "I've heard your mom is telling people one story and your friend Kathryn is telling the other." He looked over at her, a deep frown cutting folds into his forehead. "In the end, it doesn't matter who started what rumor. People are going to believe what they want, and I know that, too. What I don't know is how this is going to work, Rylee."

She fumbled behind her until she found a kitchen chair to sit down at. "What do you mean?" she asked, looking up at him.

He turned around and leaned his hip up against the counter. "I mean, us, Rylee," he told her, his voice filled with a rage that didn't match his cold expression. "How are we going to make this work so we both have a life to get back to when this is over?"

"We'll move out east—"

"No, we won't, Rylee," he overrode her in an angry voice, then drained the rest of the can and pitched it into the garbage. He turned back, every line of his body tense. "I'm done taking orders. If we have to have the arbitrator decide, then that's what we'll do. Period."

"You don't mean that, Sam," she gently told him. "We follow the plan—"

"Your plan," he interjected.

"—we move out east and start fresh," she told him, refusing to back down. "I am going to Wellesley. You can transfer to another college nearby, or finish your senior year at Northwestern before you join us." She paused, studying him to see if he was even listening. "After I graduate, maybe you will find a job overseas like Josh and we can move to Europe. That works, doesn't it?"

He glared at her for a moment, drawing out the silence as if it were his only weapon. She clenched her jaw painfully and refused to back down.

"No, it doesn't, Rylee," he finally growled. "I'm not moving out east. Period." He looked out the kitchen window and frowned. "It's been a long couple of days. I'm going to grab a shower and then dig into my homework."

With that, he turned and went upstairs. She stared after him. *Mom is telling people Sam bullied me into getting pregnant,* she thought. *What the absolute hell?*

Rylee sighed. She rubbed her belly, working to calm her heart rate. "It's going to be okay, Allison," she told the baby. "I'm not sure how that rumor got started, but I'm going to have to have a talk with Grandma *and* Kathryn!"

Chapter Thirteen

It was unusual for the entire family to gather this time of year. The annual gathering was usually held mid-summer at their grandfather's ranch in Wyoming.

Rylee walked around the great room, trying to get a feeling for why her grandfather had requested that the extended family join them. It was the end of February and the bitter cold meant everyone had to stay indoors instead of spreading out as they normally did.

Most of her cousins seemed to be in the dark as well. One or two of them had kept their distance but, for the most part, the family seemed to be comfortable with her pregnancy. Even Nana had spent time talking to her during lunch and Nana was the last person in the family that Rylee thought would approve of the baby.

"Dad has asked you to join us in his study," Chloe told her, cuddling a sleepy Patrick against her shoulder.

Rylee nodded. "Okay," she said, frowning just a bit. There was something unsettling about the way Chloe looked at her; that faint hint of smugness she unsuccessfully smothered beneath a façade of pseudo-concern. Something was off.

She found herself following Chloe out of the room, who paused only briefly to hand the baby off to her husband. Chloe and Alexander exchanged a look, and that was enough to make her nervous. Instinctively, her hand went to her belly. She didn't want to upset Allison. She might not have moved into a head-down position, but she could still pack a mean punch.

They walked down the long hallway, passing the kitchen and dining room on their way to Dad's study. Chloe paused to knock on the door, then pushed it open. Rylee reluctantly followed.

She paused, looking over the room to try and understand what was happening. Inside, her grandfather sat behind the desk, with her father standing a few steps off to the side. Nana and Mom sat on the couch. Chloe joined them.

"Why don't you have a seat?" her grandfather told her. He gestured to the leather chair closest to the desk, his usual lively expression blank.

Rylee nodded and slowly settled on the chair, adjusting a plump pillow that had been thoughtfully placed on the seat to help with her back. She cupped Allison firmly with one hand, waiting.

"I've called this meeting to discuss our financial interests," her grandfather told her.

Rylee cocked her head, puzzled. The only time her grandfather talked about money with her was when it came to the family trust. She raised her eyebrows, hand tightening around the baby. Of course. They would need to add Allison, just as they had when Patrick had been born.

Rylee took a deep breath, stealing a glance at Chloe. She didn't remember her grandfather holding a family meeting with Chloe and Alexander to discuss it, though. Of course, she hadn't been involved, so perhaps she'd missed something.

Chloe met her gaze, quirking an eyebrow at her and nodding her head at their grandfather. 'Pay attention,' she seemed to be telling Rylee.

But before Rylee could look away, a cruel smile tugged at the corner of Chloe's lip for just a second before she pursed her lips. Long enough for Rylee's heart to leap in her chest. Something was wrong. Something was very, very wrong.

Her grandfather cleared his throat, subtly bringing Rylee's attention back to him. He tapped the thin binder in front of him. He frowned, pursing his lips in disapproval. "Before we begin," he told her, "you need to understand that this action was not taken lightly. The family's financial interests *must* be protected."

"Protected?" Rylee craned her head to look first at her father, then at her mother. "Protected how?" she demanded.

"In light of your pregnancy, the Williams Family Trust has been amended," he told her, his gravelly voice sounding ominous in the sudden stillness. "You have been removed as a beneficiary."

The words seemed to suck the oxygen out of her lungs. The brightly lit room became a static-filled nightmare, almost as if she'd been transported to Hell. In a daze, she watched the almost transparent shadow of her grandfather push a spiral-bound binder across the desk.

"I'm sorry, what?" Rylee stammered, her heart hammering in her chest. "Removed?" Her gaze crawled from her grandfather to her father in alarm. "Why?"

"The board of trustees takes your pregnancy very seriously, Rylee," her father gently told her. "You are not married. It introduces an—" he paused, searching for the right phrase, "—*uncomfortable variable* into our family's business."

Rylee leaned forward, blindly struggling to grab the binder off of her father's desk. Her mom got up and handed it to her, one hand coming down on her shoulder before she sat back on the couch.

Rylee clutched the binder against her belly, feeling Allison begin to strongly butt her head against the side of her belly. *Out,* Allison seemed to be telling her. *Get me out of here!*

"Your pregnancy has opened the trust up to potential litigation," her grandfather told her. "This may sound cold, but should you die, the state will award Sam sole custody of the child." He sat back in the chair, looking pensive. "That includes managing a childhood trust fund, handling various business interests in the child's name, legal and tax compliance, and voting on financial issues that come before the family trust until the child reaches maturity."

Somehow, her grandfather's words penetrated the buzzing haze that surrounded her. "Oh," she breathed. *All of the things that Dad does for me,* she thought.

"If you had a standard prenuptial in place, this wouldn't be an issue," her grandfather continued. "However, I've been advised that marrying Maxwell isn't a possibility, and we need to take the necessary steps to protect the family."

Rylee blinked. "You're punishing my child because I won't marry her father?" she squeaked, barely able to get the words out.

Her grandfather frowned, his dark eyes narrowing. "Actually, the trustees have agreed to an addendum that transfers the current cash value of your shares to a separate trust fund that will be managed either by you or another member of the family, should you pass away before the child reaches maturity," he told her. "Before you say another word, it may be a good idea to read the amended trust agreement."

Rylee fumbled to open the spiral-bound cover, almost blinded by tears. The cover, a heavy card stock embossed with the words, 'Williams Family Trust Amendment', screamed at her. She flipped past the table of contents, trying to find the real meat.

This document, dated February 23, 2029, serves as an amendment to the Williams Family Trust, approved by the board of trustees and executed on November 11, 2001, by Albert Williams, hereinafter referred to as the Settlor.

WHEREAS, the Settlor desires to make specific provisions regarding the beneficiaries of the Williams Family Trust;

NOW, THEREFORE, in consideration of the premises and for other good and valuable consideration, the receipt and sufficiency of which are hereby acknowledged, the Settlor hereby amends the Williams Family Trust as follows:

1. For all purposes hereunder, I am specifically not making any provision for my granddaughter Rylee Annabelle Williams or her issue or for Samuel Maxwell or his issue.

2. Rylee Annabelle Williams is removed from any and all benefits, distributions, and entitlements from the Williams Family Trust. This disinheritance includes, but is not limited to, any share of the trust principal, income, or other assets.

There was more about the ratification of the remainder of the trust, governing laws, distribution, and succession planning for the next forty generations, but she couldn't continue reading through it.

"I can't," she told him, covering her eyes with one hand. "I can't believe you've disowned me."

"Nonsense," her grandfather told her firmly. "You are still a member of this family and will be treated accordingly. I'm told arrangements have been made to give you limited access to your college trust fund and that you have a well-managed portfolio to draw on. The only thing you will not have access to is the family trust."

Rylee uncovered her eyes, staring at him. She'd been counting on the annual payout to help supplement her income. She knew both Mackenzie and Chloe had received several million dollars this year and it had been a lean year due to the ongoing bear market conditions.

Her grandfather stood. "Now, if you'll excuse us, we have some additional items to talk through," he told her. Rylee looked around the room. Her mother looked away, as did Nana.

"Come on, Rylee," Chloe told her as she gestured for her to stand. "Let's get you freshened up."

Rylee stood and clutched the binder to her chest. Chloe reached out to touch her shoulder, and Rylee pulled away.

Yes, she still had her trust fund and portfolio. She could probably count on her parents to help until she was on her feet after graduation. But, otherwise, she had just become an outsider to the family.

Rylee blindly followed Chloe down the hallway. "I can't believe Papa did this—"

Chloe abruptly turned to face her, that cruel smile and glare flickering before she bit her lower lip. "Why?" she demanded. "How could you not know this was inevitable!"

Rylee stopped, gaping at Chloe. She found herself sagging against the wall. It was the only thing keeping her from falling.

"Inevitable?" she whispered. "Because I somehow got pregnant?"

Chloe crossed her arms, leaning back as she scowled at her in disgust. "You really don't understand, do you?" she taunted Rylee. "This has nothing—and everything!—to do with your pregnancy!"

"You're just jealous that I got pregnant without having to do IVF," Rylee spat. She slowly stood upright; the binder held protectively in front of Allison.

"Ha!" Chloe barked. "You have no idea what I went through!"

"Enlighten me," Rylee snapped.

"I'm not talking about the fertility treatments, Rylee," Chloe told her. "Not the pills. Not the shots. Not the six months of being inseminated with Alexander's sperm—which sucks, by the way! Not even suffering through multiple miscarriages before Patrick was born. No. It's much more than that."

"Yeah?" Rylee challenged, anger finally pushing her fear aside. "Is it because I'm not stuck with a husband with a net worth less than his wife?"

"That's a lie!" Chloe told her. "Alexander's business has taken off. Besides, the Three Sisters wouldn't exist without his construction and commercial finance connections."

"I don't believe that!" Rylee spat. "Mackenzie worked hard to line up our financing options."

Chloe laughed, a bitter chuckle that sounded more like she was gagging. "Alexander hooked her up with a few of his friends," she told her. "The financing for those first two properties was a gift. Do you really believe that our loan-to-value ratio was good enough to qualify for a decent construction mortgage? Are you really that naïve?"

Rylee took a deep breath, staring at Chloe as if this was the first time she'd actually seen her.

"Do you have any idea what it's like to fight every single day for your place at the table?" Chloe hissed. "Of course not," she said, cocking her head. "You wouldn't have a clue."

"Fight for your place?" Rylee asked, confused by Chloe's tangent. "What are you talking about?"

"Dad may be the CEO of the family business, but that doesn't mean anyone in the family wants me to take over when he retires," Chloe spat at her. "No. Women are supposed to stay home, make babies, and be satisfied working at their volunteer and nonprofit opportunities. I had to push hard to get a spot at the company. Even the mere *idea* that I wanted to work for Dad was forbidden."

"Bullshit! You're COO, Chloe!" Rylee spat back, pushing herself away from the wall.

"Papa didn't want me there," Chloe told her. "Uncle Benjamin and Liam still don't. They'd rather have Harry, Charles, Nathanial, or even Haydon, take the reins rather than allow a mere woman to put one step in their coveted C-suites. I had to fight every step of the way!"

"So, what!" Rylee hissed at her. "You made it work, didn't you?"

"I have to prove my worth, every single day," Chloe told her. "Do you know what it's like to have to hire staff to raise your own child?" Chloe demanded. "I only took off from work for two weeks before heading back into the office. We had to hire three nannies—three of them!—to provide round-the-clock care so that I can work fifty hours a week—minimum! And I still have to pump breast milk during conference calls.

"Even worse?" Chloe hissed. "Dad told me that next time, I should just use a surrogate. That way, not only do we get to choose our child's gender—and it had better be another boy!—but I don't have to step back from the company to recover from childbirth." She glared at Rylee. "He wasn't kidding!"

"What does this have to do with me?" Rylee demanded. "I don't want to work for the company!"

"You're the baby of the family," Chloe told her. "Your only job appears to be a continual embarrassment!"

"What the *hell* are you talking about?" Rylee demanded.

"Do you know how many times I had to clean up your mess while you were in high school?" Chloe told her. "At church?"

"Clean up?!" Rylee gasped.

"Yes, Rylee. Clean up," Chloe snapped at her. "I'm Rylee. I'm so sexy that I flirt with men twice my age to get them to donate money for our robotics team," she whined, trying to sound like Rylee. "I'm an influencer wannabe that flashes so much cleavage I make men who are old enough to be my grandfather blush, so they give me money to make me go away. And even though I promised Daddy that I would save my virginity until marriage at our fellowship's Purity Ball, I sleep around like a fucking whore because I'm so special. And," Chloe held up a triumphant finger, stabbing it in the air, "I didn't think twice about screwing around with some working-class nobody that doesn't deserve to be employed by our company, let alone sit down with the family for dinner!"

"What the actual fuck, Chloe?!"

Chloe smiled. "Exactly, Rylee. You're rather experienced with that, aren't you?"

Rylee saw movement over Chloe's shoulder. Nana was just coming out of Dad's office. She stopped for a moment, frowning, then quietly turned around to walk away.

"You are a pampered baby," Chloe told her. "Every member of this family caters to your every whim. 'I want a pony' and poof! You get a pony. 'I need to raise more money from the community than anyone else in the history of our robotics team!' and the family fans out, shaking down every single individual in our collective network to make you the hero at school. 'I want to go to Wellesley, just like Mom' and poof! Letters of recommendation from local business leaders and academic achievements that you didn't even *earn* flood the admissions office, including one from a senator *who never even met you!*"

Rylee gasped, backing away. She felt her way along the wall until she found the back entrance to the kitchen. She blindly found her way to the island and pulled herself onto a stool.

That can't be true, she thought, clinging to the counter with both hands. Everything she'd done in school, the classes she'd taken, the volunteer work in the community, her work on the robotics team . . . had it all been a lie?

Chloe came to stand across from her, staring at her as if she was prey.

Rylee sat up, glaring at her. "You told Papa to disinherit me, didn't you?" she demanded.

"He asked, and I gave him my honest opinion," Chloe told her. "Under no circumstances should Sam Maxwell have access to one penny of our family's wealth. Not as a 'baby daddy' and not as your *significant other*." She hooked her fingers around the words, her perfect nails raking the air to make her point.

"Why?" Rylee breathed.

"Because you could have done the right thing," Chloe told her. "You could have just gone down to Waukegan, gotten the pill, and made all of this go away. Instead, you decided to upstage me yet again."

Rylee frown. "What are you talking about?"

"I rise and grind every single day, creating every opportunity for you and Mackenzie to follow. I'm the one who gave up everything so that I could be the boy for Dad that Mom could never give him."

Rylee tilted her head at Chloe in confusion.

She laughed at Rylee again. "Oh, you didn't know?" she asked. "Dad came *this close* to divorcing Mom after you were born. He is the only man in our family who doesn't have at least one son to carry on the family name. Do you know how much that hurts him?"

Chloe searched Rylee's face, sneering at her confusion. "No? Why do you think I refused to change my name when I got married? Why do you think Patrick has a hyphenated last name? Because Alexander wanted that? No, because it was a part of our prenuptial agreement!"

"Oh."

"So, yes, I gave Papa and the other trustees my opinion about you and your little mutt," Chloe said, gesturing to Rylee's belly. "You made your bed, Rylee. Now you get to lie on it."

Rylee struggled to her feet and then pushed in her stool. "Thanks for being honest with me, Aunt Chloe," she said sarcastically. "It's good to know how much you care about me and my baby."

Chloe snorted. "It's always good to clear the air, isn't it?"

Rylee moved around the island, refusing to even look in Chloe's direction. She tried to mentally stomp those feelings of rage and anxiety under the tile as she slowly made her way to the front hall to grab her coat.

"Time to say goodbye, sweetie," she whispered, absently cupping her belly under one hand. "I guess we're no longer a part of the family."

A tear threatened to cascade down her cheek, but she wiped it away with an angry gesture. Never let them see you cry. Not now. Not ever again.

Chapter Fourteen

Rylee paused at the conference room doorway, slowly scanning the group for Devi. No Devi.

Maybe she was running late. An accident on the freeway might have caused a delay. Or maybe she was having car troubles.

Rylee sat down, then pulled out her phone and sent a quick text: *RU OK?* She stared at the screen for a long time, ignoring the conversations around her. Nothing.

She slid her phone back into her purse, concerned. Devi hadn't returned any of her texts in the last week and it wasn't like her to just ghost Rylee. Something was very, very wrong.

"Four more weeks," Emma groaned as she stretched to try and relieve some of the pressure in her back. "I can't wait to get this over with!"

Zara turned to look over at her, giving her a knowing smile. "Emma, dear," she said. "The real work starts after the baby is born!"

Emma sighed. "I know, I know," she replied. "I just need to get comfortable in my own skin, that's all." She looked over at Erin, talking to Lily by the windows. "Besides, I've already signed up for daycare. They won't take little Joey until he's six weeks old, but it's something, right?"

Brittany looked at Emma, quirking one eyebrow. "Noah and I are going to minimize the amount of time that Aaron is at daycare," she informed the group with a haughty expression. "We know what's best for our baby."

Rylee shook her head, trying to keep her expression as neutral as possible. She still hadn't nailed down her post-delivery options. It seemed unreal to even have to consider using a daycare center, but without her financial safety net, she had to rethink everything.

Erin poured herself some tea and sat down at the circle. Rylee's heart sank. That meant there wasn't a seat for Devi. Had she given birth prematurely? Was the baby alright?

"Alright, ladies," Erin said to the group. "It's time to get started. Before we begin, I have an announcement." She looked around the room, a sad look crossing her face. "Devi won't be joining us anymore."

"Did she have the baby? Oh, my God. She had the baby!"

"She can't have given birth yet. It's too early!"

"The baby has to be in a neo-natal ICU unit. We should send flowers."

Erin raised her hands, gently overtaking the group. "Give me a minute, please. I can explain."

Rylee leaned forward, trying to read the guarded expression on Erin's face. *Had Devi been sent back to detention?* she thought, her heart pounding with anxiety.

Erin closed her eyes and took a deep breath. "I can't give you a lot of details," she said, opening her eyes to look around the room. "What I can tell you is that, in light of new information presented to the Court, Devi has been allowed to return home for the remainder of her pregnancy." She hesitated and looked down. "I can't say for certain, but I believe she left for Canada yesterday."

Rylee's mouth fell open in shock. Devi had told her that she couldn't leave because that would put her student visa at risk.

"That's legal?"

"So, if I was from another country, they couldn't hold me here?"

"Wait. She's Canadian?"

"I'll bet they sent her back to avoid another international incident!"

Rylee listened to the conversation as if she was in a tiny bubble of her own. Devi had only been friendly because she needed someone to talk to. Once she was on her way home, Devi had shed her like yesterday's fashion statement.

Zara's quiet voice punctured the chaos. "Matthew told me Tyler was arrested for sexual assault," she said, glaring around the room as if she was scolding a child. "If Devi was allowed to go back home to her family . . . " Her voice trailed off suggestively.

Mia's hand went to her mouth, eyes wide in shock. Grace closed her eyes as she took a few deep breaths to calm down.

Rylee couldn't take it any longer. "Is she okay?" she quietly asked.

Erin nodded. "Better now," she said. "Going home is probably the best thing for her right now. She'll have that much-needed support and comfort from her family and close friends."

Rylee looked away, swallowing past the tears threatening to spill over. Support and comfort from her family and friends.

That's a lie, she thought. People will only tell you they love you when you've done something that makes them look or feel good about themselves. Otherwise, it's just another lie. When they're done with you, they kick you to the curb.

Allison kicked at her, demanding her attention. Rylee rubbed her belly with a firm hand. *It's just you and me*, she thought. And she had no idea how she was going to survive all alone after Allison was born.

Kathryn opened her door, her welcoming smile rapidly wilting as she confronted Rylee's unexpected rage. "What's wrong?" she asked, backing out of the way so that Rylee enter the apartment.

Rylee glared at her for a moment, then quietly stepped past Kathryn. She slowly removed her coat and placed it on one of the coat hooks near the door. The twelve-foot ceilings with exposed, antique timber beams made the space feel much bigger than it was. Her boots squeaked as she moved down the hallway, the sound echoing around her.

She stalked past the kitchenette and into the far corner of the great room until she came to the balcony that overlooked Catalano Square Park. The early March thaw had brought the usual suspects out to enjoy the Saturday afternoon buffet of activities that the Third Ward had to offer: coffee shops nestled in between art galleries, shops, farm-to-table restaurants, and of course, the sprinkle of specialty cocktail bars that were clustered along the main roads.

Kathryn followed her in, casually standing behind the couch. Rylee ignored her.

"Rylee," Kathryn finally said, her voice tentative with concern. "Are you going to tell me what's wrong?"

"What's wrong?" Rylee whispered, almost savoring her anger as she bit out the words. "What could possibly be wrong, Kathryn? Could it be something you said?"

Kathryn sighed. "I have no idea what you're talking about, Rylee," she told her. She walked around the couch until she was standing near Rylee.

Rylee turned around to glare at Kathryn. She gently cocked her head to one side, looking over imaginary glasses as if to scold a misbehaving child. A wry smile formed on her lips. Kathryn took a step back.

"Is it true?" Rylee asked, her flat tone making it less of a question and more of a statement of fact.

"Is what true?" Kathryn asked.

Rylee studied her for a moment. "Did you think it wouldn't get back to me, Kat?" she asked in a soft voice.

Kathryn blinked in confusion. "What are you talking about?" she demanded.

Rylee took a step forward. "I talked to Steven. You remember him, right? Drive team mentor for our high school robotics team?" She waited for Kathryn to nod. "You've been telling people that I got pregnant on purpose. That I didn't want to lose Sam and having his baby was the only way to ensure he didn't leave me."

"I . . . " Kathryn's voice trailed off as she gaped at her. A sudden realization flashed across her face before she tried to frown and that was all Rylee needed. She turned away to gaze at the street below.

"I kept your secret, you know," she reminded Kathryn. "All through middle school and most of high school. When you told me that you were gay, I stood by you through the whispers.

Through people making fun of you behind your back. Even when the fellowship pushed you out of our congregation."

She paused to look over her shoulder. "What I don't understand is why," she told her. "Why would you do this to me?"

"Because Sam is no good for you!" Kathryn blurted out. "He cheated on you. He used you and you still kept going back to him!"

Rylee turned around to face her. "So, you lied to people about me to punish him?" she asked. "How does that even work?"

"He doesn't love you, Rylee," Kathryn told her. She leaned forward, clenching the back of the couch in her fists. "He can't love you. Not like I do!"

It was Rylee's turn to gape. "Kathryn . . . "

"I know you stopped taking the Pill for a reason," Kathryn told her, screwing her eyes shut in pain. "You might not want me, but it sure was a convenient way to keep Sam a part of your life, wasn't it?"

"What?!" Rylee gasped. "You told people I got pregnant on purpose to get back at me for not being interested in you?" She clenched her fists at her side. "Hannah's your partner, for heaven's sake!"

Tears started streaming down Kathryn's face, and she nodded. "And I love her as much as I love you," she said in a quiet voice.

Rylee looked down at the colorful area rug, studying the overlapping circles of bright purple, green, and blue dotting the white background for a moment. Finally, she looked up. The rage seemed to drain right out of her, leaving behind an emptiness that could never be filled.

"Lose my number," she told Kathryn. "We're done here."

With that, Rylee slowly walked past her and down the hallway to gather her coat and purse. Kathryn might have been her best friend in this world, but Rylee didn't see how she could ever make up for the damage she'd caused.

Rylee stood with her back to the window, idly watching as the caterers finished setting up the buffet for the group baby shower. She'd come to the group meeting early. Not because she was asked to. No, she'd arrived early because there was nothing else for her.

Sam had finally confessed he'd been caught sneaking out to the bars, although she still couldn't believe he'd experienced anything even close to what labor felt like with that so-called 'labor simulation' punishment. Yes, she'd seen the videos online. Yes, the men howled in supposed agony, but the videos were short and their wives laughed at them. It was obvious they were overacting.

Besides, it couldn't be legal to go through pretend labor as a consequence for breaking state law, she thought as she watched the caterers bring in the last dish and get the Bunsen burners lit to keep them warm. It was all an elaborate lie, just like when that woman answered his phone during his NCAA tennis match.

If he'd been arrested, he'd have been arraigned in criminal court and he'd be up to his eyeballs in pre-trial proceedings. Instead, Sam's schedule was pretty much the same: coffee, followed by complaining about how much homework he had, followed by disappearing for hours at a time, only to whine about how little he was making while chowing down on fast food.

Zara walked through the meeting room door with Brittany, Emma, and Grace following closely behind like baby ducks.

Grace was pulling a red plastic wagon behind her that was loaded up with assorted gift bags. She wheeled it over to the gift table for the group to unload.

While they were carefully placing the gifts on the pink and blue tablecloth, Mia and Zoey appeared, herding their family members into the room. A woman, with Mia's long brown hair and interesting taste in fashion, carried two bags that bulged with assorted boxes. Zoey was directing a pair of older women who were similarly weighed down with gifts through the door.

Other family members drifted in as well. An older African-American woman held a little boy's hand, who could only be Kwame, Zara's son. Mothers, sisters, aunts, cousins, best friends. Everyone except Rylee had their plus one.

She turned away and looked out the window. This group shower was so depressing. It sounded like a great idea in the beginning. Weekly meetings had allowed them to get to know each other enough to be friends. Heck, a few might even become lifelong friendships. But they'd all split off into random clicks. Without Devi, Rylee was completely alone.

She glanced behind her. Erin was bent down in front of the gift table. She had lifted the front of the pink and blue tablecloths that draped the table and was pulling large white boxes out from underneath the table. Another woman pushed them off to either side of the table and piled them up like they were oversized children's building blocks.

Something about the boxes drew Rylee's attention. Each box was wrapped with an oversized ribbon and recipient names were printed large enough to read from across the room. Where had she seen that before?

Erin dusted her hands off, then turned to the crowd. "The Wisconsin Individual Family Education program is delighted to welcome everyone to our Motherhood Mentoring Circle's group baby shower!" she told them. "Grab a plate and help yourself to some food. After everyone's had a bite to eat, we'll get started opening up gifts!"

"I'm hungry," Kwame told Zara.

She smiled down at him. "I know," she told him. "You know that you can't have any cupcakes until after you have something else, right?"

The boy pouted for a moment. "Chocolate?" he asked.

Zara looked over to the dessert table. "Looks like, little man," she assured him. "Let's get you something to start with. I believe they have eggs and bacon."

"Bacon!" the boy said, pulling on her hand.

Rylee waited until almost everyone had filled their plates, then grabbed a small bagel with cream cheese. She wasn't very hungry these days.

Then, she took a seat in the back of the room, quietly eating as she listened to the murmurs around her. From time to time, other people in the room looked in her direction, but no one tried to include her in their conversation. It was as if she was beneath everyone's notice.

She checked her phone while she finished up her last bite. No messages.

"All right, everyone," Erin said, her voice cutting through the noisy conversation around them. "Time to move on to the gifts. Lots of them to open, and we only have the room booked until noon."

Rylee quickly got up and tossed her plate into the garbage, then returned to her seat. She was as far away as she could get from the gifts. Most of the group looked happy that the program had sponsored this. After all, many of them were poor, or nearly so.

That's why she'd thought long and hard about what she wanted to give the group. A few of them, like Brittany, were adamant about going organic all the way and damn the expense. But most of the group was much more practical, and that made it easier to decide what to buy.

"I'm going to ask everyone for a bit of patience," Erin said. "Let's get chairs set up at the front of the room so that we can pass out the gifts where everyone can see."

There was a bit of chaos as the chairs were moved so that the mentoring circle sat facing the rest of the party. Rylee took a seat on the far end, near the conference room door, so that she could minimize the chances of her being included in pictures.

The other mentor, Katie, started by passing out the smaller gift bags. Once everyone had one, they were allowed to pull out the handmade baby bibs.

Lily smiled, laughing as she displayed hers to the group. "I made each of them based on what you shared about your baby room design," she told them. "I'm going with an 'over the rainbow' theme, so I created baby lions and tigers and bears. Oh, my!" She laughed, then turned to Brittany. "You told me how much you love your princess theme, so I might have gone a bit overboard on the crowns."

Cell phones were raised as friends and families took the obligatory pictures for social media and baby books.

Rylee looked closely at her bibs. She hadn't gotten into the whole 'theme' idea. After all, they weren't staying in that apartment very long. She'd just wanted the basics: the rocking chair that had been in Sam's family for generations, a dresser her grandmother had been given as a child, a mid-century style changing table and crib. Nothing fancy. That could wait until they'd finished moving to Massachusetts.

Her bibs were bright red, blue, and green. Single-line stitching in the same color with a single snap at the back of the bib to keep it in place.

She looked over at Lily and smiled. Generic. Just like her relationship with the group. Rylee leaned off to one side and placed it on the floor next to her.

"Grab mine next," Zara ordered. The cloth bags were duly passed out to the group. Each bag had a different cloth picture book.

On it went. Hooded baby robes. A growth chart for the wall. Baby booties, socks, and onesies. Even a small bag of assorted pacifiers.

"I believe that mine's next," Rylee told the group during a lull. She saw everyone look closely at the white boxes, but she shook her head. She got up and handed a small card to each of them.

Brittany frowned. "Gift card?" she whispered to Emma.

Everyone tore open the envelopes and stared at the card. Then, Charlotte let out a happy whoop. "Diapers?" she exclaimed with a large smile, struggling to her feet. "We're going to get an entire month of them delivered to our homes?"

Brittany looked over at Rylee. "This is incredible," she said in amazement. "How did you know that I only want cloth diapers for Aaron?"

Rylee smiled, trying to force as much happiness as she could into her face. "I listened," she told her. "You talk a lot about organic and how much you and Noah are putting into sustainability. Cloth seemed to be the right choice."

She looked over at the family members milling around and chatting. The group parted and, for an instant, she spotted her mom standing next to Katie.

Rylee sat back in her chair. *Wow. So that's who the boxes are from*, she thought. Of course, they were. She should have recognized the boxes from the last gala she'd been forced to attend. White boxes with colorful ribbons? Classic Ashley Williams donation style. Simple design. Catches the eye and, even if it's just a small gift, reinforces the feeling of having a huge benefit.

She shook her head and looked away. *Whatever, Mom,* she thought.

"Our last gifts were donated by the Eternal Springs Lutheran Church as a part of the 'First-Time Mom' Celebration," Erin told them. "Go ahead and find the box with your name." She waited until everyone had moved them over to their seat. "Don't worry about how you're going to get these back to your homes," she told them. "The church will work with you to set up a delivery date."

Erin nodded. With that, the women started to unwrap the bows and tear the wrapping paper. Inside was a generic box that, when opened, had an inventory list of the items inside.

Zoey gasped. "No way!" she yelled. "An infant car seat and stroller combo? Baby monitor, bouncer, and a newborn bathtub?" She leaned against the box, crying. "I can't believe it!"

Emma and Grace high-fived each other, while Mia, Lily, and Charlotte seemed to compare notes. Only Zara and Brittany seemed to look a bit reserved. Zara, possibly because she still had some items from when Kwame was a baby, and Brittany, because she was rather picky about what she wanted to buy for her baby.

Rylee looked down at her box and carefully opened it. A pink envelope sat on top of the inventory list, her name elegantly rendered in dark green calligraphy. She carefully opened the envelope and stared at the card. A baby shower for Allison.

She calmly placed the invitation back in the box and looked up. Her mom was talking to Erin. She wasn't wearing the standard understated but expensive pantsuit she typically wore to this type of event. Instead, she'd dressed down, wearing a pair of fresh jeans and a deep purple cashmere sweater.

She made eye contact with Rylee, raising an eyebrow to ask if she felt comfortable talking. Rylee closed her eyes and gave a quick shake of her head. It didn't matter if the entire congregation had helped fund this First-Time Mom bundle or if the Williams Family Foundation had been responsible. This was quintessential Mom. Give an anonymous donation and stand back in the crowd to lap up the appreciation.

She looked around the room, sad. She knew that these donations made a difference for some of the women in her mentoring circle. This might even become a part of the family's annual charitable donations.

It didn't make up for the fact that her parents had agreed to essentially disown her and her daughter. So, no. She wasn't going to that damn baby shower, period.

Chapter Fifteen

I t took her mom only a few minutes to hunt her down after worship service was over. "Rylee, honey, why didn't you sit with us?" Ashley asked, just a moment after she poked her head into the church kitchen.

Rylee studied the generic white coffee mugs she was assembling on the counter for the Ladies' Brunch and Bible Study. They only had twenty cups, so she probably needed to do a quick headcount to decide if they needed to switch to paper cups.

"Look at me, Rylee," her mom told her. "I know you're upset about what happened, but your father and I—"

"Did nothing," she finished for her. The coffee had already been taken out by another volunteer, and the only other thing that needed to be staged was sugar and creamers. She walked over to the refrigerator, making a wide turn around Ashley as she went to get the bin of creamers.

Her mom turned to follow her movement. She looked every day of her fifty-odd years. Rylee noticed that her tightly braided blond hair was at odds with her pale green pantsuit and clashed with the platinum earrings.

"Rylee, you know that your father and I love you, unconditionally," she finally told Rylee. "But your grandfather has to protect the family's assets."

Rylee stopped piling the sugar on the cart and slowly turned to face her mother.

"It may feel like it's personal," Mom told her, almost wilting under Rylee's glare. "But really, it isn't."

"Isn't personal," Rylee spat. "Really, Mother?"

Her mom slowly shook her head. "Every single decision made about the family trust has to be fully vetted by the legal team," she reminded Rylee. "Their job is to make sure that we follow the law."

"So, you just check the box and forget about what is ethically and morally right?" Rylee asked. "I didn't realize our attorneys had that level of training!"

"Rylee, sweetie—"

"Don't 'sweetie' me, Mom!" Rylee snapped. "You disowned me and took away everything I had!"

Her mom took a few steps forward, cocking her head in concern. "Your father is working on a way to replace the amount of money you lost because of Sam—"

Rylee banged her fists against the cart, rattling the mugs. "First Kathryn and now you!" she hissed. "Unbelievable!"

"What are you talking about?" Ashley demanded.

Rylee turned to her. "Everyone here seems to be under the impression that Sam forced me to get pregnant because he didn't want to lose me," she said.

Her mom flinched. "And you think that I had something to do with it?" she quietly asked.

"Didn't you?" Rylee demanded. "This whisper campaign has your DNA all over it, Mom!" she snapped. "'Rylee is such an innocent,'" she whined, mimicking her mom's voice. "'Sam must have corrupted our poor little angel!'"

Her mom looked down at the floor for a moment.

"So, you don't deny it, do you?!"

Ashley put her hands up, almost like she was trying to push away the truth. "I don't really know how that got started, sweetie," she told her. "No one talks to me about your pregnancy."

Rylee snorted. "I don't believe you," she told her. "You are so closely involved in every single aspect of the Women's Ministry that nothing—and I mean *nothing*!—happens without you giving it the nod of approval!"

"I—I don't know what you're talking about!" her mom stammered, a guilty look creeping into her face.

"Really, Mother?" Rylee hissed. "Are you going to blame some nameless person who doesn't even know anything about me beyond your carefully curated public persona?"

Her mom shook her head again. "I honestly don't know, Rylee," she moaned. "I'd say that Wendy Maxwell started it, but since it involves her son . . . "

"No!" Rylee yelled. She held up a hand, stopping the volunteer who carefully pushed open the door to the kitchen to check on them. The woman took one look at her mom and ducked away, quietly closing the door behind her.

"Now, Mother," Rylee said, her monotone voice low. "Who have you been talking to about my 'condition'? Why have I been getting the random 'we're praying for you' comments?"

Ashley looked down at her hands, then up at Rylee. "I confided in Melissa and Jessica very early in your pregnancy," she admitted. "I never told them Sam forced you to stop taking your birth control pills!"

"I see," Rylee said, the icy calm in her voice at odds with the tears that started to stream down her face. "So, you knew what the rumors were, but decided to do nothing about it. After all," she added. "I'm just 'the baby of the family' and 'easily manipulated' by a smart boy like Sam!'"

Her mom started to say something, but Rylee sharply overrode her. "It all makes sense now," she told her. "The strange looks at worship service. The concerned way people kept an eye on me when Sam and I were in the same room. Even the way Pastor Chapman has been acting!"

She wiped her hands across her face, pushing away the tears. Then, she grabbed the coffee cart and started to make her way to the door. "It may seem like I made a colossal mistake, Mother," she told her. "But your granddaughter is a gift from God." She stopped and glared at her mom. "There isn't enough money in the world to fix this," she told her. And with that, she backed the cart through the kitchen door.

Rylee was curled up on the futon couch, watching the rom-com she'd rented. Sam clambered down the stairs, breezing by her as he headed for the kitchen.

"Where are you going?" Rylee called after him.

He stopped at the refrigerator and pulled a bottle of soda from the door. "I have a mentoring meeting tonight," he told her.

Rylee struggled to get up. Allison swam from one side of her belly to the other, making it almost impossible to sit upright. "No, you don't," she told him. "It's Thursday, not Friday."

Sam put the bottle on the counter and grabbed his coat from the back of a kitchen chair. "Theo moved it this week," he told her. "No big deal."

"You're lying!" she cried. "You're going out to that bar again, aren't you?"

Sam pulled his jacket on, looking at her with a guilty grimace. "You know that I can't afford to be arrested again," he told her. "I can't have even a sip of alcohol until after the baby's born, same as you!"

"Well, that didn't stop you from going out before, did it?" Rylee snapped, finally able to walk after him. "Or are you headed over to Lucas' place again for another off-campus party?"

"Off-campus party?" Sam glared at her. "What am I, a freshman? No, Rylee," he yelled at her, grabbing his keys off of the hook by the door. "I'm not going to some off-campus party. Midterms are coming up, for heaven's sake. No one has time for that!"

"Bullshit!" she yelled back. "You're going out to party, Sam, and if you don't stop right now, I'll call the police!"

Sam looked at her for a moment, then opened the back door and stomped his way down the steep stairs.

"This isn't over, Sam!" she yelled after him, looking wildly around the room for something to wear outside. She spotted her sweater on the rocking chair and moved as quickly as she could across the floor to get it. Then, she walked back to the kitchen, stomping her feet into her boots.

"You lied to me every single time you went out to that bar!" she yelled, carefully making her way down the stairwell. "You lie about everything! I've looked at your damn receipts and I know that you're buying alcohol with your tips!"

She got to the bottom of the stairs and pushed open the back door. "Sam!" she yelled. "This isn't over!"

Sam had already made his way across the backyard to the garage. He put his key in the door to unlock it, but turned around to look at her. "Rylee, give it a rest!" he yelled back at her. "These meetings are fucking mandatory and I'm not spending any more time in jail because you made me miss one!"

"Bullshit!" she shrieked, carefully making her way down the stoop. "Your meeting is tomorrow, not tonight! You're going down to that bar again, aren't you?!"

She walked down the icy path, glaring at him. The arctic cold was rapidly seeping past the loose weave of her sweater, but she was beyond caring. Everyone was abandoning her. Her friends. Her family. The fellowship. The hell if Sam was going to get away with leaving her, too!

"Rylee, I already told you Theo had to move this week's meeting because he has to go out of town for the weekend! What the hell else do you want?" he barked at her. "A note signed by the Court?"

Rylee moved closer, hugging the sweater closed with clenched fists. "The truth, Sam! Allison and I just need the truth!"

He looked down at her. She could see the guilty look trying to hide behind his frown. "Rylee—"

The sudden sound of a police siren in the alley startled her, and Allison kicked in protest. The backyard was suddenly bathed in the strobing red and blue lights that cut through the gathering twilight.

Sam shot her a dirty look. "See what you've done?" he muttered. "One of the neighbors finally called the police because of you."

"Me?" Rylee shrieked, glaring at him in outrage. "You're the one who started this!"

Sam turned to watch as two police officers carefully walked into the backyard. "How?" he demanded. "I was just leaving. You're the one who started screaming."

Of course, it was my fault, Rylee thought. *It couldn't possibly be that you're going out to drink again, could it?*

She turned to glare at the officers as they approached. "Good evening," the older officer said. "What seems to be the problem this evening?" His hand casually rested on his gun for a moment.

Rylee looked down at his gun, then back to his face, flabbergasted that he had his hand on his gun. Granted, it looked like the gun was meant to be pulled out by his opposite hand, but that didn't make it look less threatening.

"We're just having an argument, Officer," Sam said in his most patient voice. "I'm late for a mentor meeting and my partner doesn't seem to believe that the date was changed."

The older man looked over at her. "That right, miss?"

Rylee hesitated, then nodded

"Why don't we have a talk over there, ma'am," the younger officer told her. He gestured toward the picnic table and Rylee slowly walked over to have a seat. She could feel the chill from the wooden bench through her jeans.

The officer moved to the other side of the bench and wiped the frost off before he sat down. "Can I get your name, ma'am?" he asked.

"Rylee Williams," she replied, turning to watch the other officer guide Sam closer to the garage.

"I'm Officer Thompson," he told her. "Can you tell me what your relationship is with . . . " He gestured toward Sam.

"His name is Sam Maxwell, Officer," she told him tartly. "He's the father of our baby." She rubbed at her belly with both hands.

"So, the two of you live together?" Officer Thompson asked.

"Yes," she confirmed. "Unless he gets arrested for drinking alcohol." She paused for a moment, considering. "Again."

"Are you saying that Mr. Maxwell isn't of legal drinking age?" the officer asked.

"No," Rylee replied. "I'm saying that we're enrolled in the Wisconsin Individual Family Education program and he's already been arrested once for drinking."

The officer looked over Rylee's shoulder at Sam, frowning.

"I'm trying to make sure he's not in jail when Allison is born, Officer," she told him urgently. "He's all I have left. I can't lose him, too!" The icy wind made her eyes water, and she found herself dabbing at them with her sleeve. "Please believe me! His mentor meeting is scheduled for Friday night, not Thursday!"

Officer Thompson nodded. "We'll take a look at this, ma'am. But I do have to remind you that we can't detain Mr. Maxwell based on hearsay." She started to protest, but he raised a hand to stop her. "Until he breaks a law, there's nothing we can do."

Rylee found herself shivering. "So, he gets himself arrested—again!—and I have to raise this baby by myself? Is that what you're telling me, Officer?" she asked. "He was facing a significant time behind bars the last time we went through this!"

Her teeth started chattering, the cold finally seeping deep into her bones. She held Allison in her arms, trying to find a way to keep herself warm. "I ca-can't b-believe this!" she moaned. "He's going to get himself a-a-arrested and my baby won't ha-have a father!"

Officer Thompson stood and walked around the table. "You're going to have to calm down, ma'am," he told her. "If you'd like, I can take you inside so that you can get warm."

"No!" Rylee snapped. "I-I need to stay here!"

The officer raised an eyebrow. "Okay," he allowed. "Does Mr. Maxwell have a history of drinking? Is there something inside that you don't want us to see?"

"Oh, my God!" Rylee exclaimed. "Of course not! Why would Sam want to go down to that bar if he had brought something back with him?"

She stood up, fumbling as she tried to get her legs over the picnic table bench. "It's not like he's coming home and drinking every night in front of me!" she yelled at him.

"Understood, ma'am," he replied.

Rylee stared at Sam. He was currently huddled against the side of the garage, looking down at his phone. *Unbelievable*, she thought. *He's addicted to that damn thing!*

"Ms. Williams?" the officer said, trying to bring her attention back to him. "Do you have any immediate concerns about your safety around Mr. Maxwell?"

She looked up, studying his face. Brown eyes, full lips. An expression that was half-concern, half-doubt, and wrapped around an attitude that loudly proclaimed, 'I'm not a rookie!'

"No, Officer," she told him, stamping her feet. "I'm not afraid of Sam. I'm afraid *for* Sam!"

The other officer walked past Sam and gestured to Officer Thompson to join him. He glared first at Rylee, then back to Sam as the two huddled together, looking like two football players going over their game strategy.

After a few long minutes, the officers returned to the picnic table. The older officer gestured for Sam to join them.

"We've confirmed that you are both enrolled in the family education program," the sergeant told them, almost growling as he made significant eye contact with each of them. "Since there is no corroborating evidence of domestic violence and no outstanding warrants for either of you, we're going to issue you both a citation for disorderly conduct."

"Wait, what?" Rylee murmured, feeling betrayed as icy tears trickled down her cheeks.

Sergeant Moore held up a hand. "If we get called again, one or both of you could be arrested and face criminal charges." He stared at Rylee. "Do you understand?"

"A citation?" How was any of this her fault?

The sergeant nodded, a grim look on his face. He turned back to Sam. "I believe you have a meeting to attend. Better get going."

"Thanks, Sergeant Moore," Sam said as he fumbled for his keys. He carefully avoided looking at her, a triumphant quirk on his lips.

She walked back to the porch, slowly opening the door to finally escape the cold. Possible arrest? Did they have to wait until Sam was drunk before arresting him?

She found herself sitting on the cold steps that led to the apartment, dazed. Sam was gone. Just like the rest of the people in her life who claimed to care for her.

She slowly stood and numbly made her way back up to the apartment. She had no more tears left.

Rylee popped another bag of green tea into her mug, then poured the boiling water over it. She stabbed the bag with a spoon to force it to the bottom of the mug to steep. It had been a very long week.

Sam had disappeared again. This time, she was fairly certain he hadn't been arrested. The first thing she noticed was his laptop went missing. A few days later, she'd left the apartment to pick up some groceries and found a fresh pile of dirty clothes lying in the clothes basket in the living room closet.

She ignored it. There was no way she was going to wash his clothes again. Let him clean up his own mess.

The numbness had given way to a realization that she needed to start planning for her future—alone. The state of Wisconsin might force Sam to be a part of her and Allison's lives, but it couldn't force him to act like a man.

She stirred the tea, then fished the tea bag out of the mug and walked it over to the garbage. It was past time to take a hard look at her future. What kind of life could she create for Allison?

She sat down and stared at her mug. She was a single mother, planning a major move across the country with no support structure in place. No friends. No family.

Add in Sam. The most logical course of action was for him to leave the Midwest with her and get a fresh start on life. That didn't mean they were a couple. No, it just meant that they would have an equal place in Allison's life, just like the law said.

Instead, she would be forced to buy a condo near campus, one big enough for both a full-time nanny and a part-time personal assistant to help her stay organized. Time to get serious.

She turned on her iPad and looked over the available condos near campus. One of them drew her eye. Three bedrooms, two full bathrooms, and a living room that was large enough for a proper family room. Single garage. No mention of a charging station, but she was sure she could have one installed.

Her phone vibrated. "Mackenzie," it announced. Rylee pulled the phone across the small kitchen table and swiped left. The last person she wanted to hear from was one of her sisters.

She turned the phone over and continued her search. Maybe it would be better to buy a small house, something with a backyard for Allison to play in.

The phone buzzed again. She flipped it over, glaring as she pushed the call to voicemail. *Leave me alone, Mackenzie,* she thought. *They made it clear that I'm no longer family.*

Rylee looked out the window. Late March was a strange time in Milwaukee. Slush, followed by icy sunshine, followed by flurries. It was like Mark Twain once said: If you don't like the weather, wait a minute.

Her phone buzzed again. "Mackenzie."

Rylee got up and walked out to the family room. She sat down in the rocking chair and put her feet up. She cupped Allison with her left arm, holding the mug in her right hand.

She leaned her head back against the cushion, a wave of sadness overwhelming her. It had been apparent for quite a while that she couldn't count on Sam to be there for her or Allison. And that should have been okay because she still had her family to fall back on. Until even that was taken away from her.

The phone announced "Mackenzie" again. She got up with a sigh and slowly walked back into the kitchen to retrieve her phone. Mackenzie was the only person she knew who would just keep calling until she got an answer.

She put the mug on the counter and sat down at the table, again. She looked at the phone as she put in her earbuds. Six calls, all of them within ten minutes.

The phone rang, and this time she answered it. "What?" she demanded.

"Hey, Rylee," Mackenzie said, a satisfied tone in her voice. "Are you busy?"

Rylee put the phone back on the kitchen table. "You have five minutes before I pull the battery out of this thing," she told Mackenzie.

Mackenzie laughed. "I doubt you have the tools to open that thing," she replied. "Besides, if you don't eventually answer, I'll just be forced to call the cops for a wellness check. You are, after all, pregnant, and as a concerned family member, I have to make sure you're okay!"

"Shut up, Mackenzie!" Rylee snapped. "If I was family, I'd still be included in the family trust."

"Ah," Mackenzie breathed. "Yeah, it pissed me off when I heard they'd decided to cut you out."

"Yeah, well, Mom and Dad were absolutely fine with it!" Rylee snapped. "So was Chloe."

There was a long pause. "I heard."

"What do you want, Mackenzie?" Rylee asked.

"Mom is freaking out that you don't want to come home for the baby shower she's throwing for you," Mackenzie told her. "She invited a few folks from church and, of course, Nana and Grammy are coming. You have to come."

"No," Rylee flatly told her. "I'm not some prop she can bring out to get attention."

"Rylee—"

"I'm not family, Mackenzie!"

"Yes, you are—"

"Really?" Rylee shrieked. "Family *is* as family *does*."

"Sweetie—"

"Don't you fucking call me that, Mackenzie!" Rylee yelled. Allison kicked, hard, and Rylee put both hands around her, protectively. "No one has come to visit me once since I moved to this God-forsaken hell hole. Not my sisters. Not my friends. Not even my own parents."

"That's a little hard to do, Rylee," Mackenzie told her. "I'm back in New York—"

"Yeah, I get that," Rylee allowed. "But family obligation cuts both ways. Either I am a part of the family or I'm not. End of story."

"If this is about the family trust, I can assure you that Dad is already looking at ways to match the income you might have received from the trust," Mackenzie told her, using that familiar and soothing voice she'd used when they were younger. "There might even be a way for him to legally leave his shares to you and Allison as a part of his will."

Rylee covered her eyes, then sighed. "It's not about the money, Mackenzie," she told her. "It never was."

"Really?" Mackenzie asked, surprised. "Everything you've complained about is the family trust."

"Did you even read the addendum?" Rylee asked. She suddenly felt very tired.

"Sorta," Mackenzie admitted. "I was given brief access to an electronic version before the meeting."

"Our grandfather specifically called out Allison," Rylee told her. "He refused to make any provisions for me or my issue."

"I know," Mackenzie admitted. "But he's only trying to protect the trust. It has nothing to do with Allison."

"Bullshit!" Rylee growled. "It has everything to do with her."

Mackenzie sighed. "I'm not going to change your mind about this, am I?" she quietly asked.

"No," Rylee told her. "You're not."

"Okay," Mackenzie replied, her voice soft. "I'll leave it be. But, please don't ignore me, Rylee. I'm here for you."

Rylee nodded. "I love you, Mackenzie."

"Love you, too."

Rylee blinked back tears. *God gave me this challenge to make me stronger*, she thought. She may no longer be family, but she was still a Williams, and she knew she could build a new life for Allison out east.

Chapter Sixteen

R ylee had just put away the vacuum cleaner when the first pain hit. It felt like an intense cramp. She closed the closet door and leaned back against it, both hands around Allison.

"Deep breath," she told herself. "This can't be real labor. It's too early for that." She rubbed at the pain, grimacing as it gradually faded away.

That wasn't so bad, she thought. Maybe it was time to sit down for a while.

She slowly walked into the kitchen to make herself a cup of tea. "Allison, darling," she said, rubbing at her belly. "It's not time to come home yet."

She turned on the electric kettle, making sure the preset was right for chamomile tea. She braced herself against the worn countertop for a moment to make sure the water was heating up. Then, she slowly stood up and grabbed her mug from the dish rack.

She hadn't slept well. Maybe that second cup of green tea had been a mistake. She grabbed the box of chamomile tea from the cabinet and popped a bag into her mug, staring at it for a long moment.

She knew Sam had been back to grab some fresh clothes, but he'd left again before she could make it downstairs to check.

Annoying but not unexpected. She doubted he had moved back home. After all, he was coming back to the apartment to grab clean clothes. He was probably avoiding Wendy, too.

Of course, there was no real way to know what was going on. She hadn't been to worship service since the argument with her mom. Sam hadn't come back Sunday morning to take her and no one else had stopped by the apartment to offer her a ride. It just reinforced the emptiness of being alone, so why waste money on an Uber?

The kettle beeped, letting her know that the water was at temperature. She started to walk the few steps over when the pain hit again. This time, it started with a single spot, right in the middle of her belly, then radiated outward in an ache that made her want to double over. Her entire belly tightened around the baby.

"No," she moaned, clutching Allison with both hands. "This is not happening, Allison. Not now." She pursed her lips in anxiety. "Your birthday isn't for another three weeks. I forbid you to come home early."

Rylee smiled despite the pain. *I forbid you*, she thought. *Definitely something to put in that baby journal!* Allison responded with a defiant kick, squirming a bit before she settled down again.

She took a slow deep breath, held it for a moment, then breathed it out, trying to release that nagging pain. She found herself rocking back and forth, just a bit, as she tried to relax. *This is not labor,* she told herself.

The pain slowly faded, leaving behind a strange emptiness. She slowly rubbed her hand against her belly. Allison seemed to have fallen asleep.

Rylee grabbed the kettle. She slowly poured water over the tea bag and put the kettle back on its base. She hit the off button before she took her mug into the family room. She grabbed the remote and settled down on the couch, looking for something mindless to get her mind off the contractions.

She settled on a cooking show. The host, some generic guy, was walking viewers through how to adapt recipes for use in a slow cooker. The key was to adjust the temperatures based on cooking time.

She'd almost convinced herself that it was over when suddenly, her muscles felt like they were clamping down around Allison. Rylee dropped the remote, feeling like her skin had somehow solidified.

She took a deep breath, trying to hold it for a few seconds until she blew it out, but found herself panting with pain as the contraction continued to tighten. She felt Allison stir, almost as if the contraction was hurting her, too.

Just as quickly, the pain faded away. She looked at her phone, dazed. The last contraction had been twenty minutes ago. Maybe.

Please, God, she prayed, trying to push that panicky feeling away. *It's too early. Please let Allison be alright.*

She clutched Allison with her left hand, the phone in her right. Calling her mom was out of the question. She found herself rocking back and forth, tears threatening to spill down her cheeks. Sam, maybe? He should be here. Allison was his baby, too!

She thumbed the icon for the Phone app, then scrolled down the list for Sam's number. She stabbed the button to call. It rang twice, then went to voicemail.

"This is Sam," his voicemail said. "You know what to do."

She waited for the beep, trying to stay calm. "It's Rylee," she said in a low voice. "Something's wrong. We need you to come back to the apartment."

She sat there, waiting for him to call or text her back. It was Saturday. He had to be out making deliveries. She just had to be patient.

She looked at the time. Over ten minutes had passed. He was ignoring her. He had to be. She unlocked her phone, stabbing the icon to call Sam again. It went right to voicemail.

"Sam," she said. "Please, I need you to call me back. It's about Alison!" She ended the call and dropped the phone on the couch.

"Okay," she told herself, trying to push down her panic. "Maybe he turned off his phone because he was driving. Three more weeks until my due date. Firstborns are almost always late, right? So, he's thinking that we have plenty of time."

Rylee pushed herself up off of the couch. *Walk*, she told herself. Sometimes that would help. At least that's what she'd heard.

She slowly paced across the floor, trying to think of all of the things that still needed to be done in the baby's room. The basics were complete. The crib had arrived a few days ago and had been carefully placed near the window. The changing table was next to the closet, with the diaper pail one step away. Onesies, snuggly blankets, and assorted clothes ready for use. Diaper bag paraphernalia was ready to go.

What was missing? she mused as she moved into the kitchen. Several boxes of newborn diapers were stored in the closet. Endless containers of diaper wipes on the shelf.

A rocking chair! She turned around and studied the rocker she had set up in the family room. Of course, the baby's room needed one. Should she have it moved upstairs or have a new one delivered?

Enough of this nattering, she told herself. She crossed the room and scooped her phone off of the couch. She thumbed the Messages icon, found Sam, and texted *Allison is coming, please come back to the apartment. We need you.*

She started walking again, slowly moving into the kitchen. Her phone buzzed. "Sam," it announced. Finally. She sat down at the table, feeling that strange pressure stomach again.

"Hello?" she answered, grunting as the pain seemed to move like a wave this time, almost as if it was gently pushing Allison further down.

"It's me," Sam replied. "How far apart are your contractions?" He sounded concerned.

"I don't know," she told him, her panic bubbling up again. "Maybe twenty minutes apart?" She rubbed a hand across her belly. It might be her imagination, but the skin underneath her shirt felt hard to the touch. "But it hurts, Sam, and I'm afraid my water's going to break any minute now!" She paused, waiting for him to respond. When he didn't, she started crying. "Please, please come home!"

She could hear the sounds of traffic in the background. "Okay," he finally replied. "On my way."

She put the phone down, relieved. "See, Allison," she said to the baby. "It's going to be okay. Your daddy is coming home." She stopped, considering her words. *Home. Is that what this place had become? Home?*

The pressure had eased, so she got up and started pacing again. So far, she'd been able to walk through the contractions, but that didn't necessarily mean anything. Her water hadn't broken yet. Allison was still moving around a bit. Some of the contractions felt like the cramps she had when she got her period, but others were so strong they had to be real.

She'd just finished her tea and was slowly walking back to the kitchen when another strong wave hit her. She managed to ease herself onto her hands and knees, rocking back and forth to try to ease the spasms. It hurt so bad that she couldn't help but cry.

The downstairs back door slammed, followed by the sound of Sam running up the stairs. He dropped his keys and jacket onto the kitchen table, then hurried over to her.

He helped her off the floor and moved her back onto the couch, gently placing a few pillows behind her lower back. "When did they start?" he asked her in a quiet voice, looking down at her belly in concern.

Rylee took a deep breath, then let it out sharply. "A few hours ago," Rylee told him. "The cleaning service didn't show up today, so I decided to do a bit of vacuuming. At first, I thought maybe I'd overdone it. My muscles felt tight right around Allison, and when I put my hands over her, it felt like my skin was getting hard to the touch. So, I sat down and waited to see if it would happen again."

"Which it did, right?" Sam prompted her.

She nodded. "Yes, but they seem to be completely random and, when I have a contraction, it seems to last forever," she told him as she put one hand against the baby. "I just don't know what to do!"

Before he could reply, another contraction started, this one sharper than the last. "Oh, I think it's happening again!" she whimpered, blindly reaching for him.

"Breathe, Rylee," he told her. "Come on, just breathe with me. In and out. Nice and slow. It's going to be okay."

She found herself breathing in, watching his lips as he counted. They paused for a moment, and then he counted as they breathed out in unison. Her awareness tunneled down to the breathing exercise. For the first time, Rylee felt it was going to be okay.

When it was over, Sam pulled his phone out of his back pocket and placed it on the coffee table. He started the timer so he could keep track of the contractions. Then, he got up and grabbed his iPad from his desk to take notes.

They sat in silence for a few minutes, then Sam turned on the TV. He looked bored as he tried to keep an eye on her while he watched the show.

She snuggled back against the cushions, waiting for the next contraction to start. Sam glanced at his phone, starting to look annoyed. She began to protest; after all, it wasn't as if she had any control over what was happening when the next wave of tight pain grabbed hold.

She gasped, reaching for Sam's hand, then pushed it against her belly. "See," she whispered. "See how hard it feels?" Sam gingerly placed his hand against her taut stomach just in time for Allison to kick at him in protest.

The pain intensified, and Rylee drew a sharp breath. "Oh, my God, Sam!" she moaned. "It hurts. It really hurts!"

Sam's concerned face swam into view. "Breathe, Rylee," Sam told her in a gentle voice. "Come on, breathe with me."

She tried to focus on the sound of breathing. "In, two, three, four," he whispered. "Pause. Out, two, three, four. You've got this, Rylee."

Without warning, the contraction eased. Sam updated notes with when it started and how long it lasted. Then, he reset the timer and settled back on the couch to wait for the next one. And the next one. And the one after that.

After a few hours, Sam realized that it was well past dinnertime and got up to make them some sandwiches. As he settled back on the couch to eat, she decided she'd had enough.

"I can't take this much longer, Sam."

He looked up from his sandwich, annoyed. "Rylee, you've only had six contractions," he told her. "I'm pretty sure it's going to be a while before you're in active labor."

Maybe, she thought. *Or maybe Allison will be born on the kitchen floor!* "At least try calling the doctor," she begged.

He put his sandwich down on the coffee table and looked around. "Where's your phone?" he asked.

"Kitchen," she told him and he grabbed her phone off of the kitchen counter for her. He took another bite of his sandwich as she found Dr. Zastrow's office number, then handed it to him. He put it on speakerphone as he touch-toned through the after-hours menu.

"After-hours triage, this is Katie," a friendly voice announced. "How can I help you?"

Before Sam could respond, Rylee grabbed the phone from him. "This is Rylee Williams and I'm having contractions," she told the nurse. "They seem kind of erratic. Anywhere from ten minutes to thirty minutes apart."

The nurse started typing. "And how long do they last?" she asked.

"Almost a minute," Rylee told the nurse, frowning as Sam shook his head. *Of course, they'd been that long,* she thought. *She was the one having them!*

"Rylee, I know it can be a bit scary," the nurse told her condescendingly. "But you're not in active labor yet. You need to call us when your contractions are coming regularly at four minutes apart. Each contraction should last at least one minute and, this is the most important part, they have been following this pattern for at least one hour."

"But they are so sharp," Rylee retorted. "It feels like what they told us real labor would feel like!"

"I understand, Rylee," the nurse said, sounding as if she was trying to be sympathetic. "But until they are about four minutes apart and the contractions last at least a full minute, you're not ready to deliver. But, just to be safe, we'll schedule you a follow-up with Dr. Zastrow tomorrow morning. Can you hold while I access tomorrow's schedule?"

Sam looked at her and held up a hand to still her objection. "Sure," he told the nurse. To his credit, Sam pushed to get an early morning appointment.

Rylee sagged back against the couch, trying to find a comfortable position. It was going to be a long night.

The next morning, Sam drove her to the doctor's office. The contractions had stopped overnight. She wanted Allison to both come home today and for her to stay snuggly beneath her heart while she sorted things out with Sam.

She gingerly sat down in the waiting room while Sam checked them in. Several other patients were waiting.

"I heard that the doctor isn't even here yet," one of the women confided in her. "It was busy last night!"

"Mmm-hmm," Rylee clenched her teeth, gently rubbing the sides of her belly with both hands. Allison was restless. It was almost as if she could feel another contraction ramping up.

Sam sat down next to her, phone in hand. This time it was different, though. He wasn't as focused on whatever he was reading. Every once in a while, he glanced over to check on her. Rylee wasn't sure if she was happy that he was finally paying attention to her or simply annoyed because it took her going into labor to trigger his concern.

They sat there for over an hour. Rylee counted three contractions before the nurse called them back. One of them was so painful, Rylee found herself rocking in the chair, on the verge of tears. The others felt as if they were tiny waves of random cramping that could be soothed away with a light rub.

"Sorry for the wait," the nurse told them as she ushered them into the exam room. "We're a bit backed up right now."

Sam looked over at Rylee, an annoyed look on his face. "We know," he said. "How much longer will it be before we can see the doctor?"

The nurse smiled. "Not much longer," she told them. "Dr. Zastrow just arrived and will be with you shortly." She turned to Rylee. "Why don't you get undressed from the waist down and we'll take a peek at how you're doing?"

Rylee hung her purse and jacket up on the wall hook, which conveniently stood between Sam and the door.

"I'll come back when you're done," he told her.

"Please don't," Rylee begged in a quiet voice. "I really need your help." Sam started to protest, but she held up a hand. "Trust me, it's nothing you haven't seen before."

He reluctantly nodded, and she slipped her shoes off with a sigh. She hated this part of it. Her body was so swollen that it was difficult to get in and out of clothes these days. Compression socks helped a bit, but only if she could get them on. This morning, she'd given herself a pass because of the swelling.

It was rather amusing to watch Sam help her while trying to avoid looking at her. He'd spent so much time avoiding her that he seemed shocked to see the changes to her skin and just how swollen her ankles were.

Another contraction hit just as he was helping her get settled on the exam bed. She hissed, letting him cover her lap with the white sheet. Then, he grasped her hand in his and carefully eased her into a semi-reclined position. He squeezed her hand in reassurance, then stepped back, almost as if he was afraid of what was going to happen next.

There was a tap on the door and the nurse poked her head in. "Come on in," Rylee told her, then laid her head back against the exam table. "I'm really worried about the contractions," she said. "Please tell me that Allison's okay."

The nurse walked over to the other side of the bed. "We'll take a closer look, Rylee," she said with a smile. "But I'm sure she's fine."

Rylee looked up at Sam. He frowned as the nurse carefully folded the sheet so that her belly was exposed. Then, she squirted some warm medical gel onto Rylee's belly. She used the flat-headed wand to spread the gel around before moving it firmly downward.

Sam shifted from foot to foot, looking very uncomfortable as he intently watched the movement. It was almost as if he was expecting something to be wrong.

"Ohh," the nurse cooed. "There she is!" She pulled the screen a bit closer with one hand so they could take a closer look. It was a bit difficult to see, but it appeared that Allison had her eyes clenched and her thumb firmly planted in her mouth. 'Leave me alone,' she seemed to be telling them.

"Allison is head down, Rylee," the nurse confirmed as she moved the wand higher up on Rylee's belly.

Rylee looked from the screen back to the nurse. "Oh, that's good, right?" she asked. "She keeps kicking me right under the ribs, especially when I have a contraction."

"Perfectly normal," the nurse responded reassuringly. "Lungs are fully developed and she's just about ready to take her first breath any day now."

There was a light knock, and then Dr. Zastrow walked into the room. "Let's not get ahead of ourselves too soon," he told them. "You're in your thirty-seventh week, right?"

Rylee stared at the screen, trying to make sense of what she was seeing. "Yes," she replied. "Is my baby okay?"

Doctor Zastrow quickly changed places with the nurse. He moved the wand to the top of her belly and began to methodically trace it down the side of her belly in a zigzag pattern. "So far, I don't see any concerns," he told her. "You might be feeling less movement now. She doesn't have much room to move around."

Rylee looked up at the ceiling with a happy sigh. "That's a relief," she murmured. She felt Sam move closer to her side, staring at the screen intently. She looked up, and he frowned.

"What's that?" he asked, pointing at the screen.

Dr. Zastrow looked at Sam, then down to Rylee. "That's your baby's heart," he said in a gentle voice. "Based on what we're seeing, she's doing fine."

"Oh," Sam replied. He didn't take his eyes off the screen.

"Let's start at the top of her head," the doctor told them as he moved the wand down. Rylee tried not to squirm as he pushed the wand dangerously close to her bladder. "As I move up, you'll start to see some dark spots. Those are her ribs," he said as he adjusted the flat head against her skin to take a measurement before moving on. "Here are her knees and legs over here." He looked over to Rylee with a tired smile. "She doesn't have a lot of wiggle room anymore, but it's going to be a few weeks before she's ready."

He moved the wand again, settling on Allison's face for a moment as she took her thumb out of her mouth and yawned.

"Ohh . . . !" Rylee breathed. She was so adorable!

Dr. Zastrow pulled the wand away from her skin and handed her a disposable cloth to clean the gel off of her skin. Then, he cleaned off the wand and pulled the stool over to have a seat.

"Before you leave, I'll check to see how dilated you are, Rylee," he told her. "Based on what we see on the ultrasound, I'm not overly concerned. We still have a few weeks to go."

"What about the contractions?" Sam asked, looking worried.

"Most women experience contractions as they approach their delivery date," Dr. Zastrow told them. "First-time mothers can find them to be . . . "

Sam frowned. "Frightening?"

The doctor shook his head. "Unsettling," he replied. Then he looked at Rylee. "This is the time to try and rest up," he told her. "I know that some of the contractions may feel intense. Think of these contractions as a way of warming up your muscles, getting you ready to give birth."

Before she could respond, he held up his hand. "Let's get your feet up in the stirrups and take a quick look at your cervix," he said.

Sam moved away from the exam bed as the doctor scooted to Rylee's feet to unfold the stirrups. Then, the doctor guided one foot, and then the other into position.

She knew from experience that he needed to insert a metal speculum to take a peek at her cervix, but that didn't lessen her discomfort of having this done while Sam was in the room. She looked up at Sam. He made eye contact, then looked over his shoulder at the door. He was just as embarrassed as she was.

Dr. Zastrow quickly removed the speculum and sat back. "As of right now, your cervix is dilated less than one centimeter," he told them. "We have some time."

Less than one centimeter? "But it hurts!" Rylee protested.

Dr. Zastrow nodded. "I understand, Rylee," he said, trying to reassure her. "However, until they get more intense and, more importantly, the contractions begin at the top and feel like they're pushing down on the baby, you're not in active labor."

He smiled as he stood up. "You'll get there, I promise," he told her. Rylee closed her eyes, sagging against the exam table as the doctor guided her feet out of the stirrups. "In fact, if we don't see any progress in the next few weeks, we can always induce labor. But it's always better to let things happen naturally."

Chapter Seventeen

Rylee had promised herself that she would rest, but she spent too much time rearranging the baby's room. Allison was thirty-eight weeks along. She was running out of time.

Sam barely spent time in the apartment anymore. He spent most of his days at the library as he leaned in on his coursework while still opening his schedule as wide as possible for deliveries. If it had been just a bit warmer, she swore he'd have camped out in his car and done his homework there so he wouldn't miss out on making money.

That didn't mean he didn't repeatedly check in on her throughout the day. She had to carry her phone with her everywhere. Yesterday, she'd missed his text because she was in the bathroom and he'd called repeatedly until she answered.

She'd just finished sorting the items she wanted to take with her to the hospital when the front doorbell rang. She paused to think for a moment. It wasn't Monday, so it couldn't be the cleaner. She hadn't ordered anything recently. Most of her friends continued to ghost her and those who occasionally reached out wouldn't be caught dead in this neighborhood.

Pastor Chapman? she thought as she hid the breast pump under one of her delivery gowns. Neither of them had been back to worship service since the big fight. Maybe this was the spiritual version of a wellness check.

She heard someone coming up the steps. Of course, she'd left the lower front door unlocked when she had gone down to pick up the mail this morning. She bit back a cuss, hurrying to open the front door.

She opened the door just as her mom raised her hand to knock. "Mom?" Rylee gasped. "What are you doing here?"

"Checking on my daughter, of course," Mom told her. Rylee stared at her for a moment, confused. "May I come in?" she asked.

"Sure," she said, backing up a bit to let her enter. "Sorry, the place is a mess. Sam is working a lot of hours and I'm trying to rest as much as possible. Doctor's orders."

"I understand," her mom replied, looking around with a critical eye. "It's smaller than I imagined."

Rylee closed the door and slowly walked across the room. She eased herself into the rocking chair. "Why are you here, Mom?" she asked, looking up at her mom wearily.

Her mom walked over to the couch and gingerly sat, her purse nestled tightly against her hip. She smiled, then looked down at the assorted pile next to Rylee's go-bag. "I came to apologize," she told her.

Those were the last words Rylee expected to hear. "I'm sorry, what?" she stammered. *For lying to the fellowship about my relationship with Sam?* she thought. *Or allowing our entire family to disown me and my daughter?*

Her mom massaged her neck as she tried to find the words. "I was very upset that you insinuated that my closest friends had anything to do with the rumors that are floating around about your pregnancy," she finally told Rylee. "They've been a part of my inner circle since I married your father, and I can't imagine them saying anything like this."

Rylee nodded.

"But," her mom continued, looking down at her hands. "Discussing my . . . concern . . . about Sam was a mistake."

Rylee leaned her head back against the rocking chair's cushion, studying her mom. For Ashley Williams to admit she'd made a mistake was rare. For her to apologize for that mistake was unheard of.

"What did you tell them?" she finally asked.

Her mom shook her head. "In all honesty, I don't remember," she admitted. "I was so angry that Sam had done this to you; that he had refused to stand up and take responsibility for his actions that I . . . broke down at a Women's Ministry meeting."

"Oh, God," Rylee gasped, covering her mouth with both hands as she closed her eyes. "Sam's mom was there, wasn't she?"

"Yes," her mom admitted. "In fact, she encouraged the group to give me some privacy."

Rylee opened her eyes at that and stared at her mom. "Sam's mom showed you compassion?" she asked. She frowned in disbelief. "Really?"

Her mom nodded. "A few days later, Jessica came to talk to me about things that she'd heard Wendy was telling people behind my back. About how you had stopped taking your birth control pills because you didn't want Sam to leave you again. She swore me to secrecy."

Rylee laughed, shaking her head in disbelief. "I dumped Sam, remember?"

"That's not what the fellowship heard," her mom told her, a disapproving look cutting through her sadness.

"Figures," Rylee remarked. "So, you got back at her by talking about Sam? Is that it?"

"I wanted Jessica to know the truth about what happened," her mom snapped. "Sam would not be our first choice for a son-in-law—"

"—choice?!"

"—and you have your whole life ahead of you," her mom continued. "It should have been years before you were ready to settle down!"

"So, you lied," Rylee snapped, rubbing an idle hand against Allison. "You're the reason that I can't go back to church."

"Oh, sweetie," her mom said, leaning forward. "I didn't want to believe that you were . . . sexually active . . . " she said with a wince. "I had a very long conversation with Jessica. There have been so many rumors floating around that no one seems to know who said what." She sighed. "I am not sure what to do."

Then, she slapped both hands on her thighs and stood up. "I will figure it out, though," she said brightly. She walked over to the window and looked down. "Ah, they're ahead of schedule," she said with a satisfied smile.

"Who are?" Rylee asked.

"I made arrangements to deliver your baby shower gifts," her mom told her.

Rylee blinked. "What baby shower gifts?"

"From the group shower, of course," her mom replied. "Plus, I knew you might want a few things from home, so I had the movers pack them up as well."

"Mom—"

"Rylee, I love you and I will always love you," her mom said, tears in her eyes. "Unconditionally and without reservation. I may not always agree with the decisions that you make, but you are my baby and always will be."

Rylee stood up, tears streaming down her face. Allison started fussing, squirming around as if she was trying to get into a more comfortable position. Her mom came over and enveloped her with a hug, gently rocking her back and forth as if she were the most important thing in the world. She surrendered to her tears, loud wails of relief echoing in the small apartment.

There was a knock on the door, and Rylee quickly wiped her face as she tried to dry her tears. Her mom wiped her own tears, laughing, and let her go. Then she moved to open the front door.

"Hello, Matt," she said to the delivery man. "Rylee, can you show Matt the baby's room?"

Over the next hour, the delivery team brought in box after box. The newborn baby seat and stroller, a high chair, a bassinet, a playpen, boxes of newborn clothes, diapers, baby bottles, and the dresser Rylee had wanted from home. The team helped unbox everything and took the containers away.

They even brought the rocking chair that her mom had saved from when Rylee was a baby. Chloe had turned it down when Patrick was born because she preferred only modern furniture. But, for Rylee, it was a piece of her childhood.

They set the rocking chair up in the corner of the room, near the window. Rylee sat down, feeling the familiar contours of the wood against her body with every motion of the rocking chair. The wooden seat was lower than she remembered. Her feet were flat against the floor and just a tiny flex of her foot started the rocking.

Allison kicked, a flutter of activity as she moved around a bit. Her mom stood in the doorway, smiling as she watched her rock in the chair.

"I remember using that same rocker when I was pregnant with you," she told her as she moved into the room. She grabbed a baby blanket and folded it in half before draping it over the side of the crib. "So, what are you going to do about a nanny?" she asked. "I believe Sam is against it because of the money situation, right?"

Rylee nodded. "He's right, Mom," she told her. "We'll have a bit more options once Allison is six months old, but for now, we have to look at what Sam can afford."

"Let me noodle on that," her mom told her. "There must be some way to hire someone to help, especially in those first few months. Maybe I can set up something with our ministry."

Rylee stopped rocking. "No," she told her. "They've done enough already!"

Her mom held up her hands in surrender. "Okay," she said, her voice contrite. "I'm sorry. Let me have the attorneys take a closer look and see what we can do. Is that okay?"

Wow. Rylee carefully got up from the rocking chair and went to hug her. First, she admits she was wrong. Then, she asks for forgiveness. Now, she's asking for Rylee's permission to help.

"Of course, Mom," Rylee whispered, tears streaking down her face. "Thank you so much. I love you!"

Over the next few weeks, they built a routine around her contractions. Sam kept track of what he affectionately called the 'Countdown Log' on his iPad. This afternoon, the contractions had become more frequent but only lasted about forty-five seconds. They'd gotten progressively stronger over the last few days.

Rylee wasn't very hungry, but Sam had insisted on making dinner anyhow. They'd settled on some old-fashioned comfort food: sweet potato fries, chicken wings, and, for Sam, mozzarella sticks.

Sam was just finishing up with the dishes when another contraction hit. Rylee sat down, arching her back in pain. *This one was different*, she thought as she gripped the kitchen table with both hands. Sharper, with the pain lancing around her midsection until it felt like a painful hug.

Sam looked over. "Another contraction?" he asked.

"Mmm-hmm!" Rylee told him with a nod. Sam closed the dishwasher and picked up his phone to start the timer. She bit her lip, trying to breathe through the pain. "It feels like Allison is pushing down right up against my pelvis," she told him. "She really wants to come out."

Sam nodded back, then grabbed the air fryer bin to clean it out.

Slowly, the pain receded, leaving behind a dull ache. She felt herself sag as she released the table. "It's over," she told him.

Sam dropped the bin into the sink and then leaned over to check the timer. "That was over a minute, Rylee," he told her. "Did you want to log that?" He held up his wet hand to remind her that he was working.

She smiled, shaking her head lightly. Then, she pulled his iPad over.

"Start time?" she asked.

"5:28," he told her.

She entered the time into the spreadsheet. "How long?" she asked, not looking up.

"One minute, thirteen seconds," he said as he glanced at his phone.

"I hope this is over soon, Sam." She slowly stood up, one hand on the table to help steady herself. "It really feels like Allison is ready to come home."

Maybe it was time to pack up the go-bag, she thought, slowly moving into the living room as she gently rubbed the sides of her stomach. She moved the bag from the coffee table to the couch and eased herself down next to it. The bag was too heavy. Maybe she *had* overdone it just a bit. Did she need two delivery gowns?

Another contraction hit, a sharp wave traveling from the top of Allison's head to the very top of her baby bump. "Sam!" she called out, gripping the futon with both hands.

Sam leaned back to look at her from the kitchen. "Another contraction?" he asked.

"Yes," she hissed, clenching her teeth. "It feels like I'm being stabbed here."

She saw him toss the dishrag into the sink and grab his phone before he quickly moved into the living room. "Are you breathing?" he asked.

She rolled her eyes, slowly blowing out her breath as she dug her fingertips into her back muscles. That seemed to be the only thing she could do right now.

Sam sat down near her, looking contrite. He sat at an angle to her so they could make eye contact, slowly breathing in unison. In through the nose. Pause. Blow out through the mouth. Pause.

She groaned in frustration. It wasn't helping. What else could she do? Walking. Maybe that would help this time.

She carefully got up, trying not to stumble as she started to pace. "Dammit," she moaned. "That hurts!"

Sam watched her for a moment. "Walking doesn't help?" he asked her softly.

She shook her head. "No, it's not."

The pain cut out, leaving behind a tiny echo of discomfort. She turned around and looked at Sam. "How long was that one?" she asked.

Sam picked up his phone. "Almost a minute and a half."

"Help me find my shoes," she told him. "I don't care what the doctor said. We're going to the hospital. I need my doula. I need my phone. And my mom."

Sam gaped at her, almost as if the words didn't make any sense to him.

"Now!" she barked, rubbing at her back. Sam sprang into action, grabbing her go-bag and his backpack before dropping them in a frantic search for his car keys.

She shook her head. Yes, she knew the contractions weren't less than four minutes apart, but they were lasting more than a minute and they had been consistent for the last few hours. It was time.

Rylee grabbed her shoes from next to the couch. She carefully walked through the kitchen. She opened the back door, then sat on the stairs and methodically worked her swollen feet into her shoes.

She stood up, bracing herself against the handrail, and took a tentative step down the steep staircase. Sam burst through the open door. He had his backpack, her go-bag, his jacket, and a portable cellphone charger in hand.

"Whoa," he exclaimed as he quickly slammed the door to the apartment. "Where are you going?"

"To the car," she answered, taking another step down and then another.

"Hang on," he ordered her. "Lemme help."

Rylee shook her head, but stopped anyhow. Sam walked around her and stopped on the step below her. He dropped the pile onto the steps before putting on his jacket. Then, he slung the backpack over his shoulders, stuffed the charger into his pocket, and popped the go-bag over his left shoulder.

He grabbed the handrail with his left hand, then offered his right hand to her. "We'll take it step-by-step, okay?" Rylee grabbed his hand and together they slowly made their way down the stairs.

They were almost to the bottom stair when another contraction hit. Rylee sat down, moaning as the electroshocks traveled from the top of her stomach, down and around until it felt like she was encased in a throbbing spasm of pain.

"Another contraction?" Sam needlessly asked.

She nodded, not quite trusting her voice.

Sam waited until she took a deep breath, then started breathing with her. *In through the nose*, she thought. *Wait. Blow out through the mouth. It's going to be fine.*

The pain gradually spiraled into a dull ache in her lower back. She looked up. "We need to get going," she told Sam.

Sam helped her stand and then opened the back door for her. They slowly walked through the backyard to the garage. Sam unlocked the door and fussed until he was able to get her settled before he handed over her purse and go-bag. He whipped open the rear door behind her to dump his backpack on the floor.

As they drove to the hospital, Rylee studied him for a moment. He glared out the windshield, impatiently tapping the steering wheel with his right hand at every red light.

She grabbed her phone out of her purse, moaning as she tried to unlock it with unsteady fingers. "Come on," she whispered.

"Maybe that can wait until we get there," Sam said as he glared at yet another red light that stood between them and the birthing center. "It's not too far now."

She found her mom's number and stabbed at her phone. She put the phone to her ear just as her mom answered.

"Hello?" her mom said, distractedly. "Oh, Rylee, is that you?" Her tone changed to loving and upbeat.

"Hi, Mom," she breathed. "We're on the way to the hospital. It's time."

"Oh, my God!" her mom squealed. Rylee pulled the phone away from her ear, wincing as she yelled, "It's time!"

There was more, but she could feel another one starting. "Mom," Rylee said, trying to interrupt as Allison kicked at Rylee's ribs in protest. "Mom, I've got another contraction coming on. I gotta go." She dropped the phone onto the floor, leaning forward to brace herself against the glove box.

As the contraction powered down, it seemed to settle into that space just below Allison. She wiggled her hips a bit. There was a small spasm and then the feeling of wetness between her legs.

"Sam, I'm feeling something squishy," she told him, trying to not sound panicked. *No! Please don't let my water break here,* she thought.

"Squishy?" he asked as he glared at the car in front of him.

She managed to nod, trying to hold very still. "Mmm-hmm," she replied. "Not gushy wet like my water broke, but something very, very strange."

He spared her a quick glance, then back at the road, snarling as the car in front of them turned the corner too slowly for his own comfort. They followed, and he pulled around that car to the main emergency entrance.

He threw his car into park, swung open his door, and started to race around the car to the hospital entrance, only to have to double back and turn off the engine. Then, he pelted for the doors.

Rylee carefully opened her car door, bracing herself against the door frame to try and stand up. Her left foot got tangled with her go-bag and she kicked at it, spilling the contents all over the ground. She tried to find a clear spot on the pavement, almost crying in frustration as she pushed away from the car.

Sam raced back with a wheelchair. He came to an abrupt halt just a few paces away, glancing at the ground and then at Rylee. He stepped around the items on the ground, carefully guiding her to the wheelchair just as the emergency room attendant walked over. Then, he picked up the go-bag and started shoving things into it.

The woman ignored Sam, leaning down to catch Rylee's attention. "I hear you're in labor?" she asked.

"Yes," Rylee hissed in response. "Four minutes apart. I need my doula!"

The woman smiled. "Great!" she told Rylee. "Let's get you checked out in triage." She waited only long enough for Sam to scramble out of her way before she turned the wheelchair around and headed into the hospital.

Rylee tightly held onto her purse as they moved. She looked back, realizing Sam was still at the car. "My phone!" Rylee called to him. He said something, but it was lost as the automatic doors closed behind her.

The attendant wheeled her over to the registration desk. "She's in active labor," the woman told the nurse. "Partner is right behind me."

The nurse smiled as she came from around the desk. "Let's get you checked in," she said, bringing a tablet out. "What's your name?"

Rylee started to reply, but another contraction gripped her. "Can we hurry?" she gasped.

The nurse nodded. "Why don't we get you into a triage room?" She quickly walked around to the back of the wheelchair and pushed Rylee down the hallway to a small exam room.

The nurse assisted her up from the wheelchair and then helped her remove her sweatpants and underwear. Then, she moved onto the exam bed with a large sheet to cover her lap.

Another nurse joined them, leaving the door partially open. Sam gently knocked, then sheepishly poked his head in to confirm that he was in the right place. He slid into the chair next to the nurse.

Another contraction hit and Rylee struggled to breathe through it. The nurse ignored it, though. "Did you call your doctor or doula before you made the decision to come in?" she asked, that patronizing tone grating against Rylee's last nerve. She shook her head, trying to not pant from the pain.

"Look, Sam has been keeping track of my contractions," she snarled. "They are just over four minutes apart. They last well over a whole minute and they have been hitting me for more than an hour."

The nurse nodded skeptically. "Have you tried walking or changing your position to get some relief?" she asked.

Rylee shook her head. "Doesn't help."

"What about the baby?" the nurse asked. "Is she moving less than she had earlier in the day?"

The pain ramped down, leaving a faint echo in her lower back. Rylee relaxed against the exam bed. "Allison has been moving around less than before, but she's still kicking me right up under my ribs. My back aches from the contractions," she added.

The nurse nodded, looking over her tablet as she updated Rylee's information.

"Why can't you just admit me?" Rylee complained, struggling to sit up so she could glare at the nurse. "The pain is getting worse!"

The nurse gave her a tight smile. "Let's get your vitals and take a look, shall we?" She looked at Sam. "You may not be far enough along for us to admit you tonight." He took the hint and fled to the hallway.

Blood pressure and oxygen levels came first. "One forty-five over ninety," she told Rylee, finally looking a bit concerned. "That's a bit elevated, but no cause for alarm. Why don't you lay back and we'll take a look at how far you're dilated?"

She helped Rylee lay back and then moved around to help guide Rylee's feet into the exam stirrups. She inserted a cold speculum and, after a few painful minutes, she popped up and looked at Rylee. "Almost four centimeters," she told her. "Let me make a call and we'll get you settled."

She picked up the phone and dialed a quick extension. "It's Tracy," she said. "Active labor in Triage Three." She grabbed the tablet, cradling the phone between her chin and shoulder as she made a few updates. "Eighth floor," she confirmed. "We're on our way."

She set the receiver back and turned to Rylee. "Let's get you dressed," she told her. "I'll grab another wheelchair and we'll head right up."

Another contraction hit, forcing Rylee to accept more assistance than she preferred. Before long, she found herself being wheeled to the elevator, closely followed by Sam, still weighed down by their stuff.

The elevator doors opened. Two nurses behind the front desk looked up, and one of them came around the front to greet her. "Ms. Williams, welcome," she said with a warm smile. "Sounds like you're in active labor. Why don't we get you settled?"

She moved around the wheelchair and began to push her down the hallway. "This way, please," she said to Sam. She could hear Sam struggling to hold on to the bags. He almost dropped one of them and he quietly cussed.

About halfway down the hall, they came to a room. The nurse paused, then backed the chair into the room. "Here we are," she said as she turned the chair around to face the room. "You're currently dilated to four centimeters, so we'll need to get you changed into your delivery gown." She pointed out the bathroom. "If you'd like to grab a shower first, towels are already laid out for you."

The nurse applied the brakes to the chair and then helped Rylee stand. She was just about to leave when Rylee stopped her. "What about the whirlpool tub? I would kill for a chance to just relax for a while."

The nurse frowned. "I'm sorry, we have just the one and it's currently in use." She held up her hand. "I can put your name up on the board, but I'm not sure when it will become available. One thing to keep in mind, though. You can't use the whirlpool if you have an epidural."

Rylee looked down for a moment, then around the room. "But I was hoping I could get that done quickly." She winced, rubbing both sides of her belly.

The nurse took the hint. "The anesthesiologist should be by to visit in the next hour," she told her. "If the whirlpool becomes available before then, I'll let you know."

She sighed, placing both hands as flat as she could against the ache in her lower back, rubbing. "Thanks."

"In the meantime, why don't you make yourself comfortable," the nurse told her with a reassuring smile. "The Wi-Fi password and TV remote are on the counter. I'll be back soon."

Rylee slowly walked over to Sam and took her go-bag off of his shoulder. She placed it on the bed and started sorting through the contents, trying to find the package with her delivery gowns. *So much for being organized,* she thought. They should have been in the right front pocket.

Ah-ha! She grabbed the packet and a pair of fuzzy socks from the bottom of the pile. "I just want a nice, hot shower," she told him. It had been such a long time since she hadn't struggled to step over the side of the bathtub to get clean.

Sam nodded, already pulling his phone out of his jacket pocket. She made her way to the bathroom and closed the door. Then, she slumped against the fake wood for a moment.

"Okay, Allison," she whispered. "We're here. It's safe. You can come home now."

She sat on the white stool next to the shower and worked to get her clothes off. Soon, they lay in a pile on the floor, and she sighed. It took a while, but she got up and moved to the shower, feeling the warm water calm the raw nerves in her back. Allison nudged her, but it was only a gentle reminder.

"I know, baby girl," she said, rubbing her hand across Allison. "Hopefully, they'll get us in the whirlpool tub and we can both relax for a while."

Chapter Eighteen

After her shower, Rylee dried herself, reveling in the oversized towel that wrapped all the way around her. She studied herself in the mirror. Her face was so puffy she hardly recognized herself. Her braid was damp, and she pulled it over one shoulder so she could try to squeeze as much water as possible into the towel.

She turned away, looking over her delivery gowns. She wasn't sure which to wear. She'd brought pink, of course, along with a purple gown with blue undertones. She ran a hand over both of the gowns, then slipped the pink one on. It felt more comfortable and had a bit more give to it. Then, she picked up the socks and sat down on the hard plastic seat. She looked from the socks in her hand to her swollen feet. There was no easy way to get them on. Maybe Sam could help.

She grabbed her phone before opening the door, the honeysuckle scent escaping into the room beyond. Sam looked up from the two-seat couch under the windows as she padded across the cold floor.

"I couldn't get these on," she told him as she eased herself onto the oversized bed. "Can you help me?"

Sam studied her for a moment. "Sure," he said, putting his phone down on the couch as he stood up. He made his way to the bed and gently took the socks from her. He frowned, then got down on one knee to gently put the first one on. As he pulled the first over her ankle, he glanced up to check on her. His expression was so endearing that she chuckled.

"Isn't this where you're supposed to pull a ring out of your pocket and ask me to marry you?" she asked as she wiggled the fingers of her left hand.

"Probably," Sam replied, shaking his head in amusement as he moved to put the second sock on.

Another contraction hit, squeezing Allison on all sides. "Oh, boy," she hissed. "Where the hell is that nurse?"

Sam patted her foot and stood up. "I'll go check," he told her.

She grabbed his hand before he could back away. "No," she whimpered. "Please stay. Diana should be here soon."

"Okay," he said, lightly squeezing her hand. When it was over, he helped her get comfortable on the bed, covering her legs with the blanket before moving the recliner closer to the bed. He sat down, looking a bit lost as they waited for the next contraction to hit her.

A woman with long, brown hair streaked with dark blond highlights pushed open the door, knocking gently as she let herself in. "Hi, I'm Dr. Drexler. Rylee, isn't it?" Rylee nodded. "I'm one of the anesthesiologists on staff." She beckoned at the two young women who stood in the doorway. "May we come in?"

"Sure," Rylee murmured, grabbing Sam's hand for comfort. He gave it a gentle squeeze, then leaned back, looking at the doctor with interest.

"I'd like to talk about your birth plan," Dr. Drexler said. "But, before I begin, can I confirm your full name and date of birth?" She looked down at the tablet in her hand.

"Rylee Williams," she told the doctor. "December 22nd, 2009."

The doctor nodded. "Thanks," she said. Then, she turned to Sam. "And you are?"

"Sam Maxwell," he replied. "I'm the dad."

Rylee blinked. *He said it,* she thought. He finally admitted he was Allison's father.

Dr. Drexler smiled. "Nice to meet you, Sam." She waved her hand at the women standing beside her. "This is Janet and Bethany. They are working on their clinical rotation." She looked closely at Rylee. "So, Rylee. I need to confirm this: your plan calls for an epidural, but you'd like to defer it for now because you'd like to try the whirlpool." She paused. "Did I get that right?"

"Yes," Rylee replied. "My sister gave birth here last spring, and she was able to spend some of her early labor in the whirlpool. Chloe said it helped so much that she almost didn't need the epidural."

"We can wait," she told Rylee with a sharp nod of her head. "But just be aware that an epidural may take as long as thirty minutes to take effect once it's administered."

"Oh, that long?" No one had mentioned that!

"Yes, and we won't be able to administer it once you're fully dilated and ready to deliver," the doctor told her. "So, I'm going to recommend that you don't wait too long to request one."

Rylee nodded, blowing out her breath as the pain started to ebb again.

The doctor smiled at her. "Why don't we get that IV started? If you'd like, I can give you something to take the edge off until you're ready for the epidural."

Finally! "That would be awesome," Rylee told her, just a bit relieved. "Thank you so much."

Dr. Drexler beckoned for the student doctors to join her. "Let's get that IV set up, shall we?" One of them rolled a small metal table over while the other brought over the IV stand and hung a bag of saline from one of the hooks. "After this, one of the doctors will need to check to see how far dilated you are," the doctor added.

Rylee looked past the doctor, but Sam had already walked over to the window. He looked outside for a moment, then sat down with his laptop.

"I need you to know that I'm terrified of needles," Rylee admitted, watching one of the students casually pull a needle out of a drawer and lay it on the metal table.

The woman, Janet perhaps, nodded. "We'll use the smallest needle possible," she told Rylee. She took Rylee's hand in both of hers, gently rubbing a thumb against the veins on the back of her hand. Then, she grabbed an alcohol wipe from the tray, ripped it open, and firmly swabbed at her skin before setting it aside.

She grabbed the needle, but Rylee stopped her. "Wait, are you sure you're using the smallest needle? That looks huge!" she protested.

The other woman leaned over from the left side of the bed. "It's going to be okay, Rylee," she told her. "I promise."

Rylee looked from one to the other, feeling another contraction starting to build. "Wait!" she moaned. "I can't . . . !"

"I've got you," the woman said, holding Rylee's other hand. At that moment, Janet plunged the needle in, and Rylee jumped.

"Ow!" she yelled, trying to pull her hand away.

"You're doing fine, Rylee," Janet told her unapologetically. She quickly taped down the flexible tubing along Rylee's arm as the other woman hung a smaller bag on the stand. The tube was connected to the IV, and the drug started dripping.

After the pain had ebbed, Rylee glared at Janet. "I was having a contraction," she hissed. "Why didn't you wait?"

"The sooner we get you hooked up, the quicker we can help turn down that pain," Janet told her.

"There you are," Dr. Drexler said, turning to study the IV for a moment. She looked over at Janet with a frown, then back to Rylee. "It should take effect in a few minutes."

"Thank you, Doctor," Rylee replied. She wiped her face with her left hand, then laid back against the pillow to wait for the medicine to take effect.

There was a slight tap at the door and then Diana peeked in. "Diana!" Rylee squealed. Diana quickly moved into the room and gave Rylee the squeezy hug she so desperately needed.

"I'm sorry I'm late, dear one," Diana finally said, moving to sit on the edge of Rylee's bed. "Lactation visits can be just a bit time-consuming, especially when it's twins!"

Rylee smiled. "Oh! Are the babies alright?"

"Perfect little angels," Diana told her reassuringly. "Just a bit challenging to breastfeed in tandem." She studied Rylee's face for a moment. "I was told that you were about four centimeters dilated at the time of admission. How's the pain?"

She frowned, struggling to not sound so bitchy. "Real intense," she told Diana. "I can't have the epidural until after I try the hot tub and I can't try the hot tub because it's in use right now!"

"Did they give you something for the pain?" Diana asked.

"Just now," she told her.

Diana smiled. "Well, I'm sure it will take effect soon," Diana told her.

There was a knock, then the door opened. A small group of nurses stood in the doorway. Diana nodded, then stood up. "Well, why don't I get out of the way, Rylee," she said. "We'll know more once they've verified how dilated you currently are." She looked over to Sam. "Let's step out into the hallway."

Sam looked up, frowning. Diana waved a hand at him and then walked out of the room. He glanced at Rylee and then followed. The door closed behind him.

"Hi," the lead nurse said. "My name is Kristal, and this is May, Debra, and Candace. How are you feeling?" One of them pulled the privacy curtain closed and then moved back to the group.

"Better, I guess," Rylee told her.

"I'm here to get a baseline on how things are progressing," Kristal told her. "Is that okay?"

Rylee nodded, relaxing her head against the pillow. She ignored the group as they pulled out the obligatory stirrups, guided her feet into place, and adjusted her blanket.

While they were working, Kristal pulled the rolling stool out of the corner of the room and pulled on some dark blue gloves. "I'm going to touch your inner leg, and then insert the speculum," she told Rylee. "I know it's uncomfortable, but I'll be quick, I promise."

Rylee squirmed, hating the feel of that metal prong as it was inserted. *How many times did they have to do that?* she wondered.

Just as quickly as it was inserted, Kristal removed it. "There we go," she said with a smile. "Holding steady at just over four centimeters. Plenty of time before you're ready to give birth. We'll let Doctor Zastrow know."

Rylee lay there for a moment, thinking. Now that she was here, she felt so much more relaxed. Diana was here. Sam was here. It was going to be okay.

The door slowly opened and Diana and Sam came back in. She sat up a bit and sighed. "Whatever they gave me is starting to work," she told them. "I need to walk."

Diana nodded approvingly. "Sounds good," she said. "We'll need to stay on the delivery floor, though."

Rylee frowned. "My mom expects me to check in, Diana."

Diana smiled, slowly shaking her head. "You can call or text them, but they aren't allowed to visit," she reminded her. "The Birthing Center has a firm rule. You're only allowed to have your partner up here. If they're not available, only one other family member can join you. And you're not allowed to leave delivery."

"So, it's just us for now?" Rylee asked.

Diana nodded. "Once you're moved to the post-delivery floor, close family members will be able to visit. Just not all at once!"

Part of her was relieved. No need to listen helplessly as her mom argued with the doctor about how her labor was progressing or pushing away the ice chips she didn't want.

She groaned, stretching her back as much as she was able to. "Oooh . . . my back is killing me. I need to walk." She reached out for help and Diana moved around the bed to help her get up.

Rylee grabbed the IV stand and took a few tentative steps toward the door just as another contraction hit. She tried stretching her back a bit to ease the pain.

Diana frowned in concern, then looked at Sam. "Sam, can you walk with Rylee?" she asked him. "I'm going to check to see when they expect the whirlpool tub to become available."

"That would be awesome," Rylee said, trying to breathe during the contraction. "Thank you so much, Diana!"

Sam switched places with Diana and tentatively held Rylee's hand as they moved to the door. It felt a bit clammy, so she dropped his hand when they got out into the hallway. She put her right hand up against the hallway wall and pushed the IV pole with the other hand as she slowly walked.

Sam stood there for a moment, then followed a step behind her, almost as if he was afraid she was going to fall. It was mildly annoying, but she was glad to have him there.

"I hope Diana can get me time in the whirlpool," she told him as they moved around another woman who was standing with her back against the wall, panting through a painful contraction. "Once I have the epidural, I know I won't be able to move around anymore." She thought about it for a minute. "Normally, I'd text my mom, but I don't want to. As much as I love her, I kinda feel like this needs to be just us, you know?"

"Why just us?" Sam asked, sounding curious.

She bit her lip, trying to decide how to talk about what happened with her family. "I know she's still struggling to accept what happened," she confided. "But like it or not, my parents are going to have to accept that their baby girl is growing up. And that means accepting you're always going to be a part of my life. Of *our* lives."

Sam snorted. "It's a nice thought," he told her. "But they're never going to accept me, Rylee. You know what happened at church."

"Yeah, Mom's BFF got it in her head that I was too innocent to enjoy sex," she replied. "Either way, there's going to be a baptism in our future." Another contraction hit at that moment and she stopped, eyes closed as she tried to slowly breathe through the pain.

It didn't help, so she put her hands up against the wall, leaning forward as if she were going to do a modified push-up. Sam came to stand next to her, one hand tentatively rubbing at her lower back as it spasmed in pain.

She thought about heading back to the room, but Diana joined them. "Rylee, I have great news," she said. "They're almost done cleaning the tub out. By the time we get there, it should be ready for you."

She took a deep breath, opening her eyes as she slowly pushed away from the wall. "That's the best news I've had all day!" she told them.

Diana gently took the lead, her hand just above Rylee's as they slowly pushed the IV stand down the hallway. "At the end of this hallway, we'll take a right," Diana told her. "The hot tub is in the room at the far end."

It didn't take long, but Rylee still breathed a sigh of relief when they made it to the room. An oversized whirlpool tub sat in the corner, flanked by two oversized wooden spa chairs on one side and an automated bath lift on the other. Shaded windows surrounded the tub.

Diana walked Rylee toward the side with the bath lift. "Why don't you have a seat, Rylee," Diana directed her. "I'll get that tub filled."

Rylee sat down. Diana moved around to the other side and started running the water. She made a few minor adjustments until she was satisfied with the temperature. Before long, the tub was full.

Sam sat down in one of the spa chairs, then uncomfortably turned his back while Diana helped her remove her birthing gown. Then, she used the automated bath lift to help Rylee settle into the warm water. It was as if the water melted into the muscles cramping in her lower back, and she moaned in relief.

"Chloe was right," she told Diana. "This feels *so good* against my skin."

Sam slid his phone out of his back pocket. "My dad's here," he told them. "I should go out to see him."

Rylee nodded. She laid her head back, submerging as much of herself as she could, except for her right hand. With any luck, the heat would make the contractions stop being so damn painful. The medicine the doctor had given her only had a minor impact on the pain.

She thought about warning him about her parents, but decided against it. He had to know they were already in the family waiting room, eager to get any updates they could. He was a big boy, right? He was going to have to learn how to deal with her parents sometime.

Rylee wiggled around in the water, another wave of contractions tightening around Allison. "Wasn't this hot tub supposed to help reduce the pain?" she moaned.

"It is," Diana told her, moving from the seat next to the tub to the side where Rylee lay. "What are you feeling?"

Rylee slowly took a deep breath. "It's a stabby pain underneath my skin," Rylee said. "It's like the heat only relaxes the top layers, and the pain is really, really deep."

The contraction crept further down with a sudden spike in pain. "Oh!" Rylee exclaimed. Something popped deep within her, followed by a sudden gush of fluid. The water around her inner thighs felt hot for just a moment before the temperature stabilized.

She turned to Diana in amazement. "I-I think my water just broke."

Diana smiled. "It's time to get out then," she told Rylee. "I don't want you to risk an infection."

"But, Diana—"

"It may be time to get your epidural started," Diana reminded her.

Rylee nodded and sat up. Diana grabbed a few towels out of the cabinet for Rylee to wrap up in. Then, she moved the automated lift into position to help Rylee out of the tub. As soon as she was out and reasonably dry, Diana helped her dress.

"Let's get you back to the room," Diana told her after she got Rylee's socks back on. "I'll let the nursing team know so they can have a look before they drain the tub. It looks clear to me, but they'll need to check, just in case."

"Okay," Rylee said. She was disappointed she couldn't spend more time in the tub, but the pain was getting worse. She needed to lie down.

Diana let the nurse's desk know that Rylee's water had broken, so by the time they got back to Rylee's room, a small group of doctors were waiting for her. They got her into bed and double-checked her cervix before Sam made it back.

He took another look at the room number before coming in. "What happened?" he asked, concerned, as he moved around to the other side of the bed to join Diana.

"The whirlpool didn't help," Diana told him. She dropped Rylee's hand and gestured for him to come closer. "Rylee has asked for the epidural. Switch places with me."

He moved closer to the bed, looking around in confusion. Rylee reached out blindly for Sam's hand and he gently squeezed back.

One of the nurses brought a pair of wide elastic straps attached to electrical pads. "What are those?" Sam snarled. Rylee looked at them in confusion.

"This?" the nurse asked as she looked down at the straps. "We're just hooking up the fetal heart monitor, that's all." She cocked her head at Sam and he pulled his hand away, rubbing his palms against his jeans.

Rylee looked up at him, then back to the straps. Why did that upset him?

Another nurse placed a blanket over her thighs, then flipped her gown up to expose Allison. She smiled down at Rylee, then moved to her feet and adjusted the blanket to cover her toes.

"I'm Madison," she told Diana as she handed the straps to her. "I'll help pull Rylee up if you can get this underneath her," she said. Then, she held out both of her hands to Rylee and pulled her forward while Diana placed the straps on the bed, with both ends hanging over either side.

Rylee laid back down. She wiggled a bit, trying to feel if another contraction was starting. So far, so good.

"This is called a transducer. We use it to listen to the baby's heartbeat," the nurse explained. "That way, we can detect any fetal distress." She grabbed a small bottle of clear gel and squirted it onto Rylee's belly. Then, she placed a large, light blue disc onto the gel. The disc was attached to a small monitor.

The nurse wiggled it around until she found the right spot, then pointed at the screen. "Ah, 120," she told them before attaching the transducer to keep it in place.

"That's a good number," Diana said, distracted, as she stared at the monitor. "Normal range is 110 to 160."

Next, the nurse held up a dark gray disc. "We use this one to measure your contractions, Rylee. It will give us a much better picture of how productive your labor is." She quickly attached the gray disc to the lower strap.

Rylee wiggled around as she tried to get comfortable. "Are the straps too tight?" the nurse asked her. "I can adjust them."

Rylee closed her eyes for a moment. "No," she told her. "I think we're good."

"Alright," the nurse responded, "then, I'll leave you to it." She turned away.

"Wait," Rylee said, concerned. "Where's the anesthesiologist? I asked for an epidural."

The nurse almost dismissed her concern with a quick shrug of one shoulder. "We put in a request, Rylee. They should be along shortly," she said and quickly left the room.

Rylee looked over to Diana, who frowned with concern before she sighed. "Could you turn on the TV, Sam?" she said. "We have some time before Allison is ready to arrive."

Sam looked at Rylee, then shrugged. He walked over to the TV and grabbed the remote control. He turned it on and then handed the remote over to Rylee before he went to sit down on the couch.

Rylee thumbed through the menu, trying to find something interesting to watch. There were certainly enough channels. Problem was, she couldn't find anything to take her mind off of the contractions.

She looked over at Diana, who nodded before she brought over her oversized bag. "I thought you might enjoy something light, like a rom-com," she told Rylee as she laid a handful of movies on the bed. "You choose."

Rylee picked up the closest disc, giggling. "Some of these are older than I am!"

Diana took the disc out of her hand and held it up. "*Groundhog Day*, it is!" she proclaimed.

Sam closed his laptop and stood. He looked restless. "I'm hungry," he said. "I'm going to take a walk."

Rylee rolled her eyes. Hungry? Was that the best he could do?

But Diana smiled. "That's fine, Sam," she reassured him. "I'll text you if something changes."

They were about halfway through the movie when Dr. Drexler returned, three trainees closely behind. "Sorry about that," she told Rylee as she entered the room. "We had a bit of a backlog this evening."

One of the trainees wheeled in a cart. It included an incredibly long needle, a long but slender tube, and other random things that made Rylee cringe.

A sudden contraction grabbed hold, and Allison kicked in response. She reached for Diana's hand in panic, desperately needing reassurance. *Maybe I should have called Mom*, she thought.

"It's going to be okay," Diana told her. She moved closer until she blocked Rylee's view of the cart. "Just look at me and we'll talk you through this."

Rylee nodded, clenching her eyes shut.

"The first thing they're going to do is roll you onto your side, Rylee," Diana told her. "They'll cover your back with something called a sterile drape, which is just a fancy name for a surgical-style paper cloth to help minimize the risk of infection. Then, they'll clean your lower back with an alcohol wipe. Okay, so far?"

"Uh-huh," she managed to respond.

"Then, Dr. Drexler will give you the tiniest shot of a local anesthetic to numb the area before they insert the catheter," Diana told her. "Did I get that right, Doctor?"

Rylee opened her eyes, wildly looking around for the doctor. Dr. Drexler came to stand next to Diana. She gave Rylee a reassuring smile. "Exactly right," she said. "Are you ready to get started, Rylee?"

She took a deep breath and nodded. Diana dropped her hand and stepped back. "I'll be right outside the door," she told her reassuringly. Rylee followed her with her eyes as she walked across the room, then pulled the privacy curtain to block the view from the hallway.

A nurse helped Rylee roll onto her side, then carefully placed a pillow between her knees to help her stay in position. A nurse pulled her gown up above her shoulders, laid the blue surgical drape across her, and swabbed her back. The sudden cold made her shiver.

Another nurse came over and grasped Rylee's hand. "You're doing great," she told her. Rylee nodded, feeling the contraction starting to ebb.

Dr. Drexler moved behind her. "I'm going to numb the area and then we'll get started," she said in a warm, reassuring voice.

"Okay," Rylee responded, closing her eyes and squeezing the nurse's hand. The woman tightened her grip in response.

"Good," the doctor told her. "Now, you may feel a pinch for a few seconds, and then a feeling of pressure when we start the medication."

There was a sudden stab in her lower back. Rylee gasped in pain, but the pain almost immediately faded as the entire area went numb.

"How are you doing?" she asked Rylee.

"I'm scared," Rylee said, her voice just above a whisper.

"I know," Dr. Drexler said in a soothing voice. "Here we go."

A sharp stinging sensation pierced the numbness. "Oww . . . !" Rylee shrieked. "That hurt!" She clenched her hand around the nurse's hand, trying desperately to hold still. There was a strange almost-feeling while the doctor did something to the needle.

"How's it feel now?" the doctor asked.

"Better."

"We're ready to start the epidural, Rylee," the doctor told her. "You should feel a bit of pressure . . . now."

A cool sensation slowly flowed down her back and around her sides, almost as if her muscles were relaxing in spite of her. "Oh," Rylee exclaimed. "That feels so strange!" The doctor taped the tubing down her back, but Rylee felt very little of it.

"Let's go ahead and get you on your back, Rylee," Dr. Drexler told her. Two nurses helped her roll over. Before long, she was in a comfortable position with the baby monitors back in place.

"You should feel some relief in about twenty minutes, although it may take a bit longer to feel the full effect." The doctor raised her voice and said, "You can come back in now."

Rylee looked over to the door. After a moment, Diana and Sam appeared behind the gaggle of nurses and student doctors clustered around the bed. Diana grabbed Sam's arm and gently pulled him forward. He looked concerned.

She smiled. "It's weird," Rylee said. "My legs are starting to feel all warm and watery like they're falling asleep." She thought about it for a moment, then laughed. "No, more like they're still in the whirlpool!"

"The epidural isn't supposed to completely numb you," Diana reminded her. "It just pushes the pain aside so you can work with Allison when she's ready to come out." She looked over at the TV. The main menu had come up when the movie ended. "Now, what movie do you want to watch?"

Rylee leaned back against the pillow. She felt emotionally spent now that the needle was in. "I don't care, Diana. Dealer's choice."

Diana walked over to the counter and picked a movie at random. "*Ghost*, it is, then!"

Chapter Nineteen

Rylee brought her knees up, ankles wide as she rocked back on her tailbone. There was an intense feeling of pressure against her pelvic bones, almost as if they were being split apart like a wishbone. Her lower back whimpered in sympathy with every single contraction.

She looked out the window. She didn't know what time it was. Over the last few hours, she'd watched the monitors as her contractions had gradually gotten so powerful the muscles below her skin felt as hard as steel. Halfway through the third movie, she'd had Diana turn it off because she couldn't stand the noise anymore.

A nurse came into the room and turned on some of the lights. "How are you feeling, Rylee?" she asked.

"I don't know," Rylee muttered, looking up in confusion. "There's this pressure down there like my pelvis is being stretched apart. It doesn't exactly hurt. I need . . . I don't know what I need!"

"Her contractions are about a minute apart," Diana told the nurse.

"Why don't we check how you're progressing?" she asked in a low voice. She smiled, looking down at Sam, who was dozing in the recliner. "You may be in transition."

She quickly pulled on a glove and added a dollop of gel to her fingertips. Then, she pulled the blanket up over Rylee's knees and carefully inserted two fingers inside of her. It was the strangest feeling as the nurse quickly probed her cervix.

The nurse pulled her hand out and replaced the blanket. "You're fully dilated," she told Rylee. She removed the glove, carefully turning it inside out before throwing it into a nearby medical trash can. "Let me page Doctor Zastrow."

Transition? Rylee gulped, looking from Diana to Sam and back again. Diana stood, her hand moving to massage Rylee's neck.

"Sam!" Rylee whispered. Sam stirred but didn't open his eyes. She reached out, squeezing his arm with her left hand. "Wake up!"

He groaned, struggling to open his eyes.

"She's coming, Sam!" she told him, her voice trembling with anxiety.

He opened his eyes wide, staring at her in confusion before he briefly looked over at Diana.

"Sorry," he said as he struggled to sit up. "Didn't mean to fall asleep."

Rylee laid her head against the pillow. She closed her eyes, focusing on that strange feeling between her legs as Sam and Diana's banter flowed past her. It felt like she was sitting on a strong magnet that was slowly pulling Allison out.

Her heartbeat felt heavier in her chest. "Oh, I think I'm having another one," Rylee whispered. She flipped up her delivery gown and pulled Sam's hand onto her belly. Allison was lower now and the muscles around her flexed as if protecting her from an unknown danger.

"You're doing very well, Rylee," Diana told her. "So is Allison." She pointed at the fetal heart monitor.

Sam stared at the screen. "Is Allison in distress?" he asked, sliding his hand out of hers as he stood. "Where's the doctor?"

Diana smiled at him. "Allison's heart rate is absolutely normal, Sam," she told him reassuringly. "And the doctor is making his rounds. He should be back to check on us very soon."

Rylee pushed her feet wider, that feeling of pressure increasing. "Oh, I think I feel another one!"

Sam sat down and reached for her hand. "It's going to be okay, Rylee," he told her. "You've got this. Just one contraction at a time."

"Is it time to push yet?" Rylee asked with a groan. The pressure was building.

Diana gently pulled Rylee's legs straight and began to massage them with long strokes of her hands. "Not yet, dear one," she told Rylee. "It's not quite time for you to push."

Rylee shook her head in frustration. "But it feels like it's time," she told Diana. "Really, it does!"

"I know, sweetie," Diana told her. "But we're almost there." She moved closer and rearranged the pillow under Rylee's head. She pulled Rylee's delivery gown back into place and pulled up the light blanket.

Rylee shook her head from side to side in frustration, moaning as she planted her feet solidly on the bed.

"It won't be long," Diana told her. "Breathe with us." She sucked in her breath in two short bursts, then panted it out in two short but hard exhales.

Rylee stared at her for a moment. She wanted to push, not breathe!

"You can do it, Rylee!" Diana told her. Then, she nodded at Sam, and he followed her lead. Of course, he did.

Fine, she thought, *I'll breathe, but I still need to push. It's time!*

She gripped Sam's right hand and slowly rubbed at her belly with her other hand in a slow, circular motion. She sucked in her breath and blew it out again. The breathing seemed to ease the feeling of pressure, but not enough to make a difference. She wiggled her toes, fighting the urge to bear down.

The door opened and Dr. Zastrow pushed past the privacy curtain. At least, that's who she thought he was. Hard to tell with the surgical mask. Several nurses closely followed behind him. Sam tried to pull away, but Rylee held firmly onto his hand.

"Hi, Rylee," the doctor said warmly. "It sounds like we're just about ready for you to deliver."

She pushed a stray strand of hair out of her eyes with a nod. "Are we done yet?" she asked plaintively.

"Let's take a closer look," he told her as he gestured for the nurses to help. Sam got up and pulled the recliner out of the way as the nurses moved in. She heard a metallic click as one of them pulled the boot-like stirrups into position and a pair of nurses helped her scoot farther down on the exam bed. Someone guided her feet into the padded boots as the bed was moved into a reclined seated position. The pillow and blanket were set aside.

The nurses retreated, and Sam made his way to her side. She grabbed his hand, feeling the cool skin against hers.

Dr. Zastrow pulled the rolling stool into position between Rylee's legs and sat with a flourish. He studied the space between her legs intently for a moment, then looked up.

"Rylee, you're doing great," he told her. "I can see the baby's head. It's time to push."

Push? Rylee blinked at him, angry but confused. "What?" she asked. She turned to Diana. "I wanted to push before, and you told me not to!" she yelped.

"Rylee, honey, it's okay," Diana told her in a quiet voice. "It's time now."

Rylee flopped back against the bed. "I'm so tired, Diana," she complained. "I can't anymore. If he can see the baby, can't they just pull her out?"

"No, sweetie," Diana replied in a firm voice. "You need to push now. Allison is exactly where she needs to be. And you'll hold her in your arms very soon."

Diana took Rylee's right hand in hers. "Now, with your next contraction, we're going to breathe like we practiced, right, Sam?"

Rylee looked up at Sam. He nodded, squeezing her left hand. "You've got this, Rylee," he told her.

"Here's another one," Diana announced, her eyes on the monitor. "Breathe in, Rylee. Now push, Rylee! Push!"

Rylee bore down, grunting as she struggled to push. After a long time, she laid back. "I can't, Diana!" she said, panting as she tried to catch her breath.

Sam squeezed her hand, trying to get her attention. "Yes, you can, Rylee," he told her. "Push!"

"It's too hard," she whimpered, shaking her head in frustration. *I can't,* she thought. *I just can't!*

Sam moved closer until his face was her whole world. "Come on, Rylee!" he told her encouragingly. "It's time for the big push, remember? Breathe in and tighten those abdominal muscles, just like we practiced in class! You can do this."

Rylee sagged against the mattress, closing her eyes. "The big push," she repeated. Fine. She moaned, almost snarling as she pushed down.

"Good job, Rylee," Diana said. "The contraction is subsiding. I need you to breathe with us, Rylee. Breathe . . . "

Sam leaned down, slowly breathing in as he stared at her. He nodded, encouraging her to take a deep breath with him. Then, he slowly counted to four before forcing the breath out of his mouth.

After a few more breaths, Diana gently squeezed her hand to get her attention. "I need you to open your jaw for me, just a bit," Diana told her. "Let's see if we can get you to relax into this next one."

"Relax?" Rylee found herself giggling. "It feels like I've got a beach ball down there, and it's stuck!"

"I know," she replied, trying to reassure her. "Okay, we have another one starting. Deep breath. Now, push for me! Push for Allison!"

Rylee leaned forward, pushing as hard as she could. She growled deep in her throat and this time she refused to lie back until it was over.

The doctor was intently staring at the baby. She couldn't tell how the baby was doing, so she looked at Diana.

Diana gave her a soft smile. "Now, with the next one, I need you to remember to focus on relaxing your pelvic floor while you push," Diana told her. "We're going to take deep relaxing breaths."

Rylee moaned, shaking her head slowly from side to side as she tried to blink the sweat out of her eyes.

"Another one is starting," Diana told them. "Take a deep breath. Let it out. Now take a breath and push into the pressure. That's right!"

Rylee clung to their hands as she tried to pull herself into a sitting position. Sam's hand came up between her shoulder blades, his left hand firmly squeezing her hand.

"Almost there, Rylee. The baby is crowning," Dr. Zastrow told her. "I'm going to need you to relax and stop pushing for a moment."

"What?" she moaned, panting as she tried to catch her breath. "Why?!"

"We're going to let your perineum stretch a bit," he gently told her. "Otherwise, I'll need to do a quick episiotomy to reduce the chance of a tear."

She let exhaustion pull her back against the mattress. "First, you tell me to not push. Then, I have to push. Now, you tell me to stop!" she complained. "I need to push! I need this to be over with!"

Diana slowly moved forward until her forehead was touching the side of Rylee's head. "I know, dear one," she said. "Let's breathe through this. Nice and slow." She stood; eyes half-closed as she breathed in deeply.

Rylee found herself whimpering. *Don't leave me, Diana,* she thought.

Sam gently squeezed her hand, bringing her attention back to him. "That's right, Rylee," he told her. He took a light breath, then blew it out. "Come on, Rylee," he said, gesturing with his other hand. "Breathe with me."

She found herself relaxing as she breathed with Sam. It was as if that feeling of unending pressure had paused under the weight of their combined breathing.

"Rylee," the doctor told her, his gloved fingers gently poking at her cervix. "Get ready to push again on the next contraction. We're just about there."

Sam smiled at her as he slid his right hand under her shoulder. "It's going to be okay, Rylee," he told her. "Just a few more minutes."

Rylee awkwardly squeezed his left hand in hers, pulling their hands against her cheek for just a moment.

"Alright, Rylee," Diana said. "Take a deep breath. Now, let it out. Take another and push!"

Rylee found the strength to pull herself up on their hands, loudly grunting as she gave it everything she had left. She felt Allison slide out, leaving behind a sudden emptiness in her wake.

There was a shriek of newborn outrage. "Oh, my God," Rylee breathed as she lay back. "It's over, right?"

Diana squeezed Rylee's right hand. "For the most part, yes," she gently told her. "Just a few more pushes to deliver the placenta."

She heard the nurses move Allison to the electronic bassinet in the corner. "Initial Apgar looks good, Doctor," the nurse reported. She couldn't see much from her position, but it sounded like Allison was still fussing as they gently wiped her down and wrapped her in a blanket.

Suddenly, the machine pinged, and Sam chuckled. "Sounds like she's done, Rylee," he told her.

Rylee smiled, then pushed. She felt something else come out. Placenta? "So am I," she said, laying her head back against the bed.

"Apgar is a solid ten," the nurse told the room. She brought Allison over. "Time for some skin-on-skin cuddling, Rylee," she said.

Diana pulled the front of the delivery gown. The cool air caressing her skin was quickly replaced by the warm feeling of Allison settling against her swollen breasts. "Oh," Rylee breathed.

Diana covered them both up with a soft blanket. Allison snuggled in, one clenched fist near her mouth. Sam stepped back, almost as if he wasn't sure if he should be a part of this moment.

"Sam?" Rylee asked. "My mom's going to want some pictures. Can you . . . please?"

Sam nodded. He grabbed his phone off of the couch and snapped a few close-up pictures.

"I can send these to our parents," he told her with a tentative smile. "Are you okay if I duck out to give them the good news?"

Rylee nodded. "Have fun," she said with a tired yawn. She closed her eyes, feeling Allison's heart beating against hers.

"Welcome home, baby girl," she whispered.

Rylee felt the blanket move. "Rylee, it's time to get Allison dressed," a soft voice whispered to her.

"No," she whimpered. "She's sleeping. Leave us alone."

"I'm sorry, dear one," the voice said. "We need to get Allison into a diaper. You don't want her to poop all over you, do you?" There was a light chuckle, then a moment of cool air as Allison was scooped up from her bare chest.

Irritated high-pitched cries ruptured the quiet as Allison protested. A soft voice whispered reassurances as they carried her away.

"Allison?" Rylee said, struggling to open her eyes. "Where are you taking her?" Her body ached down to her core. Tired, as if labor had wrung the last ounce of energy that she had to give, leaving behind a limp rag.

"It's okay, Rylee." Diana slowly came into focus. "The nurse is getting Allison dressed. Then, both of you need to rest. You worked hard today."

Somewhere nearby, the angry cries gave way to a quieter whimper of dissent. "It's okay, Allison," the nurse told her. "I know, but you're going to be so much more comfortable once we get you into this onesie, I promise!"

Rylee heard the door open, and the soft tread of sneakers as Sam returned. He stopped near the heated caddy, watching as the nurse finished dressing Allison. She wrapped her up in a blanket with a pink stripe along one edge.

She handed Sam the baby and stepped back with a smile. He turned to Rylee, looking a bit confused as Allison settled into his arms and the whimpers gave way to a soft cooing sound. He took a few tentative steps toward Rylee and smiled.

Rylee could barely keep her eyes open. She smiled, feeling herself drift into that place where she wasn't quite awake, but not yet asleep.

"Allison," she heard Sam say in a soft voice. "Allison Isabelle Williams Maxwell." She heard him move across the room to the window.

Part of her wanted to force her eyes open. *Isabelle?*

Allison Isabelle Williams Maxwell. She let the name slowly roll through her thoughts. Sam was finally making a connection with Allison. It was going to be okay. She let go and allowed exhaustion to pull her into the sleep she so desperately needed.

It was early evening before everyone had finally taken the hint and left for the night. Just watching Wendy and Ashley as they tried to be nice to each other in that almost cliche 'Church Lady' kind of way was exhausting. Add in all-important grandfather bonding-while-passing-the-baby-to-the-next-relative-in-line, and an overtired Patrick throwing an epic temper tantrum because he wasn't allowed to hold the baby, and it made for a very long afternoon.

Rylee looked over at Sam. He was slouched in the recliner and looked like he was going to pass out at any moment.

"Sam," she whispered at him.

He looked up, widening his eyes as he tried to wake up. "Hmm?"

"Go home," she told him. "Allison's fine. I'm fine and I won't be able to sleep until you leave."

Sam blinked at her. "But what if she wakes up?" he asked. "I should be here, right?"

Rylee smiled. "If I need help, I'll call a nurse," she told him.

"Are you sure?" he asked again. He was beginning to sound desperate.

"Yes," Rylee told him. "In fact, why don't you bring Allison over here? That way, I don't have to get out of bed if she wakes up."

Sam sighed, pushing himself off of the recliner. He padded over to the bassinet and carefully picked up the baby. Allison stirred, then snuggled deeper into his arms as he slowly walked across the room and gave her to Rylee.

"Okay?" he asked.

"We're fine," she told him. "Go home."

Sam bent down and lightly kissed the knit cap that covered Allison's head. "See you in the morning," he said. Then, he grabbed his backpack and slowly made his way out of the room.

Rylee adjusted the bed slightly, so she was sitting up. The occasional afterbirth contraction added to the general ache in her core. It made her wonder how long it would take before she felt normal again. What would normal even feel like?

She looked down at Allison. Both of her hands were cupped around her mouth, her tiny tongue moving like she was nursing. It was both adorable and scary as hell.

Rylee closed her eyes, leaning her head back against the pillow. Suddenly, everything she thought she knew about caring for a newborn was gone, replaced by an overwhelming urge to call Sam back to the room. How the hell was she going to take care of Allison when they went home tomorrow?

There was a quiet knock on her door. "Knock, knock . . . " a voice called from the hallway.

Rylee quickly wiped her eyes, sniffling as she tried to swallow the tears that threatened to spill out. "Yes?" she called.

Nana poked her head in, smiling as she saw them. "There's my little namesake," she said.

"Hey, Nana," Rylee said. "You didn't have to come back tonight."

Nana smiled, shaking her head as she came to stand near the bed. "I'm exactly where I need to be right now," she replied. "May I hold her?"

Rylee nodded, carefully handing Allison to her grandmother. She took a deep breath, trying to relax.

"Firstborns are the most difficult," Nana said as she sat down in the recliner. "Boy, girl, it doesn't matter. Everything is a first, both the good and the bad. The first time she latches on. Her first bath. That first time she won't stop crying because she's overtired." She looked over at Rylee. "You're going to doubt everything you think you know and you're not going to feel confident enough to ask for help."

"What—"

"You're a Williams, my dear," Nana told her. "We're stubborn to the core. Especially little girls named 'Allison'."

Rylee looked down at the baby and nodded.

"Since I'm here, there's something we need to talk about," Nana said. "I didn't bring this up earlier because I didn't want anyone butting in."

Rylee's heart leaped into her throat. *Oh, God,* she thought. *Please don't talk about the family trust!*

Nana got up, a stern look on her face. "I don't agree with your grandfather's decision to remove you from the family trust," she told Rylee as she started to slowly walk across the room, a slight bounce to her gait. "If that law firm we have on retainer can't figure out how to safeguard our family's money, then they're not worth the money we're paying. No, what's bothering your grandfather is good old-fashioned misogyny."

"Nana!" Rylee gasped.

"Well, what else would you call it?" Nana asked, turning around to walk toward the door. "The only advice he ever gave your uncles when they were young was 'to use protection', but when it came to his daughter and granddaughters? Well, he expected them to wait until marriage!" She snorted. "We started dating in 1967 and I can tell you that was the last thing on his mind!"

Rylee covered her eyes with one hand. Why was Nana telling her this?

"My point is that he shouldn't be holding you to a standard he couldn't keep himself," Nana told her. "My best guess is that he's also in a tizzy about Sam, too. He doesn't come from money. Take away his phone and he doesn't seem to know a thing about socializing. He's not even going to an Ivy League school."

Rylee dropped her hand and glared across the room. "Wellesley isn't an Ivy League school, either," she reminded Nana.

Nana stopped pacing and smiled at Rylee. "No, it's not. And that's okay."

Rylee groaned. "I don't understand, Nana!"

"I know," Nana replied, slowly walking back to Rylee. "Men can be difficult to figure out, even when they're honest." She arched an eyebrow at her, then laid Allison back in her arms before sitting down again. "The Lord works in mysterious ways," she told Rylee. "There is a reason that He gave you Allison so early in your life. It's not our place to question His wisdom."

"I know, Nana," Rylee told her with a sigh. "I just don't know how I'm going to take care of Allison by myself."

"You're not alone," Nana reminded her. "You have family to help."

"I will be alone when I move out east," Rylee told her. "Sam doesn't want to change schools. Am I supposed to put my life on hold until he graduates?"

Nana shook her head. "Sweetie, don't wait for him."

"I can't do this by myself!"

"You're a Williams girl," she told her. "We don't wait for the prince to save us. We can slay our own damn dragon!"

"Nana!" Rylee blinked. She'd never heard Nana swear, ever!

"I'm serious, Rylee," Nana said, leaning her head back against the recliner. "Don't wait for Sam to step up. You are strong.

Intelligent. Fearless. I've seen you accomplish great things in your young life, and I know you can do anything you put your mind to."

Rylee took a deep breath. "But we're still disinherited," she told Nana. "How am I going to explain this to Allison when she's older?"

Nana grimaced. "I don't know," she admitted. "But, until then, you need to focus on what's important: getting your education so you can move on to the next phase of your life." She slowly stood up. "Let me put Allison back in the bassinet," she told Rylee. "For the next few months, you're going to need to sleep when the baby sleeps."

Rylee gave the baby to Nana and laid back against the pillow. Was she the type of princess that could slay her own dragon?

Something was tingling against her wrist, pulling Rylee from a deep sleep. She fumbled against the tangled covers for a moment. *What time is it?* she thought.

She slowly opened her eyes. Time to get up. She reluctantly pulled her hands out from under the covers and tapped the 'stop' button on her watch. Then, she pulled the covers up over her head for a moment.

Six hours of sleep. That's it. Just six hours of sleep.

She pushed the covers back and sat up, feet firmly planted on the cool hardwood floor. *Time to get up*, she told herself. Sam had probably been up all night again with Madam Fussy.

She grabbed some clothes and made her way to the bathroom to get ready for the morning. Then, she padded down the stairs.

It was quiet. She paused at the foot of the stairs, savoring the sight of Sam giving Allison her bottle. He looked tired, his two-day-old beard making him look a bit scruffy this morning.

But he held Allison with a confident hand and that meant so much to her.

"There she is," Rylee breathed, content. "Coffee?"

Sam nodded. "I started some as her bottle was warming up," he said.

Rylee walked to the kitchen. This had become a part of their morning routine since their very first morning as parents. Sometimes Sam got it started. Other times, he was so busy with Allison that she made the coffee. It gave them just a bit of time to start their day together.

She grabbed their mugs out of the strainer and carefully filled them from the drip coffee maker. Cream for her. A dusting of sugar for him. Then, she made her way back into the living room and placed both mugs on the coffee table before settling down on the rocking chair next to the windows.

She leaned forward to grab her mug. "How'd she sleep?" she asked, blowing on her coffee before taking a careful sip.

"Pretty good," Sam told her as he yawned. "She woke up a few times but quickly settled down, so I was able to get a few naps in."

Rylee nodded, a tired smile playing on her lips. "Still think that having a nanny is a bad idea?" she asked. The only thing standing between them and some well-timed assistance was Sam's stubbornness.

He looked down at Allison as if considering it, then sighed. "Look, I know that this is hard, Rylee, really I do," he slowly said. "But handing our daughter off to some stranger—"

"A carefully vetted stranger," Rylee interjected.

Sam rolled his eyes at that. "Fine," he responded. "A 'carefully vetted stranger' brings a whole set of worries that I'm just not comfortable with."

Interesting. Was this something she could work with? she thought as she took another sip of coffee. "Tell me," she said in a quiet voice. "All of this would be so much easier if we could get some help around here."

Sam repositioned Allison across his lap, one hand cupping the back of her head. "We can't afford a nanny," he told her, a thread of bitterness tinging his voice. "Yes, I know that you have access to money from your trust fund and this wouldn't make a dent in what your parents gave you."

Rylee took another sip of coffee, closing her eyes to hide her frustration. *If only you knew*, she thought.

"It doesn't matter how much money you have," he reminded her. "We have to split our finances evenly. And, every single receipt, every deposit, everything that we spend every month has to be reported to the guardian ad litem until Allison is six months old."

He looked down at the baby. "They know how many hours I work and how much I'm able to provide. We're barely making ends meet now, Rylee, because I can't pull more hours, help with Allison, and get my homework done. Can you imagine what could happen if the Court found out you were paying for a nanny?"

Allison pushed away the bottle with her fists, fussing at him. Rylee put her mug on the coffee table and stood up to stretch. "Here, let me take her," she told him quietly. "She might be a bit gassy now."

She carefully settled Allison against her left shoulder. Allison gave a bit of a wiggle, her wet lips settling against Rylee's neck. She reached up and gently rubbed the baby's back with her other hand and slowly walked across the room.

It may have been the lack of sleep, but now might be a good time to talk this out. "My mom and dad have offered to pay for the nanny," she finally told him.

"What?" Sam's mouth dropped open. "That can't be legal, Rylee!" he complained.

She turned around and walked back across the room. She could feel Allison starting to relax into a light drowse. "There's nothing in the current law that prevents it," she told him in a quiet voice. "The money wouldn't go to us. It would directly go to the nanny as their employee."

Sam frowned. "What about the whole 'grandparents can't raise their grandkids' thing?" he asked sarcastically.

Allison interrupted her with a well-timed burp, and Rylee laughed. "Good girl," she crooned as she swayed her hips from side to side. Time to open negotiations. "Technically, it would still be us raising our daughter. Just with some well-timed assistance. Think about it, Sam. Most daycares accept six-week-old newborns. What is the difference between dropping her off at a center or having someone come here to take care of her during the day?"

"We can't afford that, either," Sam groused.

Rylee shook her head, then sat down in the rocker. She moved Allison to her lap, facing Sam. Allison's tiny fists closed around her fingers and she gently bounced them up and down for a bit of sensory play. Diana had recommended it during her last lactation visit as a comforting way to encourage two-week-old Allison without overwhelming her.

She looked at Sam intently. "At our current income, the state provides a subsidy allowance for daycare, Sam," she reminded him. "We could afford a few hours per week and have a nanny take care of her the rest of the time."

Sam stood and glared down at Rylee. "No nanny. Period."

"Why not?" she demanded. What the hell was wrong with him? "This is a very simple solution. Allison gets a bit of social interaction, and we can get on with our lives!"

Sam grabbed the baby bottle and his mug. "It always comes back to that, doesn't it, Rylee?" he growled before he walked to the kitchen. "Allison is not just a speed bump on your way to Wellesley. She's our daughter!"

"What is that supposed to mean?" Rylee demanded. Her sharp tone startled poor Allison, and she began to wail. "See what you've done?" She glared at Sam as she pulled Allison up onto her left shoulder again. "It's going to be okay, baby. Momma's got you . . . " she crooned as she began to slowly rock in the chair.

She watched Sam load his mug into the dishwasher, then carefully clean out Allison's bottle and place it in the drying rack.

Sam turned to look at them. "I'm transferring to Marquette in the fall," he told her. "You're still planning to go to Wellesley. I can't imagine that your parents will pay for a nanny when you're not here."

"What are you saying?" she demanded, her voice soft. "The nanny will stay with Allison, no matter where we live." Wasn't that obvious? She glared at him, slowly rubbing Allison's back as she calmed down. It might be time to put her down for a nap.

Sam walked back into the living room, grimacing as he stood against the wall. "Do you really want to have Allison move every month so that she can have equal time with both of us when you move out east?" he asked quietly.

"No—"

He cut her off. "If you push for the nanny, I'll insist that Allison come home every other month so that I keep joint placement."

"You wouldn't!" Rylee softly snarled. She brushed by him as she stalked into the kitchen. She carefully placed Allison in the baby bouncer on the floor near the table, pausing only long enough to strap her in before turning to glare at him.

Sam walked back into the kitchen and sat down at the table. He looked down at Allison, who was happily munching on her fist, then looked up intently. "There has to be a way for both of us to get what we want, Rylee," he told her. "And it starts with not having a nanny in our future."

Rylee walked over to the coffeemaker and poured herself a fresh cup. She hid a smile as she carefully stirred in some cream. If she didn't know any better, she'd say that he'd picked up a bit of the Williams negotiation tactics. Nice assertive opening salvo, but he'd left himself with very little strategic leverage for the inevitable compromise.

Let's do this, she thought as she carefully set her spoon down in the sink. She moved to the kitchen table and sat down, cuddling her hot coffee mug in both hands. "Fine," she said before taking a careful sip of coffee. "Let's talk."

Epilogue

Rylee took one more look in the mirror, then clicked on the link to join the video call. *No pressure*, she thought as she waited for the connection to be made. Her legal team had hammered out the best deal they could. All that was left was judicial theater.

Truth be told, she was just the tiniest bit nervous. The outcome of this call would determine the next four years of her life. Yes, the arbitrator had recommended that Rylee be allowed to move to campus before the probationary period was over. But that could just as easily be taken away if Sam balked at the last minute.

Once the picture came up, she quickly looked around the room to see if she could spot Allison. Attorneys, guardian ad litem, arbitrator, mentors. Ah, Sam sat on one side of the oval table, the carrier on the floor next to him. She frowned in disappointment. She could only see a small sliver of her baby's black hair.

Rylee stared at Allison for a moment, then pulled out her phone to double-check her afternoon schedule. Her phone had become essential to managing her life when she hit campus. The irony was not lost on her.

A door opened and Judge Olson entered the room, closely followed by the stenographer. The conversation quieted as the judge sat down at the head of the table.

Rylee glanced at the small window that showed her image on video and smoothed her braid over one shoulder. She set the phone down on her desk to give the judge her full attention.

The judge looked around the room, nodding at Rylee, before she opened the folder she'd brought with her. "Mr. Mueller," she said in a quiet voice. "The settlement we have before us is quite unusual. Are you certain that you are in agreement with it?"

Rylee turned up the volume on her computer as she strained to hear the conversation.

"Yes, Your Honor," he replied. "I believe this is in my client's best interests."

The judge turned to the arbitrator, who sat on her left. "Ms. Rodriquez, as the arbitrator assigned to the case, can you walk us through the agreement at a high level?"

"Of course, Your Honor," the woman replied with a smile. "This case was unusual in that, while both parties are enrolled in universities, one of them has been accepted out-of-state. This complicated the usual placement rotation."

Judge Olson gestured with one hand, a silent command to continue.

Rodriquez cleared her throat. "Both parties have agreed that Ms. Williams Maxwell, aka Allison, will live with Mr. Maxwell until Ms. Williams has completed her undergraduate program at Wellesley University," she said. "During this time, Ms. Williams will pay 100 percent of their child's financial expenses. This includes half of Mr. Maxwell's housing expenses, reasonable child care expenses, and all of Allison's food, clothing, medical, and educational allowance."

The judge cocked her head to one side. "Educational allowance?" she asked.

The arbitrator looked down at her notes. "Educational books and toys, Your Honor," the arbitrator read. "Both parents have expressed an interest in Ms. Williams Maxwell learning a foreign language."

"Ah. Continue."

Rodriguez cleared her throat again. "During this time, Ms. Williams will have to return home during school breaks to assume custody," she said. "Once Ms. Williams has completed her undergraduate program, Allison will move to her mother's residence until she's ready to attend elementary school. This will allow Mr. Maxwell to travel, if he chooses, or pursue employment outside of the country. He will, however, be responsible for 50 percent of their child's reasonable expenses during this time."

"Interesting," Judge Olson said, tapping her pen against the folder almost impatiently. "Why is Mr. Maxwell responsible for only 50 percent?"

"Because Mr. Maxwell has agreed to remain in the state so that Ms. Williams Maxwell is able to regularly visit with her grandparents and extended family," Rodriquez advised.

"Anything else?"

Rodriquez nodded, her finger pointing out a specific paragraph in the agreement. "Both parties have agreed to a weekly video call so that Ms. Williams Maxwell is comfortable with both parents and annual reviews with the guardian ad litem, in person, to ensure that they remain in good standing with the program," she said.

The judge turned to a man wearing a plain, white t-shirt. "Mr. Petropoulous, any concerns?"

Rylee studied him closely. That had to be Sam's mentor. He smiled, giving Rylee a sly but relaxed grin as he looked up at her. "Is there a no-nanny clause, Ms. Rodriquez?"

Oh, my God! Rylee thought, her cheeks burning with embarrassment. *What had Sam told that man?*

Judge Olson glanced up at Rylee, then back to Petropoulous. "Is there something I should know, Mr. Petropoulous?" she asked, one eyebrow arched in amusement.

Sam brought his hand up in front of his mouth so she couldn't see what his expression was, but both Sam and his mentor shook their heads in denial. "No, ma'am," he finally said. "Sorry. Just a private joke, Your Honor."

The judge laughed. "Someday, someone's going to let me in on the joke, right?"

"Absolutely, Your Honor," Petropoulous said.

Then, the judge turned to Erin, Rylee's mentor. "Any concerns, Mrs. Meyer?"

Rylee's mentor glanced up to look at her, then shook her head. "None, Your Honor."

The judge turned to Sam. "Mr. Maxwell, do you have any thoughts that you'd like to share with this Court before I make a final judgment?"

It was difficult to tell from this angle, but it looked like Sam pursed his lips for a moment. This was it. The make-or-break moment where she either stayed on campus and worked her ass off to build her future or lost everything.

"Your Honor, this has been a wild ride," Sam told the judge. "In all honesty, I never expected to become a dad this early in my life and I never expected that I would fall so completely in love." He looked down at Allison as if to prove his point.

"Children will do that to you," the judge replied with a satisfied smile. She glanced at Rylee. "Okay, Ms. Williams, do you have anything that you'd like to add?"

Rylee found herself sitting up straighter, smiling anxiously as she tugged at her long French braid. "I'm just glad that we were able to come to a reasonable accommodation, Your Honor," she said. "I agree that Allison's placement and the financial support are exactly what our little family needs to have in place to ensure her future."

The judge nodded, then took one last look around the room. "Does anyone have any other information that needs to be taken into account before I issue my final ruling?"

At that moment, Allison woke and started fussing. Rylee bit her lip, watching helplessly as Sam pulled the baby out of her carrier and settled her on his lap to face the judge. She blinked back tears. Sam had dressed her in that adorable Dolce & Gabbana red rose outfit she'd sent for the court hearing. It was perfect!

"Ah, you're awake, Ms. Williams Maxwell," the judge said, leaning forward to talk directly to Allison. "Do you have anything to add?"

In response, Allison spit out her pacifier and yawned.

Judge Olson laughed. "Alright, then," she replied. She turned her attention back to the group. "Based on the feedback I've received, this settlement goes into effect today, October 8th, 2029. Both parties are expected to meet with Ms. Williams Maxwell's guardian ad litem, annually, to make any necessary changes to placement and financial support until she has reached twenty-one years of age. So, ordered. Case closed."

Rylee closed her eyes in relief, listening as people started to gather their things to leave. She swallowed, taking one last look at Allison. "Thank you, Your Honor," Rylee said. The video abruptly ended.

She stared at her computer screen for a moment. She couldn't sort out what she was feeling. She wasn't free. No. Some part of her would always be tied to Sam. First steps. First words. First day of school. Endless parent-teacher conferences. Graduations. Allison's wedding. The inevitable grandchildren.

Rylee stood up and walked over to the window. Her second-floor room overlooked the courtyard, and she watched as other students walked along the cement pathways on their way to class.

She took a deep breath. She had to be strong. Fight for what was hers. Network her ass off so that she could give Allison the life she deserved. No one, not even Sam, was going to get in her way.

Stay updated! Join my mailing list at www.mewright.com to receive notifications about new releases, exclusive giveaways, and exciting updates. By being part of our community, you'll be the first to know about upcoming projects.

If you found my book engaging, please take a moment to leave a review. You play a crucial role in reaching a wider audience and encouraging fellow readers to explore my work.

There are two sides to every story...

Curious about Sam's experience with the Wisconsin Individual Family Education program and Rylee's pregnancy? Here's the first chapter of **The Fatherhood Mandate**.

Sam stood on the rocky beach, watching the small waves lap against the monochrome shoreline. It was late August, but the wind coming off Lake Michigan was a bit chilly. *Probably should have brought a jacket*, he thought as he shoved his hands deep into his front pockets.

He kicked at the pebbles that littered the beach, then pulled his phone out of his back pocket to check the time. 8:10 am. It was too early for this shit.

Sam shaded his eyes as the sun momentarily poked through the somber clouds, then slid the phone back into his pocket and glared at the horizon. Of course, Rylee was late. She was always late.

He sighed. Rylee was the kind of girl that you could love one minute and hate the next. Bright blue eyes that just drew you in. Long black hair and a saucy smile. Curves in all the right places.

She knew what to say, when to say it, and what it took to get her way.

And that was the problem. Rylee always got her way.

Not this time, Sam thought as he kicked at the sandy pebbles at his feet. No more meaningless late night texts. No more screaming fights over some imagined insult. No more scheduling and rescheduling his life around her ever-changing wants and needs. It was over. Done.

He heard her cuss as she stumbled across the damp rocks and pieces of driftwood that littered the beach, her complaints almost lost in the mindless hiss of the surf as she slowly made her way across the deserted beach. He ignored her.

"Sam, I'm cold," Rylee said when she finally reached him. That telltale whine warned him she was already in a mood. "Can't we go someplace else?"

Sam felt her tentatively reach for him. He pulled away and shoved his hands into his front pockets again. "Just tell me what you want, Rylee," he said, eyeing the darkening clouds that threatened rain out over the lake. "We broke up. It's over. There's nothing more to say."

"It's really chilly out here," she whimpered. "I can't talk when I'm freezing to death!"

She sniffed as if she was holding back tears. He turned and one look was enough. Melodramatic expression. Bloodshot eyes. Blotchy skin from crying.

That was the last thing he needed that morning. "Let's go," he muttered. He grabbed her arm and forced her to walk toward the trail that threaded its way through the woods surrounding the beach behind them.

Sam felt her stumble over a small piece of driftwood and glanced down. Soft leather flats peeked out beneath a long dress that were more at home on a riverboat cruise than on sandy terrain. No matter how many times they'd been to Tietjen Beach, she just couldn't take the hint and wear sensible clothes.

He released her arm as they slowly made their way through the overgrown trail to the stairs. Wild grapevines, goldenrod, and assorted weeds crowded the entrance to the limestone steps and made it almost impossible to reach the rough, wooden handrails as they climbed.

They approached the top of the bluff. Sam headed for one of the benches that used to overlook the beach below. Now, trees and small brush huddled against the hill, creating an almost impenetrable view.

He sat down. "Tell me what's going on," he asked as gently as he could. Sometimes it was easier to just go with it.

Rylee slumped onto a nearby bench. Almost on cue, tears started rolling down her cheeks. "We can't break up, Sam," she whispered. She brushed her long, black hair away from her face. "I need you."

Sam turned away, staring at the clouds that randomly filtered through the foliage around him. It was definitely going to rain. He could smell it in the air.

"Rylee, it's over." Sam ducked his head, staring at the sandy ground. "You broke up with *me*. We're done."

"No!" Rylee stood, fists clenched, as she screamed at him. "You don't understand. We made a mistake!"

Sam leaned back and wearily looked up at her. "How many times do we need to break up before you finally accept that it's over, Rylee?" he asked, lightly mocking her. "Two more times? Five?" He searched her face for any bit of understanding. "Breaking up was your idea." He paused for emphasis. "Both times!"

Rylee screwed her eyes shut and turned her face to the sky. "I was wrong," she whispered. She opened her eyes and wiped her face with both hands. "Things have changed, Sam."

"What things?" Sam demanded. "I'm really tired of this, Rylee! Tell me what's going on!"

She sat down and slumped against the bench, covering her eyes with one hand. "It doesn't matter, Sam," she told him. "I'm probably worried about nothing."

Sam sighed as he stood up. "Fine," he growled. And, with that, he walked away, trying to ignore the quiet sobs behind him. He had better things to do than to deal with the drama queen.

Don't miss out on the next chapter of The Unborn Child Protection Act series. Get your copy of *The Fatherhood Mandate* today!

Author's Note

April 13, 2024

The novel *The Motherhood Mandate* is set in a dystopian future in the year 2028. A place where pregnant women who are either unmarried or, in the midst of a divorce, are detained if a fetal heartbeat is detected. Where the State of Wisconsin takes the idea of personal responsibility to such an extreme that pregnant women have been reduced to 'fetal host' status. A place where society is ill-prepared for the consequences imposed by the state legislature and the United States Supreme Court.

So, how did we get here? Our story begins the moment that women in the United States lost their right to self-determination.

On June 24, 2022, the United States Supreme Court overturned Roe v. Wade, the landmark ruling that made access to abortion a federal right in the United States. This decision dismantled over fifty years of legal protection, paving the way for individual states to restrict or outright ban a woman's right to bodily autonomy.

Justice Alito delivered the High Court's opinion[1]. "We hold that Roe and Casey must be overruled. The Constitution makes no reference to abortion, and no such right is implicitly protected by any constitutional provision, including the one on which the defenders of Roe and Casey now chiefly rely—the Due Process Clause of the Fourteenth Amendment. That provision has been held to guarantee some rights that are not mentioned in the Constitution, but any such right must be 'deeply rooted in this Nation's history and tradition' and 'implicit in the concept of ordered liberty.'"

Prior to 1973, abortion had been illegal in 30 states and was only legal under specific circumstances in the remainder. Justice Alito pointed out that common law had long recognized abortion as a criminal offense, in at least some stage of pregnancy. Common law as early as the sixteenth century declared that abortion was a crime, at least after 'quickening'—i.e., the first movement of the fetus felt in the womb.

Other federal rights that relied on the Fourteenth Amendment were also put in jeopardy by the ruling, including interracial and same-sex marriages, as well as religious and gender-related discrimination.

---

1. The Associated Press. June 22, 2022.
   https://apnews.com/article/abortion-us-supreme-court-health-racial-injustice-gun-politics-e38479715c763a4972a85cc4003d73f9.

Following the Supreme Court ruling, Wisconsin abortion clinics halted elective abortions[2]. Many of them relocated over the border in neighboring states, as women who needed abortions traveled across state lines to receive them. Planned Parenthood launched a mobile abortion clinic initiative to cut down travel time, and the costs associated with seeking abortion care.

Governor Evers called a special session of the Wisconsin State Legislature on October 4, 2022. He requested that the legislature create a pathway to repeal Wisconsin's 1849-era criminal abortion ban. In response, Wisconsin's Senate convened for 15 seconds, long enough to gavel in and adjourn without taking action.

Milwaukee County circuit judge Janet Protasiewicz's election to the Wisconsin Supreme Court in Spring 2023 tipped the Court to a 4-3 liberal majority. However, the election of conservative Dan Knodl[3] handed Republicans a supermajority in the state senate. This injected a high degree of uncertainty into state politics, as this would allow Wisconsin's senate to impeach state officials, including a state supreme court justice.

---

2. McCabe, Samantha. Here's what to know about abortion access in post-Roe Wisconsin, Wisconsin Public Radio, September 9, 2022.
https://www.wpr.org/heres-what-know-about-abortion-access-post-roe-wisconsin.

3. Levine, Sam. Wisconsin senate supermajority win gives Republicans impeachment power, The Guardian, April 5, 2023.
https://www.theguardian.com/us-news/2023/apr/05/wisconsin-senate-supermajority-impeachment-power.

By early 2024, the Comstock Act – enacted by Congress in 1873 to ban the mailing of 'lewd' materials – was raised as a viable dissent in Alliance for Hippocratic Medicine (AHM) v. Food and Drug Administration (FDA) case before the U.S. Supreme Court. [4] If successful, this lawsuit will effectively ban the use of misoprostol in the United States.

These events are the foundations that *The Motherhood Mandate* is built on. From here, we move into the dystopian future that may come to pass. History may diverge as the story unfolds.

In this universe, the state legislature declined to repeal or amend the 1849 Wisconsin Criminal Abortion Statute, which had been in place shortly after Wisconsin had been admitted to the Union as a state. The statute[5] reads in part:

Any person, other than the mother, who does either of the following is guilty of a Class E felony:

(a) Intentionally destroys the life of an unborn quick child; or

(b) Causes the death of the mother by an act done with intent to destroy the life of an unborn child. It is unnecessary to prove that

---

4. Doshi, J. (2024, March 26). What is the Comstock Act? The 151-year-old law mentioned in SCOTUS abortion pill case. ABC News. https://abcnews.go.com/Politics/what-is-comstock-act-supreme-court-abortion-pill-case/story?id=108395444

5. Wisconsin State Legislature Statute 904.04: https://docs.legis.wisconsin.gov/statutes/statutes/940/i/04

the fetus was alive when the act causing the mother's death was committed.

A series of lawsuits were made against the state and individual legislators, claiming that the statute clearly stated abortion was legal before sixteen to twenty-four weeks of gestation when movement could be felt. Others pointed out that the statute allowed medicinal abortions, as the mother could voluntarily ingest medications that would end her pregnancy. The medications prescribed for this, mifepristone and misoprostol, are generally considered to be safe to use up to the eleventh week of pregnancy.

Due to legislative inaction, the legal question of abortion remained in place until the 2024 election. In response to retaining a veto-proof supermajority in both Assembly and the Senate, Republicans replaced the 1849 abortion bill with one that declared life began at conception and outlawed abortion if the pregnancy was viable. This included pregnancies due to rape or incest. Once a fetal heartbeat was detected, there were very few options available to protect the life of the mother.

In December 2024, a video captured a prominent pro-life state legislator's daughter as she was transported by ambulance to Illinois to undergo a life-saving abortion following an unexpected complication late in her pregnancy. The video went viral and prodded the legislature to take action. The law was amended to include that ectopic pregnancies and specific instances where the embryo or fetus is determined to not be able to survive to be medically necessary.

It's important to note that according to this legislation, the health and safety of the mother were secondary considerations. Women were routinely denied cancer treatment until after they had successfully delivered their babies and women died because care was delayed until their life was confirmed to be in danger. In addition, it did not include severe birth defects that would result in the newborn dying after birth.

Section 1 of the state constitution was amended to reinforce the state law that life began at conception: *All people are born equally free and independent, and have certain inherent rights; among these are life, liberty, and the pursuit of happiness; to secure these rights, governments are instituted, deriving their just powers from the consent of the governed. The term 'person' or 'persons' shall include every human being from the moment of fertilization, cloning, or the functional equivalent thereof.*

By early 2025, the legal age of 'adult' was standardized to occur at age twenty-one. Legally, anyone under the age of twenty-one was no longer allowed to vote in local or state elections, or allowed alcoholic beverages, to purchase tobacco or CBD products, or even marry without parental consent.

A measure to raise the age of consent for statutory rape from age sixteen to eighteen was introduced. It was a difficult law to pass, but the need to protect children was heavily used in advertising and media talking points.

Wisconsin's birth rate began to increase, straining the already shaky healthcare system. This especially impacted the poorest residents, who were unable to afford to travel outside of the state for abortions. More fathers found themselves taken to court for child support, but the standard guidelines remained paltry: only 17% of income for one child, 25% for two children, and 29% for three children. As child support did not cover all of the costs of raising a child, the number of fatherless families applying for FoodShare Wisconsin and other state support programs dramatically increased around the state.

Various tax measures were considered—and rejected—in response to the increased pressure on the state budget. Instead, the legislature passed a series of measures in early 2027 which were designed to reaffirm the core principle of 'personal responsibility'. These included:

- Act 292, also known as The Unborn Child Protection Act, which had been originally designed to allow pregnant individuals to be detained if they were suspected of substance abuse, was amended to allow unmarried, pregnant women to be taken into custody to determine if they posed a risk to their embryo, provided that a fetal heartbeat was detected.

- Unborn citizens gestated by an unmarried woman, or one who was suing for divorce, automatically became a ward of the state. This was designed to prevent women from traveling outside of the state for an abortion.

- Child support guidelines were replaced with one that called for each parent to contribute half of all offspring's reasonable expenses until age twenty-one. The exception was if either parent was convicted of rape, domestic violence, or was deemed to be a risk to the life and safety of the child. In this case, the convicted parent was responsible for 100% of their offspring's reasonable expenses.

- The Wisconsin Individual Family Education program, which had been a voluntary program designed to facilitate an unmarried couple's transition to parenthood, was made mandatory under most circumstances. This

included couples that were in the process of divorcing
and those that were pursuing adoption after their child
was born.

- The 'No Means No' initiative changed all rape charges
  to state felonies. No misdemeanor charges remained in
  state statutes. Rape kits were required to be processed
  within seventy-two hours, or three calendar days, of
  the reported event and the state's attorney general was
  required to provide a quarterly report on the progress
  the state made in securing rape convictions.

Conservatives felt that these measures were a good start, but
didn't go far enough. A new bill was introduced to codify the
idea that every child was entitled to have a father and a mother.
Backers knew that they couldn't force unwed couples to marry,
but felt that cohabitation during the child's first months of life
might improve marriage rates.

Under the new law, unmarried couples were required to live
together from the third trimester of pregnancy until the child
was six months old. Courts could wave this for several reasons,
including but not limited to a history of physical or emotional
abuse, where rape is suspected but not reported, and in very
limited child support and custody cases. In all things, the child's
needs were placed above the needs of the parents.

The state was immediately sued, and the case was fast-tracked
to the Supreme Court. In anticipation of the conservative majority prevailing, staffing for family courts around the state
greatly increased and the number of guardian ad litem positions
tripled.

In May 2028, SCOTUS declined to hear the case and Wisconsin began immediately enforcing the new laws. And this is where *The Motherhood Mandate* begins.

Acknowledgements

In August 2023, we lost my mother after a brief illness. Before she passed away, I had the opportunity to brainstorm with her on my current project, *The Motherhood Mandate*. Every one of Rylee's challenges and every victory is a gift from my mom. She insisted that no matter how bad things got for Rylee, I needed to show what a strong young woman she was.

To my loving husband and daughter, thank you for your unwavering support. Your belief in me has been the fuel that kept me going during the long hours of drafting and editing. I am grateful for your patience, understanding, and unconditional love.

A big shout out to Heather Flanagan, my friend and compatriot who planted a seed with Patreon. Many thanks to Dave Boucher, who gave me the much-needed support on pastors and prayers. To Renji and my Cafe Crew at Immersed's VR coworking space, I hope you enjoy the Easter Eggs you helped create. And, to #TeamWright, who gave me feedback on that all-important first draft: you guys rock!!

About the Author

M.E. Wright is a Midwest native with a passion for delving into dystopian and speculative fiction. As a social scientist and writer, she starts each project with a simple question: 'What if...'

She doesn't shy away from the brutal realities of a world shaped by shifting ideologies. With a knack for social commentary and a talent for creating characters you can't help but root for (or against), M.E. is all about crafting stories that make you think, laugh, and maybe even cringe a little.

On a personal note, she prefers soda to pop, measures distance in the time it takes to get there, rather than in miles, and has been known to secretly cheer for the Bears even though she live in Packer country.

Her website is www.mewright.com